AWAY GAME

by Michael Jacob Rochlin

Unreinforced
Masonry
Studio
Los Angeles

Special thanks to Theresa Powers, Feather StandingBear and Ayofemi Folayan

Typeset and printed in the United States of America

This book is printed on recycled paper.

Published by Unreinforced Masonry Studio
P.O. Box 33671, Los Angeles, California 90013

Rochlin, Michael Jacob
Away Game/Michael Jacob Rochlin
p. cm.
ISBN 0-9648304-0-X
1. Athletics—Fiction. 2. Women basketball player—Fiction
I. Title

96-090296
CIP

To the memory of

friend Shirley

and

Uncle Leonard

SAN FRANCISCO

Pro League? Prologue

Smaller and older than the Forum, yet newer and larger than the Olympic, the Los Angeles Sports Arena, built in 1960 to house the Democratic National Convention, thirty-six years later, was available for rent at fairly reasonable rates. Theresa "Terry the Taxi" Taktikabian, coach of the Exposition Park Exiles had bargained well for the two-day, single elimination tournament. Promoting an up-coming summer tour, she had pulled together half a dozen Western Conference College teams to participate. With all the publicity from the Olympics, the first day was packed, or at least, packed for a Women's game which meant about half full. Players, parents and fans from all over the state were anxious to see how their kids would fare against the barnstorming "Exiles". Unfortunately, on the tournament's final day, a heat-wave struck the basin raising temperatures to one hundred and three. Only the truly faithful and fanatic showed up and with half-time almost over, Theresa's team huddled.

"Now I know this is an easy game and the crowd isn't too big—"

"Big? Terry, if my mom hadn't come, attendance would have been down twenty per-cent."

Daisy pushed Patty. "Will you give her a break. She can't control the weather."

Terry referred to her clip board and tried to keep the team focused. "Okay everybody, just like the first half. Iris posts and Villa is point. Patty stay to the right. Dahlia and Claudette play the wings. On defense, were staying with the 3-2."

Claudette pulled out her jersey then tucked it back in. "Terry, Iris is taking care of business underneath. You hardly need me. I'm not doing anything."

Peggy, the replacement center and Claudette's best buddy chimed in. "She's right Terry. The 'Horn-ettes' are even smaller this year than last, if that's possible."

Claudette chuckled. "Do you want me to float?"

Theresa looked concerned. "Alright, alright, if you want to try it, that's fine. But we're not letting them back in this one. This isn't Pomona."

Patty rubbed her eyes. "Don't remind me. Ooh, that game was boring. Even the referees were yawning. It was sad. The gym didn't even—"

"Okay Patty, I'm sorry I reminded you."

Claudette tapped Theresa's shoulder to confirm instructions. "So, I should float?"

"If you're free—"

"I'm free."

"Then go ahead. Break away if you can, but be careful."

Starting forward Claudette Goodwin stood two inches above the tallest Hornet. At twenty-eight, she was a solid veteran: three years all-city high school, four years Division I NCAA, two years in the Italian League, one year coaching teenagers and now two seasons with Terry. Her boyfriend would tease her that it was time to retire, but this league didn't interfere with teaching, it was fun, kept her in shape and brought in a small, but steady salary. As long as her right ankle—the weak point of her career—was carefully wrapped and taped, she would be able to play several more years at this level. The strongest defensive player on the Exiles, Claudette oddly enough, rarely stole the ball and almost never cherry-picked. She did, however, play the boards with authority—her powerful hips and low center of gravity providing the leverage to control her zone. This made her invaluable to Iris at center, but in this game her size and agility were hardly needed and she found herself shooting, passing and even dribbling once when Dahlia had been trapped.

Now, she was drifting down court, grabbing outlet passes and laying-in gimmies. Several minutes into the second half, Claudette again found herself all alone and began waving her arms and shouting. Patty spotted her and let go the bomb. Claudette took off smiling—the only other player was four steps behind and she planned to make this look good. She caught the high pass, took the needed one and one half steps and left the ground for the lay-up. The pursuing Hornet guard leapt up and tangled Claudette's legs forcing the two of them to fall together, Claudette coming down on the side of her bad foot. She heard a pronounced crack inside her ankle and screamed.

"Oh no!" Theresa jumped up from her seat and ran out.

Patty was there first. "Can you get up?"

Claudette looked at her like she was crazy. "No!"

Iris eyed the guilty Hornet guard. "You got to watch out for these young players."

Coach Taktikabian arrived and took her player's hand. "How is it Claudette? Are you okay?"

She was crying. Claudette never cried. "No, I'm not okay. It hurts." Terry believed it. After the two had come down, the big forward had pounded the floor, dragged her own body several feet and howled in pain. Her face was pale and twisted like a dish rag.

"Okay, just try to relax. I'll call Flor and she'll look at it later on. Take your time. Just let us know when you're ready to help you up."

Play didn't resume for ten minutes when finally Claudette—a player under each arm—was carried to the bench. It put a damper on an already depressing outing.

"Now what are we going to do?"

"I'm not sure yet Patty."

"Terry, we need Claudette."

"Well we don't have her anymore. Even if nothing tore, she won't be playing this season. I'll talk to Flor about it tonight. I guess we'll have to recruit someone new right away."

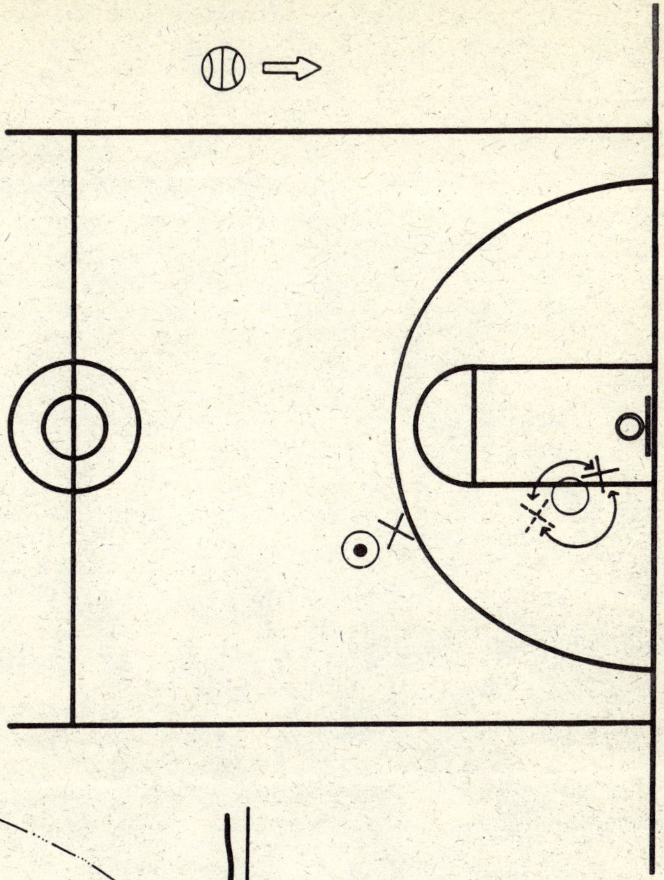

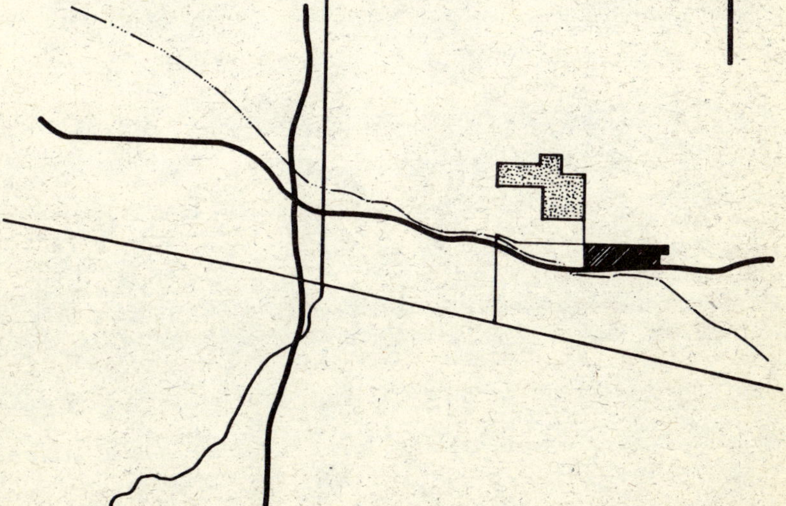

APPLICATION FOR EMPLOYMENT
PERSONAL INFORMATION
AMARYLLIS
9920 LASAINE
SANTA CR
(818)88

Turnoff for the Workhouse 1

The bus came to the end of Van Nuys Boulevard and headed west on Ventura. The turning alerted the tall young woman out of her daze. She was lost—definitely—no question. And what did she expect? The night before, descending into the forty-mile-wide basin, she'd stared down at those dark hills, that black ocean, that crisp shoreline, those elegant curving red lines of freeway and that endless grid of orange lamps. Damn! Awesome! Impressive! But how's anyone supposed to find their way in all that?

She'd have to ask someone for directions, but who? The passengers of MTA #561 sat like bent-over statues—serious and silent—motionless in their wrinkled shirts, ironed blouses and dusty black shoes. Had they ever spoken? Who knows? Not a word had been muttered since she'd stepped on ten minutes ago—a rolling wax museum. She leaned forward. Might as well start with the closest.

"Excuse me, do you know where this bus is headed?"

The balding man turned around and grinned. "At Sepulveda, it gets on the freeway, but I'm going to Topanga." He pointed up and read: "Look! 'Topanga—place where the mountains meet the sea'."

She followed his glance to a bus placard map entitled, Indigenous Place Names. "Is there a mall in Topanga? I'm looking for Fashion Square."

"There's a mall everywhere, but that one is a Plaza, not a Square. Topanga Plaza, Tujunga Center, Cahuenga Mall." He made his eyebrows go up and down. "Look! 'Cahuenga—place in the little hills'. See, it says place names end with the suffix 'nga'. What kind of place are you looking for?"

"A donut shop. I'm applying for a job."

"Then you might try looking for 'Donutnga—place of baking junk food' or 'Fashion Squarenga—place of Muzak and credit purchases'." He breathed a phony laugh and reached out. "Just playing. My name's Nick. What's yours?"

"Amaryllis." She shook hands and felt his grip tighten. "But really, do you know if I'm heading in the right direction?" She pulled to free her hand.

Not letting go, he referred to a different placard in the series and began lifting the fingers of his other hand one by one. "I'm not sure, but I think you've got *pukú...wehé...pahé* more stops to go. Don't you get it? Look! *Pukú* means one, *wehé* means two and *pahé* means three."

Amaryllis Benjamina Seltzer squinted. All she had wanted were directions. You know, like, point and say, 'It's back there,' or unfold a bus schedule and mark an X, or look out the window for the right street, or even ring the bell and step out the back door exclaiming, 'Follow me!' What was the stand-up routine for?

"Excuse me, would you please let—"

"*Majár* means five. *Papáhe* means six. *Watsá kaviyá* means seven..."

Amaryllis' week had gone well so far. She'd gotten her act together, painstakingly built her confidence, crammed for nights on end and aced three finals in one day—Alternative California History; Anthro 203—Societies and Their Structures since the Industrial Revolution; and Contemporary Political Theory—Post World War Two Trends and Tendencies. Then, the next morning, she'd jumped up, and in the 5:30 a.m. darkness, packed her belongings, caught the airplane, hopped on the shuttle and before noon was met at the door by her stuck-in-the-sixties daddyo, Max Seltzer. And what did Max have to say after not seeing her for two years?— "Geez, look at that, just what I wanted to be, six feet tall." Everyone's a comedian.

"*Wehés watsá means* eight. *Mahár kaviyá* means nine. *Wehés mahár* means ten..."

Now she was stuck holding hands with Crazy LA Dude. Crazy, just like her dad and his hippie bear hug. No question, after that third degree, he was proud of her. But how did she feel? This morning, all she felt was the need to find a job. It doesn't matter where. Get me an interview! Sell donuts in a mall? Sure, be right down.

"*Wehéhes majár* means twenty. *Páhes majár* means thirty..."

Yeah, dad was different then she'd remembered. How many times had she seen him in the last eight years—maybe a half a dozen? Even on those six, she must not have been looking very hard because she never remembered him as a fat slob. Maybe the radical life was not all it was cracked up to be. If that's how you end up: piles of collected trash, mountains of dusty videos, half-eaten frozen dinners and a floor full of dirty clothes. Yeah, maybe she would rather be like Mom after all: full-time job, friendly luncheons, hilarious cynical attitude and a dry resignation to only a few important social causes. Max—how sad—he'd tried to hold on to them all: "Save the Redwoods," "Stop Nuclear Testing," "Legalize Hemp"—the list was too long for anyone to handle. Uh-uh, after seeing that blob asleep in the reclining chair in front of the TV, the nine-to-five life suddenly seemed just fine.

"Please let go—"

"*Watsáhes mahár* means forty. *Maháres mahár* means fifty and *pukú pa aviyá mahár* means sixty."

She let her arm hang limp and looked out the window to the flags and banners of the used car dealership. Maybe she could borrow Max's Dodge. Then she'd leave this tribe of pass and transfer holders behind. Right! And gloriously escape into the ranks of bumper-to-bumper freeway traffic. It's all messed up down here. In Berkeley, having a car is an option, but in L.A.?

"*Áwkut* means crow. *Shuyót* means star."

Great. He'd gone on to Indigenous Nouns. Maybe she could drift back in time a few minutes to when she hadn't yet realized she was even lost. What was she thinking about then? Oh yeah, one of her favorites, the very thing she was trying right now to reclaim—her hands. Her hands were good and they were all hers. Good hands.

"Kokít means fog. *Akwíkin* means rain."

Rain? That's a coincidence. It had been raining the day she first realized her hands were good. So long ago, during that big storm (the tropical kind, those loud ones, you know—inches in minutes), quite a contrast to today's cloudless skies. In Grandma's living room, the television blasting its lightning-interrupted news reports: flooding in the Valleys, landslides in the foothills, ten-foot swells off the South Bay. Amid a symphony of sounds: the aluminum awning booming like a kettle drum, pianos of water falling from mile-high windows, rivers slurping down the gutter and roaring out the spout. Sitting on the rug, back against the sofa, leaning over to work on a jungle jigsaw puzzle—that realization, like a new island, surfaced. Just like Natalie said, "You've got good hands." Out there, on the playground, she had stopped for a moment and just looked at them, the fronts and the backs and it was true. They were good. Good, good hands. She had tried to tell Grammy, talking her own melodic language into the phone, but what was the use?

"*Támit means sun. Ahíkan means* wind. *Xáyiy* means mountain."

Sun, wind and mountains had beckoned her that day, strengthening her desire to be outside playing in that fresh, crisp just-after the storm smog-free air. Outside, embraced by the cold and leaning into warm Nat; pushing rib cage into curvaceous shoulders. Outside, with the clouds and the schoolyard shouts and the passing traffic and the smell of Nat's salty skin. Just wanting to be with her buddy had made her remember, "Good hands." Good because they were skilled at blocking Nat's shots and quick with long fingers for stealing the ball away during her dribble. Good on "D" babe! Good guarding Nat. And Nat was the best so that made them good against anyone. "Good Hands."

"Let go!" she grunted, yanking away. Surprised, the man became quiet and turned around sheepishly. Another man, from the next row, stood up and stopped by her seat. He wore a black sports coat with large sweat marks under each armpit.

"Fashion Square is across the street from Sunkist Tuna." He pulled the cord and stepped off the bus.

Uh-huh. Where is Sunkist Tuna? And don't they sell oranges? She sighed and looked to the other row. Maybe the old guy knows.

"Excuse me, I'm looking for Sherman Oaks Fashion Square. Do you know where it is?"

"What?"

"Do you know where Sherman Oaks Fashion Square is?"

"Sherman Oaks Fashion Square? That's on the corner of Riverside Drive and Hazeltine Avenue. Riverside Drive, like its name says, is by the river. And Hazeltine is where the fence of the old wheat ranch had its gate. Oh that was a nice spread. Wheat, walnuts and oranges, then they subdivided the property. This whole valley used to be nothing but farms and ranches. You see, I came out in thirty-eight with my wife..."

"But do you—"

"She's a brunette and used to like to dress up like a Spanish lady with a hat and a cape. That used to really tickle me. At one party, she told everyone that her great-aunt was married to one of the original Dons. Can you believe that? She had long hair that she combed sixty strokes three times a day. Do you girls these days take care of your hair like she used to?"

He was waiting for an answer. She nodded.

"I did a little of everything back then—herded sheep, plowed the soil. Did you know that I even had a bit part in an old Western? It was filmed out in Thousand Oaks and—"

Someone was tapping Amaryllis' shoulder from behind. "Don't listen to Old Faithful."

"Huh?" She turned around.

It was a large woman in a security guard's uniform placing her index finger to her own head. "He's not all there. We all call him Old Faithful because he rides this bus every day, back and forth. Is he going anywhere? Nope. He just waits for anyone to talk to him so he can start jabbering on about walnuts and wheat. If you ask me, I think that's about all he's got left up there. Don't you listen to him or no one else on this bus. If you want to know something, you go ask the driver." She cupped her hand by her mouth. "Hey driver, did we pass the mall?"

"Up ahead. Last stop before the freeway. Have your checks ready. If you need a transfer, come up and get one, but next time ask for it when you get on. And turn down that radio."

Radio? What radio? A small woman with dark hair smiled innocently and beckoned to Amaryllis. "Fashion Square?"

"Yes, do you know where it is?"

"Sí, sí, ahí compre una blusa para mi nieta. Tenía flores por en frente y Winnie the Pooh por detrás. A ella le encanta. ¿Sábes que me dijo? 'Abuelita, Winnie the Pooh es mi favorito.' ¡Que linda es! El Fashion Square esta a un lado del freeway Ventura. Ya la pasamos." She pointed towards the driver. *"Este enojon no sabe, pero nada."*

The bus came to a stop in front of the mall. Amaryllis pushed on the hydraulic handles and stepped down. Behind her stood a young girl wearing a Perma-press fast food service uniform. A string of beads hung from her neck and each ear bore studs, rings and small feathers. Her face looked both worried and angry. Amaryllis smiled at her compassionately and spoke.

"Do you happen to know where Donut Basket is?"

"It's in Sherman Oaks Fashion Square. This is Sherman Oaks Galleria. Cross the street and get back on the bus in the opposite direction."

"Back on the..." Amaryllis glanced across the street and saw a bus pull away. "Couldn't I walk?"

"It's pretty far, but if you keep going that way to Hazeltine and then turn left, you'll find it eventually."

"Thanks." Amaryllis took a deep breath, headed towards the corner curb and waited for the light to change. She looked out at her first obstacle, the intersection. Sidewalks, high-rise offices and twelve lanes of traffic (left turn on arrow only) looked strictly ordered and unormanmented except for a small polished tile mural directly ahead.

Crossing, she stepped onto the opposite sidewalk and came face-to-face with the mosaic facade of Mission Home Savings and Loan. A robed and hooded Junipero Serra, cross-bearing fist overhead, blessed basket-bearing children, his dark brown garment matching the color of their skin. Amaryllis leaned against a weathered bell-shaped marker that read, "The King's Road—*El Camino Real.*" Bus placards and history finals still fresh in her mind, she no longer felt lost. Modern as this asphalt intersection may appear, beneath it lay dirt trails of soil, oil, rock, root and bone.

El Camino Real, two hundred years ago, her professor had said, connected Missions San Gabriel and San BuenaVentura. San Fernando del Rei, set near the foothills in the abundantly fertile valley later to bear its name, from this corner, lay ten miles due north.

The choice of public art commemorating this turnoff made Amaryllis slightly sick. Catholic Fathers and basket-bearing children? California was a Spanish colony (like Cuba or Nicaragua or Puerto Rico). Padres were directed to oversee the servicing of the Military, not host Bring-Your-Own-Basket Potlucks.

They enslaved the Fernandeño. Children may have been blessed, but then were held as lure to their families. Baskets were not quaintly received, but confiscated; their makers, punished. Tribes were commandeered away from their villages and forced into daily work regimens as long and monotonous as the Mission's "picturesque" arcade.

Adobe block by block, the Fernandeño erected the church's thick imprisoning walls. They were forced to pitch the roof then top it with disapproving statues and threatening crucifixes. Native hands were directed to install the bells that tolled as their people, along with every other California tribe that fell captive to the Missions, disappeared.

Amaryllis looked at the line of cars beneath the red arrow. They don't know what they're doing. Waiting for the signal to change, staring up at the street names, they didn't see the irony. From BuenaVentura ("blissful good fortune") to Sepulveda ("place of burial") was what this turn meant to the subjugated original residents of Topanga, Tujunga and Cahuenga. Disease, forced labor, torture and death awaited. This was the turnoff to the Workhouse.

Amaryllis shook her head then found a fallen branch and picked it up. Beginning her walk, she ran it across the fronts of stores and restaurants. Doubts surfaced in her mind and a pang of regret struck in her stomach. She had forgotten just how depressing the Valley was. After months of strolling the wooded Berkeley campus, staying up nights in airy libraries and cozy study rooms, what had convinced her to come down to this grid of sad roads and minimum wage opportunities? Maybe that recruiter had misled her. Was she really ready to play for a professional barnstorming team? She was just a third-year college forward. Her mind drifted back to the night the draft scout had sat in the bleachers staring and taking notes.

It had been a gloomy "Golden Bear Classic." With just over six minutes remaining, Stanford's Tanya Banning (the Division I probable "Player of the Year") sunk turnaround bank after turnaround bank. Banning always went on a terror in the second half. Thick and muscular, she was seemingly unstoppable, drawing fouls and widening the scoring gap. Time-out was called after "Player of the Year" sunk yet another bank shot over Berkeley's All-American center, Janis Tanichek.

Coach Jack Paroni took his favorite player by the arms, "That's it, Janis. I don't want to do it, but you're coming out for a while."

"But I only have two fouls."

"Even so, we can't let them open up like this."

"It's not my fault. Give me another chance."

"That's not what I want to hear." His Mr. Understanding Coach routine was slipping fast. "First it was, 'Just give me room, I can handle her.' Then it was, 'Back off and don't get in my way.' Or do you forget the last time-out?"

"But nobody is helping me out."

"Janis, everyone is helping you out!" he shouted, then, trying hard to regain his patience, softened his voice again. "She's scoring on you both sides, up and down, top and bottom."

His sleeve was tugged on by Assistant Coach Cheryl Fergueson. The only woman on the coaching squad, Cheryl was respected for her intelligent strategy and last-minute clutch cool. "Amaryllis," said Cheryl into Paroni's ear. It wasn't kosher for Coach to receive instructions from his assistant, however, in pressure situations, he relied heavily on Fergueson's advice. It was rumored that Paroni would never have made it to the playoffs last year without her.

Tanichek, ignored the assistant and pled her case. "If Tina could help me out down low, I'd stand a much better chance. I'll try playing her close."

Fergueson shook her head. "Amaryllis," she repeated.

Paroni, irritated at the two vying for his decision, resumed shouting. "Tina can't help you down low. Rene can help you down low, but you two aren't even speaking to each other. You tried playing her close last half. It didn't work then either." He gave Fergueson a quick, careful glance, then returned to Tanichek. "I'm sorry, Janis. I don't want to lose this one. I'll put you back in as soon as possible."

"Jack," said Cheryl. "Amaryllis is our defensive specialist. We've been training her for just this situation. Now's our chance to use her."

Paroni glanced to the far end of the bench at his least favorite player. "She's a forward, not a center. She can't shoot. She can barely dribble."

"Jack, at this point, you're not looking for someone to shoot or dribble. You're looking for someone to stop Banning. She'll eat us up if we let her go on like this. She's just about their only shooter. Stop her, and their whole game will collapse. We'll take over easily, just like in North Carolina."

"Oh yeah?"

"Yeah. Amaryllis won't shoot or dribble. She'll just pass it off to Rene."

The logic seemed to penetrate. Paroni considered it briefly as the time-in buzzer sounded and Cheryl instructed six-foot, mop-headed Amaryllis Seltzer to rise and remove her jacket.

Amaryllis moved slowly, having been benched the entire game and also most of the season. Her lack of playing time was not a reflection of her ability. It was a result of her obstinate attitude. She had refused to submit to Paroni's tirades and had remained rebellious throughout the season, clowning around whenever the opportunity arose. Twice she had walked out during a postgame lecture. Every practice, she had rolled her eyes, made faces and asked ridiculous questions: "Where do we change? Can we keep our uniforms? Do we handwash them or have them dry-cleaned? When we travel, do we get a room all to ourselves?"

Cheryl massaged the back of the girl's neck as she guided her over to Paroni. "Just like we practiced," she whispered in her ear. "Front her. Don't let the ball in. If she does get it, arms up, but no fouls. When you get in trouble, let everyone know—don't wait." Amaryllis nodded absently, having heard the same instructions at least a hundred times. "Hustle. Bend your knees and stay on the balls of your feet. Block the passing lane and remember—box out." Cheryl shook down a pair of long arms and squeezed two muscular shoulders. She smiled into Amaryllis' face. "Okay, now shut your mouth and nod your head until you're in the game."

In the bleachers, the band quieted down and on the floor, the cheerleaders cleared off. The time-in buzzer sounded. Paroni took #24 by the arms. "I want you to listen carefully. No shots. Not even a lay-up. As soon as you get the ball, you pass it off to Rene." She nodded silently as she received instructions from a man she both feared and disliked. His pedantic, insulting tone continued. "I think you know the rest, but in case you don't, it's easy to remember. You shut down Banning!"

Ventura Boulevard was longer and wider than any street in Berkeley (where Amaryllis dormed during semesters) or Santa Cruz (where she lived with her mother the rest of the time). Traffic roared by and a white pickup truck sounded its alarm and flashed its tail lights. The sun warmed her skin and a slight breeze blew through her curly dark hair. With bladder full and pressing, she knocked on the window of a gas station and felt her skin grow hot from the reflection off the two-inch plate glass.

"May I use the toilet?" she asked. The attendant shook his head and pointed to a restaurant down the street. She headed towards its entrance.

The manager of Chez Bernard was handsome. His long brown hair was slicked back and he wore a shirt and tie patterned with old newspaper headlines. He surveyed Amaryllis' fashionable, loose linen slacks and matching oversized blouse. "Good! You're here," he said enthusiastically before she could speak. "Go back and see Patricia. She'll tell you where to put your things."

"But, I just want to use the toilet."

"Yes, she'll show you. Go on. She's waiting."

Walking towards the back, she ducked inside the bathroom, relieved herself for rapturous seconds, washed her hands and face, took several deep breaths and a long look in the mirror, then decided to brush her teeth and comb her hair as well. Swinging open the bathroom door, she nearly crashed into a stunningly beautiful young woman with glowing dark eyes. The woman's astonishing figure bore a pair of standard black waitress pants and a near see-thru white blouse. Amaryllis looked down. "Are you Patricia?"

"Yes."

"I'm not who you think I am."

"Who do I think you are?"

"I don't know. But, I tried to explain to that guy in front that I just wanted to use the toilet, but he kept shouting at me to go see you."

"Steve thought you were the new waitress? He never listens. You're six inches taller than she is. I told him she was nice-looking, so I guess he thought you were her." Amaryllis lowered her head and smiled at the compliment. "Yeah, you're just his type. Don't worry. I'll explain to him. You can get out through that door. But if you ever want to work as a waitress, I know you could get a job here."

Amaryllis opened the rear exit door, walked through the parking lot, took one look back, then continued her sidewalk course. When she came to Hazeltine Avenue, she headed north to Riverside Drive. And finally, nearly an hour after getting off the bus, Amaryllis reached her destination—Sherman Oaks Fashion Square. The walk had done her good. She felt revitalized, enthusiastic, ready to get that job.

The donut decorated door the man had described was right off the entrance to the mall. The owner, short and stocky, grinned at her. He was holding a tray of plastic forks, half-eaten food and Styrofoam cups. "Can I help you?" he asked. A feeling of foreboding overcame her. Her confidence vanished and she became tongue-tied. Now hold on. Why was she letting a balding, five-foot six-inch mall tenant intimidate her? She could handle some of the best college centers in the NCAA and she'd proved it that same night against Stanford.

"Number 24 Amy Seltzer now in the ball game for the Golden Bears replacing Janis Tanichek," the deep-voiced broadcasting grad student had announced.

She took her position guarding man-to-man against Ms. Most

Likely to Be Player of the Year. Leaning heavy into Banning's chest like a fresh dance partner, she could smell her opponent's breath and body, yet avoided her stare. Head down, she momentarily studied the muscular thighs and strapping calves. Some said Banning looked like a guy; others, like a guy you wouldn't want to meet in a dark alley. Amaryllis admired this fine opponent and savored the opportunity to tame her. The label "Player of the Year" only added to the challenge. To Amaryllis, too much publicity took away from a player's prowess. What did the PR department know? Something perverse made her feel confident that she could, and would, "shut down Banning."

Stanford passed the ball crosscourt and back while Banning posted up at the edge of the key. Having witnessed each of her fourteen rebounds from the bench, Amaryllis knew she had to keep her away from the basket. Banning knocked down Amaryllis' extended arm to receive a pass. She immediately tossed it out, but then signaled that she wanted it back.

"Front her! Front her!" yelled Cheryl from the sidelines. Amaryllis shifted her position as the players swirled and jockeyed. The Stanford point was looking to lob, but instead passed it to the wing. "Get back! Get back!" yelled Cheryl. Amaryllis swung back behind Banning and braced herself. Banning turned and bolted. Ready, Amaryllis shifted with her, preferring to remain face-to-face (giving up any chance at a rebound) rather than allow her assignment to penetrate the key. A shot went up. By the disappointed expression in Banning's eyes, she knew the Bears had the ball.

Number 24's next job was to rebound and set pics for Cal's shooters. She rolled off Stanford's frenzied guards, relieving the pressure on Rene. A bounce pass went out to the side for a three-point attempt. The ball ricocheted off the rim, and Amaryllis angled in for leverage. She sprang straight up, came down with the offensive rebound and passed it back out to Rene, as instructed. Amaryllis rolled again and set another pic clearing a lane down the center. Rene did not use it, so Amaryllis rolled back out of the key to avoid a "three seconds" violation, planted her feet to the side of the point guard at the top of the key and yelled out, "Come around! Come around!" Rene, her defensive assignment blocked, was then free for her favorite ten-foot jumper. Angry from being scored on, the blocked guard shoved Amaryllis off her and screamed at her teammates in frustration, "Call out pics, damn it!"

By now Tanya was livid and wanted the ball right away. Once in her grasp, she slapped on it as if punishing a child. Her elbow hammered Amaryllis' ribs. Her hips and rear rested on Amaryllis' upper leg. This was bad news. A moment later and Cal's #24 would be singing, "You dropped a bomb on me," as Tanya banked in another one. What was there left to do but yell for help?

"Help!" shouted Amaryllis loud, reaching in and trying to keep a hand on the ball.

Rene, leaving her assignment to double-team the giant, managed to get a jump ball, but Stanford retained alternating possession. This gave Amaryllis a few seconds to think. She knew she could not stand still, but instead, like Cheryl had said, must "hustle, block the passing lane and box out." Tanya couldn't score if she couldn't get possession. Amaryllis, on the balls of her feet, deflected the inbounds pass. There was a scramble and the racing Stanford point grabbed it back. She gave a frustrated "Who is this chick?" look to Banning who returned a "Don't worry—I'll take care of it" nod.

Hustling back inside the key, Amaryllis was late and found herself again face-to-face with Banning. Knee's bent, she jabbed forward to get a hand on the ball. Banning threw an elbow and rocked her hips preparing to shoot her famous bank. Amaryllis' only remaining option was a block.

"Pass it off!" she hollered as a ploy to quicken the attempt. "Pass it off!"

It worked. Banning double-pumped twice, then turned for the shot. Ignoring the fakes, Amaryllis timed the jump and deflected it back just as it was released. Tanya, regained possession but was embarrassed and angry hearing the standard "Get that shit ooout!" taunt from the fraternity crowd. She slammed in again, bouncing her hip hard off of Amaryllis' upper leg and began rocking back and forth again.

"Ball! Ball! Pass it off!" shouted Amaryllis. The shot came again. Blocked. Tanya grabbed it back and drove, foolishly rolling left, putting the ball on the floor. Delighted, Amaryllis immediately yelled for help, as much as she could get. "HELP! HELP! HELP!" she shouted. The zone converged in on the giant, Rene rushing in from behind, slapping the ball from Banning's grasp, scooping it up and fast-breaking three-on-two for a triple-pass lay-in "and one." The crowd grew loud and obnoxious and remained that way as their home team caught up and passed the rival visitors. Kept scoreless for three minutes, "Player of the Year" was subbed out furious and frustrated.

During the Stanford time-out, Paroni substituted his famed center back in without delay. "Okay Tanichek, you're back in. Tie it up!"

Ignored by her coach, #24 took her seat breathing heavy and sweating buckets. Fergueson nonchalantly paced over to the far side of the row of plastic chairs, pinched Amaryllis' knee and flipped a towel over her shoulder. "Relax Ms. 'D', you might have just changed the 'Player of the Year' selection for the season."

"Who me?" laughed Amaryllis between breaths. She wiped the sweat from her eyes, mouthed sounds and made strange faces. The playing time had had a giddying effect on her. She could just barely keep herself from acting like a complete jerk.

Fergueson knelt down like she was watching the game. "I have a surprise," she said into her player's ear. "There's someone who wants to talk to you after the game."

"Oh goody. Did he bring a box of chocolates?" she asked wide-eyed, tongue out.

"No, *she* didn't bring a box of chocolates. And you might want to act your age for a change. This might be a nice opportunity. It's Flor Ortega."

Amaryllis' clowning expression disappeared. Her smile fell and her eyebrows furrowed. She grabbed the assistant coach by the arm. "*The Flor Ortega?*" Cheryl Fergueson nodded and pointed to a woman with a clipboard sitting directly behind the typing statistician. "Flor Ortega wants to see me?" Cheryl nodded again. "Why?"

"She's recruiting for the Exiles."

"The Exiles?" She said the words softly.

Cheryl eyed the empty seat next to Coach Paroni. She had to get back. "Maybe she'll have to be the one to explain."

Amaryllis' watched the game momentarily, but couldn't help squinting towards the mysterious visitor. What could women's basketball pioneer Flor Ortega want with her?

The donut shop owner cleared his throat. "Young lady, can I help you?"

Amaryllis took a deep breath and spoke up. "I'm applying for the cashier's job. I called you this morning."

The owner tipped the contents of the plastic tray into the green trash bag. His face became stern and unforgiving, disdainfully staring at the new applicant. "I thought you said you were twenty-three."

"I am twenty-three."

"Really?"

"Yes."

"Where are you from? Why do you want to work here?"

"Well, I was born in Los Angeles. I used to live with my grandmother on the other side of the hill. Well actually, I kind of lived on both sides of the hill." She was becoming a bit chatty from nervousness. "Since then I've lived with my mother up north. I'm down here for the summer to play basketball. I need to buy a car and pay for team and travel expenses."

"Do you have experience working with food?"

"I helped prepare meals at home. You see, we live—I mean my mother and I—in a communal house in Santa Cruz. Everyone takes turns in the kitchen. Also, during semesters I volunteer at a health food co-op in town—off campus in Berkeley, that is. You see, I'm still in college. I washed the vegetables, stocked the shelves and cleaned up. I applied for work-study, but—"

"So you have a high school diploma?"

"Yes."

"Really?"

"Yes, I even graduated a semester early."

"Then sit down and I'll be with you in a few minutes." He stood peeking out the glass door. When he was satisfied that whoever he was looking for wasn't coming, he went to the register to pull out an application and a standard yellow pencil. "Are you good with numbers?"

"Yes, especially #24," she joked. "You see, that's my number when I play. Luckily, no one on the Exiles—that's the team I'll be playing for—has that number, so I can keep it down here too. The thing is, though, I can't understand why they—"

"Have you almost finished college?"

"No."

"What year are you in?"

"I just finished my junior year."

"There, I got you! If you're twenty-three, why are you only a junior?"

She bit her thumbnail. Why was she only a junior? "Basketball practice takes up a lot of time and energy. I only have a few classes each term." She pressed her fingers to her chest. "I try to keep politically active as well. Also, I can't make up my mind what to major in."

"You can't make up your mind?"

"There are so many things to be. You see, my dad wants me to study politics. My mother is in favor of something more practical like medicine, but really—this semester—I did best on my history final. For now, I'm out of school and this summer is going to be a real challenge! Getting out into the real world," she said, deliberating a moment, "and trying to apply what I've been reading and memorizing and discussing—"

"Apply?"

"Yeah, you know, all those theories and formulas and arguments. How do they really help you to deal with people and everyday life?"

"Everyday life? Apply?"

"Yes, apply. Apply myself. I'm not timid, really. I like to get involved in difficult situations. Try new things. Meet new people. Become totally immersed, use all my senses and feel the world living and breathing around me. And for my occupation, I'd like to work in a field I can really wrestle with. Have a job I can grow into. One that has meaning." She thought a moment. "I guess I just want to learn how to think for myself. How to confront the world instead of appease it. So many of my friends keep saying they're so powerless to make any kind of change. But, it all depends on what it is. Maybe people can't change the whole world, but within our own spheres of influence, I believe it's still possible. Things are changing all the time. Life is change. And that's what I want—to make change."

The owner was staring out the glass door again. He cleared his throat. "What's that? Ah yes—make change. Would you come over here a moment please?" She stood and joined him at the register.

"If the customer eats two dollars' worth of donuts and gives you a ten-dollar bill, how much would you give him back?"

She looked from side to side, to the door, then answered. "Eight dollars."

"Very good." The owner made a check on his clipboard. "What if it was one dollar and twenty-nine cents and they gave you a five-dollar bill?"

"Three dollars and seventy-one cents."

"What if it was four dollars and forty-seven cents and they gave you a fifty-dollar bill?"

She calculated. "Forty-five dollars and fifty-three cents."

"Seven dollars and eighty-nine cents and they gave you two hundred and ninety-one dollars and sixty-nine cents?"

"I would ask them why they were giving me so much money."

"But how much would you give them back?"

She went blank. "Doesn't it say how much to give them back on the register anyway?"

"Very good! That's just my point. Never do the counting in your head. You'll make a mistake. Always use the register." He pointed a finger. "Never try to do it in your head. Never, never."

"I didn't realize."

"It's very important. But not only that. We'll soon officially be a franchise and the company policy is that you can only be late twice. On the third time, you'll be terminated. Can you get here on time?"

"Yes."

"Really?"

She nodded.

"Okay then, fill this out and don't leave anything blank."

She took the paper and quickly removed her recently purchased Job Application Pen. She stared down at the form and grimaced. Damn, stuck on the very first anwser.

Looking over her shoulder, the owner spread out his hands and turned his eyes to the ceiling. "It's not hard. It's easy. Just put your name inside the blank space."

"Well, legally my name is still Amaryllis Seltzer, but my mother unofficially changed my last name to her maiden name after she divorced my father."

"So you have two real names. Now I've heard everything. Please just put your legal name."

Amaryllis began filling in the form: name, address, city.

"You live in Northridge? You must have really got it during the Earthquake." His voice was loud.

She didn't respond but wrote quickly, detirmined to finish. Finally, she clicked her pen shut, sat up straight, and handed over the completed document.

The owner sat down and kneaded his jaw. "If you are such a sports superstar, why do you want to work here when you could have a multi-million-dollar contract instead?"

"I wish. Actually, like I said before, I'm just trying to pay my team expenses and save up for a car." Trying? She had to do it or it was back to Santa Cruz.

"This is an off-season offer," Ortega had begun. "The NCAA won't allow direct payment. Travel expenses, room and board will all have to be your responsibility. Do you have any relatives in Southern California?"

"My dad lives in Northridge."

"That's close enough. See if you can live with him. You'll only run with us for ten weeks. It won't be worth your while to get your own place. Do you own a car?"

"No. I'm against air pollution."

"Huh?" Ortega twisted her face. "Well, you'll need a car. Does your father drive?"

"Yes."

"Do you think he'd let you borrow his car during the week?"

"I don't know."

"We're scheduled for two local exhibitions and three away games. We practice three times a week, so if your father can't loan you his, you'll have to get your own."

With this opportunity of playing for a professional team, the day-to-day logistics just hadn't seemed important. It was not until she had been picked up at LAX and arrived back at Lasaine Avenue that some of the excitement had worn off. There amid old newspapers, dirty dishes and stale smells, she had first understood the necessity of getting out and getting a job.

She raised her head. The owner was staring at her body. "Just how tall are you?"

Yes of course, why should he leave out her favorite question. The one she'd only been asked three thousand times since her growth spurt in the last year of high school.

"I'm six feet tall."

"Do you smoke?"

"No."

"Drink?"

"No."

"Take drugs?"

"No."

"Are you a U.S. citizen?"

"I told you I was born in Los Angeles." She was losing patience.

"Are you married?"

"What?" She forced a smile. "How many more questions are you going to ask?" If the answer was other than just one, she would leave.

"Just one." He came uncomfortably close. "What kind of place is this?"

"What kind of place is this? You mean what would I call it?"

"Yes, that's right. What would you call it? What kind of place is this?"

"It's a donut shop."

He slapped his hand against his forehead. "No! No! No!"

"No?"

"No! Look around. Look. What kind of place is this?"

She avoided his eyes, tapped her foot and looked around—glass shelves, coffee pots, fiberglass seats and tables, linoleum floor, donut decorated door. Then she spotted something—the little window to the parking lot.

"Drive-thru donut shop."

"No."

"Home delivery donut shop."

"No. No." He held his breath then grabbed a roll of paper towels and tore off a handful. "I want you to look around carefully. Here is the microwave. Here is the hot dog cooker. Here is the soda fountain. Here is the coffee area. The disposable utensils are here. This is the napkin dispenser. These are the salt and pepper package containers. This is the tea display. And here, are the donuts. Now, what kind of place is this?"

She put her index finger to her lips. Her boyfriend, Harold, would really be sarcastic if she couldn't even get a job at a donut shop. She raised both hands in the air. "Donut...Basket!" Who knows, maybe he was looking for an applicant with team spirit.

"Wait. Lets try this another way. Which direction did you drive from?"

"I didn't drive. I walked from Ventura and Sepulveda."

"Didn't drive? You walked all that way?" He was mystified, but then something important occurred to him. "Then, that means you went down Ventura Boulevard, right?"

She nodded.

"Well, what did you pass?"

"Oh," she muttered, realizing the correct answer. If she hadn't stopped to clean up and use the restroom, she might not have gotten it at all. Her stomach began to turn. She closed one eye and grimaced. "A restaurant?"

"You've almost got it. What kind of restaurant?"

She tried not to leave anything out. "N...n...nice, plush, f...f...fancy, upscale restaurant?"

He inhaled, sighed, then humbly confessed to a slightly lower category. "Donut Restaurant."

"Donut Restaurant," she repeated robotically.

"Fantastic!" he exclaimed clapping his hands together. "You're just right. You start tomorrow at six."

Already hearing the early-morning alarm and bus brakes screeching to a halt in the five a.m. darkness, Amaryllis started towards the door. She pushed it half open, then paused and turned back for one last look. The shelves and microwave, the linoleum floor and soda dispenser, the hot dog cooker and the fiberglass tables all seemed to be urging her to speak. "Before I do, may I ask you something?"

"Of course, always ask. There is no such thing as a dumb question."

"I'm sorry to be the one to tell you this, but, this isn't a restaurant. This is a donut shop. I'd like to work for you, but I'd probably last about as long as the last employee if I tried to pretend this place is Chez Bernard instead of Donut Basket." She hesitated a moment. "Look, if you misrepresent yourself, people resent you for it. If I tell someone I work at a restaurant and they come here, they'll laugh and call me a liar. But if I tell them I work at a 'donut shop', they'll come here and be proud of me. Now, wouldn't that be better?"

Amaryllis soon found herself walking down the street having to use the toilet again and unemployed just like before. Out there among the signs, the apartment complexes, the corporate headquarters, the flood control channel, the freeway overpass and the traffic, she felt suddenly very lonely, missing the beautiful campus up north, the hikes in the hills, the exciting lectures, stimulating rallies and alluring excursions into the city. To top it off, this was summer break. She should be taking it easy playing backgammon with her mother on their porch overlooking Santa Cruz Bay. What was she doing here?

"Mom, the guy was nuts. Donut Basket!? You know what I should have told him..." She was talking to herself. "I should have told that egomaniac to take his donut basket and..." Yeah, yeah, yeah, but even so, what was there to do now? Go home and call Harold. He wouldn't understand. After he got through laughing, he'd probably just say, "Stick with it. You can do it." Yeah, thanks Harold. The bus pulled up just ahead of her. She ran and shouted but was too late. Well, if nothing's going right she'd better just take it easy a while, walk, view the distant mountains, breath the sweet Valley air.

Ambling down the long sidewalk, she soon came to a large park with a perimeter of several miles. Its large, open fields spanned the space between two major streets and she was immediately sucked in by the grasses and tall trees. Still unemployed, discouraged, she walked through the set of baseball diamonds and soccer fields, strolled by the tennis courts and swimming pool, then doubled back to the basketball gym.

Pushing open the double latched doors, textures blurred and sounds echoed. After being in the bright sun, the interior colors seemed dead. She felt a knot in her throat. The place looked like it hadn't gotten a good cleaning in years. Dust coated every surface. The buzzing wire-enclosed sodium lamps shone a pale light, turning the air a creepy yellow. The chocolate-colored doors and dirty beige stage curtains added to the uncared-for appearance. At one end of the thick hazy space, a lanky eleven-year-old with a new crew cut taunted his small challenger who was dressed in a green NBA jersey extending to his knees. "Scared to shoot, halfpint?"

"In your face, wus!"

They'd been at it for hours. "Screw you shrimp."

"Eat this beanpole."

Amaryllis sat down on the courtside bench, stared up at the walls and rafters, and commenced a mental voyage back in time. Like Kane dying in Xanadu, she uttered a single word, "Natalie."

The only girls on the City Park/Rec. team, elbow to elbow, knee to knee, they had played in gyms just like this, each, the other's only away game security. On their own turf, however, it was a different story. Day in and day out, hour after hour, they had practiced; one game ends, the other begins.

"What do you want to do?"

"I don't know. What do you want to do?"

"Wanna play one more?"

"Yeah, okay."

And so, the day's after-school occupation would last into the night. Their parents might have worried if they hadn't undoubtedly known exactly where the two could be located. Buckets to 16. Baskets to 36. How can you defend against someone who had every move in the book: underhand finger-roll, double-pump fake fallaway, reverse mini-skyhook, three-pointer from the very edge of the paint—anything was possible. Cards, magazines, books, media guides, stat sheets, NBA T-shirts, official starter jackets, fluorescent wristbands, a collector's item red-white-and-blue ABA ball, beautifully smooth espresso brown skin and shiny tight black braids—Natalie had them all.

From age ten to thirteen, they held the deed; the shady outdoor court by the fence was their personal property. Hang out, play a few games, practice new moves or whatever: "Tip-in", "Twenty-one", "Spin the ball on one finger longer than me", "Consecutive free throws in a row", "W.H.O.R.E.S". (Horse), and of course, hours and hours of "One-on-one".

On the team together, they made twelve-year-old history, and slo-mo instant replayed it again and again: last-minute shots, slick passes, smart come backs to manic foul-mouthed deluded dads that posed as weekend coaches. The time when Natalie stole the referee's whistle (after he bawled her out for nothing), hid in the storage room and blew it every ten seconds during the game—stopping play every time. The time during "First three to make it" when Natalie missed the whole backboard after Klutzy made his shot, just to show him how much she wanted *not* to be on his team. The time they tried to make personalized sports trading cards from their own photo booth pictures. Brushing against Natalie's smooth skin, bouncing off her back, leaning on her shoulder, waiting for her next trick shot—that would always be Amaryllis' "Rosebud".

Beanpole burped. "Take that in here again fool and I'll slam your punk ass."

Halfpint burped back. "You couldn't swat a fly you too tall turd."

Amaryllis looked down, rubbed her forehead, rose and left. Sun hit her and she shielded her eyes until they were readjusted. Still savoring her pleasant recollection, she began to plan ahead for life's next trick play. Drop in on a department store personnel office? Temporary employment agencies? Telemarketing? Data Entry?

She headed back towards the hills along Ventura. Time passed quickly and soon in the distance, she spotted the black-and-white facade of Chez Bernard. What about that offer? Maybe Patricia had really meant it. It was much fancier than a donut shop. "Hold it, I might get tips too!"

Amaryllis walked a brisk two blocks and arrived at the canopied entrance. She swung open the lavish plate glass door and disappeared inside. Ten minutes later, she emerged with a new uniform inside a shiny black box.

The bus arrived. She climbed aboard, placed the box on the seat next to her and settled back . It was just turning dark and the tinted windows dully mirrored the interior. In the reflection, she spotted those same placards floating above and recalled that angry and worried young girl who'd given her directions earlier. Suddenly, there, staring back at her, eyebrows furrowed, eyes glaring, jaw clenched, was another face, just as tense—her own. "Why?"

Street lamps switched on in groups, emitting their eerie orange glow and blurring storefront details into twilight. Doors slid shut and wheels rolled away from the curb as the bus headed towards Northridge—her summer home.

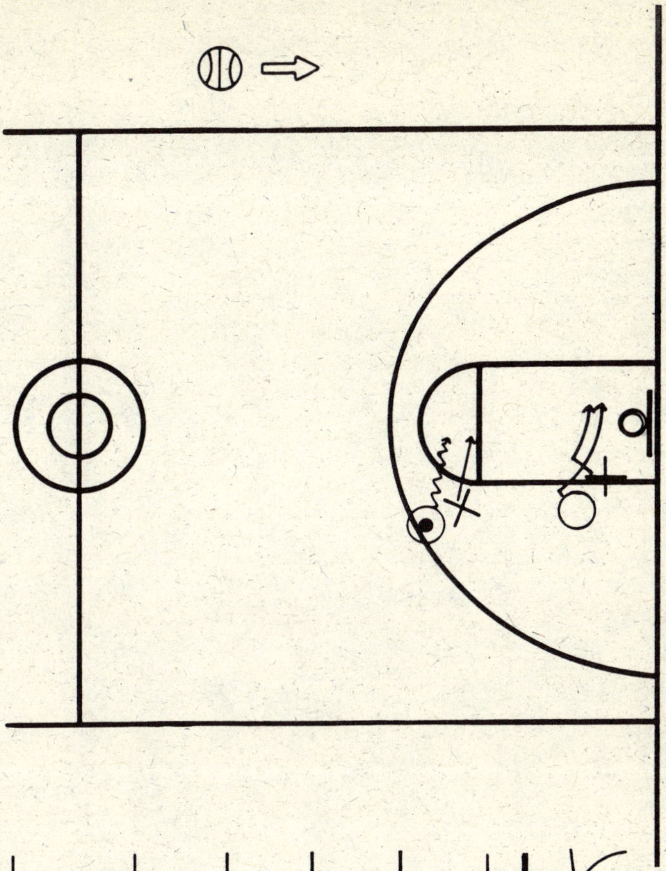

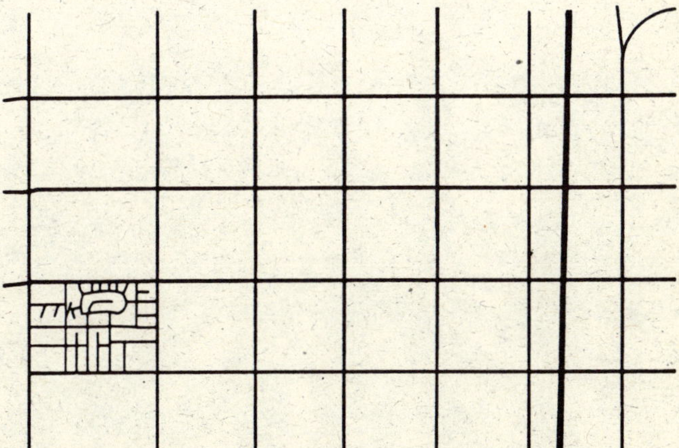

1/17/94
M
A
X

Eight-Lane Drain 2

Max pressed the VCR play button with his toe. He tilted back into the recliner and stared at his foot propped up in front of the screen. With the thriller movie soundtrack moaning in the background, his crooked digits, flaking skin, bulging varicose veins, gray toe hair and protruding ankles, inspired an eerie question: how could a pair of feet age faster than the body they were attached to? He considered pursuing the mystery further in front of the bedroom mirror, but dismissed the idea, pressed the stop button, grabbed the TV remote and began changing channels.

The front door creaked open. Amaryllis walked in, threw down her bag and collapsed onto the sofa. "Hey, guess what."

Eyes glued to the screen, Max ate a handful of microwave popcorn. "What?"

"I got a job at Chez Bernard!"

"Is that stuffy place still in business?"

"Stuffy? It seemed pretty stylish to me. Maybe they've remodeled. I start Friday night and get minimum wage minus eighteen per-cent during training, plus half my tips. Here's my uniform." She showed him the black-and-white checkered box. "The manager said I didn't have to pay for it now. He'd just take the cost out of my first paycheck."

"Did he tell you how much 'cost' he'd take out?"

"No, but he seemed real nice—a sharp dresser too."

"Did you open the box to see whether the uniform was new or used?"

Amaryllis opened the box. "They must have made a mistake. This is a see-thru blouse. I thought only the hostess had to wear one. Sheesh, what a day." She replaced the garment and sighed.

"I've been asleep." He switched channels.

"Are you feeling okay? You haven't left that chair since I got here. And you snored so loud last night. I couldn't sleep."

"I went out earlier this afternoon—to the supermarket and the ninety-nine-cent Chinese buffet." He rubbed his belly. "Thanks for your concern, but early retirement suits me just fine. Twenty-two years of Patient Transporting finished—over! No more wheelchairs. No more elevators. No more techs, nurses, doctors or administrators. Just lots of free time." He stretched and yawned. "Today, I cleaned out the garage. You wouldn't believe the stuff I found." He reached down to the coffee table and picked up a dirt-stained photo album with a large yellow Smiley Face on its cover. "Have a nice day," he said dropping it onto his daughter's lap.

"Wow!" she exclaimed, turning the pages. "I remember you used to take some pictures, but these are beautiful." She studied the eight-by-ten action glossies. "Wait, I know who that is—Robert Kennedy."

"And John Kennedy and Hubert Humphrey and Pat Brown and

Tom Bradley. Yeah, back then, I was an aspiring world-class photojournalist. I covered all the local happenings, running all over. Marches, protests, assassinations, suicides, murders, overdoses, speeches, uprisings, concerts—I was there for all of them, snapping my little heart out."

Amaryllis turned to a photo of a bearded man, camera in hand, with squinting eyes and a broad dimpled smile. All the traces of newfound freedom—curly hair waving in the wind, easy going loose striped T-shirt, political button above the pocket—shone from the high-contrast self-portrait. "This is you!"

"Yeah," he replied watching the screen. "That was after graduation, when I was working for the alternative press—1965. My mother wanted me to study medicine, but I spent all my time in the darkroom."

"You were a full-blown hippie!" she exclaimed. "Not bad, Max, not bad at all. I bet the women loved your beard."

"They liked the hair on top of my head too, when I had it. But that's all over now—finished, gone, kaput. Just like everything else—what we said, what we did—lost, all lost, all over now."

"Everything's over? What are you talking about?"

"Just look around you. Where's the hope? Where's the outrage? Where's the protest? Everyone is numb to their surroundings. They can't even be shocked anymore. Look at this video." He leaned forward, pressed the remote with his thumb and the VCR play button with his toe. "I haven't seen this in thirty years." He adjusted the volume. "*Psycho was the most* upsetting, frightening movie of its day. Now, I bet the shower scene wouldn't even make a fourth-grader flinch.

"Maybe it's just because they've copied it so much."

"It's our whole society. What was shocking then is common today. It can't even be called a 'thriller' anymore. It's more of a documentary. Employees stealing from employers, people driving around in their cars alone, police asking questions, insulting salespeople ripping you off, mentally disturbed killers cleaning up after themselves—all the elements are there in plain view, it's just like everyday life."

"Ah come on, Max. I thought horror movies were supposed to be fun. You're not supposed to analyze them to death. You're just supposed to scream at the top of your lungs."

"Fun? This is dreary. Even the director's famed dark humor has become passé and boring. It doesn't matter how you analyze the plot, it doesn't hold together anymore. No one would trust a strange man in a lonely motel. Everyone today assumes you're a mass murderer already."

Amaryllis smiled and patted her father's shoulder. "Lighten up a little. Maybe you've just seen it too many times. Change the channel if you don't like it. Watch a cartoon."

"A cartoon? All right then." He flipped through the stations. "Look here—Disney. Now he has his own channel." Max slouched over. "I've been propagandized by that man my entire life. Every birthday we made straight to the movies to see the latest sicko adaptation of American literature. Grad night and prom, we'd drive right out to that huge

Anaheim parking lot. Magic Kingdom? Ha! Try insidious right-wing mind-control concentration camp!"

"I kind of always liked the Peter Pan ride. You get to fly through Wendy's bedroom and—"

"But don't you see how sickening the whole thing is?" He turned away from the screen and waved the remote at his daughter. "Don't you see how we've become conditioned? We'll pay a week's wage to drive through traffic, park in a grid of slots, march in line down a Main Street that never existed and sit in a circular plaza that would be fenced off if it did."

"Max—"

"Then we get lost in their themed shopping lands and become completely disoriented in their storybook sermon rides."

"Max—"

"And finally we get so tired and hungry, all we can do is search for a place to sit down and stuff our guts. And if the children object or say they're not having fun, we slap their faces."

"But Max—"

"We're all Norman Bates—peeping into little girls' bedrooms, hooting at pirate rape scenes, tisk-tisking the sight of burning settlers' cabins—all the while stirring up our own hatred, racism, sexism." Max continued louder. "We're supposed to teach our children a lesson! Teach them to stand in line quietly? Teach them to consume endlessly? Teach them to stereotype instead of consider?" He stood up. "Thirty years ago, Martin Luther King, Jr. marched in protest because they wouldn't let his daughter into Funtown; now it seems like the only place people will march is inside of it. I give up! I give up!" He sat back down.

Amaryllis got up, went to the kitchen and poked through the assortment of take-home leftovers inside the refrigerator. "But Max, if it's racist, why do so many people still go there? The lines are so long."

"People have been desensitized while corporations have mixed racism and classism. Now they give an ' Equal Opportunity' to anyone who dresses by their codes and can afford the price of admission. Try going there wearing baggy pants and not spending any money. You'll see how equal they treat you."

"What do you want—Bum-O-Land—spin around in Whirling Wine Bottles and shower off the vomit in Splash Gutter? People need to escape. Companies need to pay their bills."

"I've raised a robber baron. It's all over. My own daughter is like everyone else. You think if you don't have money you're not good enough to set foot in 'The Greediest'—uh, I mean—'Happiest Place on Earth'!"

Amaryllis was beginning to see that her objections were just fanning the blaze. And anyway, she hadn't eaten all day. "Look, so your radical past seems to be resurfacing. Let's drop it a while, sit down and stuff our guts. I'm starving!"

"Yeah, Melissa used to always end arguments like that too. You've really grown up to be a lot like her."

"Mom? What's mom got to do with this—oh, nevermind. How about we go out to dinner before your next video selection. Maybe getting out of the house for a while would cheer you up. I bet you haven't even gone into the backyard. Vines will be growing on you soon."

"Speaking of vines, tomorrow will be the day that I finally start fixing up the old garden. As for tonight, I'm fine just where I am. I think I'll order a vegetarian cheeseless pizza." He began changing channels again. "I saw a documentary this morning about the additives they put in foods. Did you know that margarine is a petroleum product? Did you know they put dyes in meat, inject BGH into dairy cows and feed hormones to chickens? Did you know they irradiate oranges?"

"Did you know donuts are an entree. Listen, If you give me the keys, *I'll* go pick up that pizza. And by the way, Flor, the team trainer, told me I'll need to be at practice three afternoons per week. Would it be all right if I borrowed your car then?"

"No problem. Just leave the keys on the telephone table when you're through."

"Are you sure that sharing the car won't interfere with your plans?"

"The only plans I have for this summer are weeding, planting an herb garden and catching up on twenty years of videos."

The next day, Amaryllis drove for the second time in seven years. She felt a guilty detached exhilaration as she passed pedestrians on side streets and zoomed along on freeways. But whatever her feelings might be, she was determined to begin the regimen that Exiles trainer Flor Ortega had recommended—a six-mile jog every day and two hours on the court. After the run and the stretching, she walked over to the college.

The L.A. Valley men's gym sat across the street from two smaller Quonset huts that formerly served both men's and women's teams. In 1956, the men moved out to a new gym leaving the huts to the women. It was only within the last twenty years that the Lady Monarchs got a gym of their own. During the daytime in summer, it's the men's gym that is left open. And with a June temperature of eighty-nine degrees, players escaping the heat filled the floor with games of five-on-five.

"Traveling!" hollered a thick-armed, six-footer wearing a tank top.

The accused, six inches shorter and fifty pounds heavier kicked the ball up into the rafters. "Forget this! How can you keep calling that shit! I quit!"

The first man outstretched his arms. "Just give it up."

"No way! I'm not giving this one up. I'm not giving this one up." He turned his back and returned to the half-court line to restart the game, but neither side would give in. The players sat down, got drinks, slapped the bleacher seats, stomped on the floor, shouted in each other's faces, and finally "shot for it."

It had been quite a while since Amaryllis had played pickup ball with men. Dividing a college schedule between studying and practice left little time and she couldn't stand the inevitable arguing. Should she put on her "game face" or just stick to the sidelines and sink some jumpers? As the battle raged in the background, a rather short, large-bellied man wearing wraparound sports glasses approached her court. He had a strange two handed pitch for a shot and a nervous too-quick dribble. He was probably in his forties, married, an office worker, and escaping from his family. He had too loud a laugh, wandering eyes and would attempt a conversation at any moment.

"Wow, you must play for a college team. Ha. Ha. Ha."

"UC Berkeley," she answered, expecting more questions, possibly the entire third degree.

He stared at her body. "You must be an All-American. Ha. Ha."

"No."

"Ha. Just down for the summer?"

"Uh-huh."

"Wow, how tall are you? Ha. Ha. Ha."

"About six feet."

He tossed the ball to himself. "When does the college season start up again?"

"November."

"Will you be playing any games in the off-season?"

"Five."

"Wow, with who?"

"The Exiles. It's a barnstorming exhibition team."

The man made a clown face. He stopped dribbling and looked around the gym. "HA! HA! You play for a barnstorming exhibition team?" He held the ball below his stomach, leaned forward and stood motionless, mouth opened wide. "Wow! Why don't you get in there and show these guys a thing or two. You can't take them seriously. You know, teach them a lesson. They're really just a bunch of babies." He turned around. "Hey, Danny!"

"What you want, chump?"

"Come here. This girl says she plays for the Exiles. Play her one-on-one."

Amaryllis stopped shooting. "Listen, I just came to practice."

"Ah come on—just one. You can beat him." He turned around again. "Come on, Danny. Come here."

"Go home, chump." Danny was in the middle of a game.

"Alright, alright," said Chump. "I'll play. Let's go to sixteen."

"No thanks. I got to get going soon."

"But you're an Exile. You should be able to take on anyone."

The ornamental white stepping-stones, red roof rocks and black asphalt driveway of 9344 Lasaine Avenue all grew hot in the noonday sun. Arriving home, Amaryllis followed a frayed brown extension cord out the rear sliding glass door, across the cracked concrete patio and over dry patches of grass until it connected with a rainbow portable party 45 record player. Daddy's scratchy selection: "Feeling Fine" by the T-Bones.

"Max, you have it on the wrong speed. It's playing too slow."

"Oh yeah." He scratched at some crabgrass with a hand shovel. "Only a few were still playable. I got tired of turning them over. They last longer that way."

"Last longer?" Amaryllis surveyed the carpet of dry pine needles, the piles of brown leaves, the dead bushes and the overgrown trees. "You really think you can fix this yard up?"

"I got the idea from watching public TV. Hydroscape's the way to go. This part will be my herb garden."

She carefully sat down on a rusty wrought iron chair. "I remember when it used to be so magical. The benches and the fountain and the big rocks. Where did you put those little animal statues and the dwarf with the wheelbarrow?"

"Don't worry. Squirrel Land is in the garage."

"How about the goldfish pond?"

"Evaporated." He picked up a pair of clippers. "I found Jack's tools in the storage shed. This was his dream garden. After Melissa left, it just withered away."

Jack Cohen (Melissa's father) wanted a "Sunset Western Garden Book" garden. A place for entertaining and for the children to enjoy. Forty years ago, when he first visited the Valley with his wife Rita, it was a spacious patchwork of farms growing oranges and truck crops. There was a small airport, a new college and an old mission. Scattered tracts were already up near Reseda Boulevard and there were plans for a freeway to be built along Sepulveda. It was February and the couple had been waiting for the rain to subside before they began navigating the flooded streets and puddles to a roadside vendor famous for asparagus, winter radishes and giant artichokes. Chestnut horses lounged in rectangular corrals sorting through moist allotments of hay. Black Angus cattle grazed along dewy slopes. The occasional freight train clanged by on its way to Oxnard. Children in cutoff pants sailed homemade rafts by the shores of miniature lakes.

"Jack, if we got a house out here, we could have garden parties. You could serve drinks from your very own bar. The kids would have more room to play."

"It would sure beat the city."

In 1964, the Cohens chose the house on Lasaine. Rita liked the French name and Jack loved the mature perennials lining the street. The backyard, naturally, he was going to do his way—lay in the sprinklers, spread the manure, plant the sod. Over the years, little by little, he planted fruit trees and wildflowers, built a gazebo and arranged huge boulders and little paths. The slumpstone property walls were lined with Mexican orange bush and benches were surrounded with Chamomile. Filling in that wide lot wasn't going to be easy.

"The garden looks so pretty, Jack. When are we going to throw a party to show it off?"

"Not yet. There's still that big empty space by the gate. And I haven't finished around the pond either."

But for more than fifteen years, no matter how he picked, pruned and dragged ten-gallon pots from here to there, the wide lot was never filled.

"Honey, I never dreamed the back could look so beautiful."

"Beautiful? I'm sick of it. Let Melissa and the freak move in. At least our granddaughter should have a place to play. As for me, I'm ready for a condo. I'll never be finished with this yard."

By the time the young Seltzer family moved in, the whole Valley had been entirely overbuilt. Throughout the sixties and seventies, tracts as large as five thousand houses might be put up within a five-year period. In some cases, entire districts were the work of a single company—razing orchards, paving wheat fields and reorienting street grids. A modern dream of semi-rural homesteads within commute time of the high-rise city had become merely a blander and wider version of the city itself.

Wide, wide, wide, why in Northridge is everything so wide? The houses, wide; the lots, wide; the streets, wide; the boulevards, enormously wide! Even Jack's cherished garden, which he filled with every tree, shrub, herb, and vine in the nursery, was always just too wide.

It was a friend of Max's that ended the mystery. One of those talkative geology majors, the kind that can lull you to sleep with facts about the earth during a simple trip to the supermarket. "Why are the streets so wide? They're wide because they're not streets, they're drainage routes. On a floodplain, if you can't dig deep, you need a wide surface to run off all that water. The whole Valley is one big drain. The streets drain into the channels. The channels drain into the river. The river drains..."

Max's wife, Melissa, left the drain in 1982 and reverted back to her maiden name, insisting her daughter do the same. Max's daily commute then included dropping his daughter off at his mother's four-unit apartment building in Fairfax, going to work, picking up his daughter and shopping for groceries on his way back to the Valley. The garden, during this time, remained ignored and unused. Four years later, when guardianship of Amaryllis was transferred to her mother, leaving Max alone with some free time for gardening, he opted instead for TV. But now, since his daughter's return, he'd gathered some energy to begin tending to it again.

Amaryllis looked concerned. "How long have you been out here?"

"Let's see. I got back from the library at about—"

"Max, you got of the house!" She clapped her hands together. "That's great!"

"It was a disaster. I watched the latest video exposé on Marilyn's murder. What a tragedy."

"Yes, she was so vulnerable."

"Not her death. What I mean is that I tried to check out a book on her instead of a video, but these days you have to read them at the reference desk because they keep disappearing. That's the tragedy."

Amaryllis knelt and picked through the hot gravel. "Why do you want to read about her anyway? It's so depressing."

"I'm just reminiscing. Marilyn, Manson, Morrison, Martin, Marley—you know, in my day I photographed them all." He looked up from his weeding. "A guy's allowed to relive his glory days, isn't he? Today I stuck with the letter 'M'; tomorrow, maybe I'll do 'D' for Angela Davis or 'H' for Patty Hearst."

"What about 'P' for you ate all the pasta."

Her father did not laugh but instead got up and tried pulling down oranges from the tree. "Just can't seem to reach the high branches like I used to. Maybe I *should* go on a diet."

Amaryllis stood and jumped up to grab them. "Hey, I have an idea. Maybe you could join a gym."

"You mean a Spa? Like Jack LaLanne?"

"Yeah, something like that. I'm going to visit Grandma and then return my uniform to that restaurant. Come along and I'll drop you at Valley Fitness Emporium while I go over the hill. You can take their Introductory Workout Tour.

"This is our step and bicycle room. There is a fifteen minute limit, but you can avoid that by becoming a VIP. Our weight room is to the left and men's lockers are to the right." The trim trainer guided Max through the glass doors and out into the main room. "We have sixty classes a week at all different levels—Jazzercise, Burnin' Abs, Step and Slide, Aquatic Conditioning, Work Your Buns Off..."

"Excuse me just a second." Max rushed outside. "WAIT!" he shrieked as his daughter and his blue Dodge pulled away. Head down, he turned and headed back inside. He shoved his clothes into the Formica-paneled locker and trudged out to the treadmills. Lights flashed. Beepers beeped. His legs began to stride beneath him.

A large-hipped woman on the next machine leaned over. "You have to push the pedometer. It will tell you how far you've gone."

Max sucked in his stomach. "This is like NASA training."

"That's a new one. You were an astronaut?"

"No, but I once photographed Neil Armstrong at USC. That was his alma mater."

"If you think this is space-age, try the Electro-Muscle Stimulator."

"I'd prefer a mudbath."

"What do you think this is—La Costa?"

Max huffed and puffed. "No, I think this is—pointless. It reminds me of life—walking and walking and getting nowhere."

"If you don't like the treadmill, try the aerobics workout."

"Not me. That's more my daughter's speed. She's a professional athlete. In perfect shape. Endless stamina."

"Well, take the Introductory Class."

"Introductory Class!" Max objected. "I'm not ready for that."

"Just stay to the back—in the 'Low Impact' section."

Max walked over and shyly poked his head inside the aerobics room. "Bend your back! Uh-huh! That's it! Come on!" The instructor bounced around on a small stage. "Kick it out! Lets go! Do it! Do it!"

"I can't! I can't!" Max closed the glass door and made a beeline for the dressing room, but the instructor's amplified voice followed him to the lockers. Not even the spray of the hot water could drown out the pounding aerobics rhythm. Alone in the showers, he rocked his head back and forth and tried to remember a time when he enjoyed dancing. His mind drifted back to a get away weekend of free-flowing movement in the Golden Gate Panhandle. Scoffing the restrictive ballroom couple dances and rejecting the pseudo rebellious Twist, his movement was an expression of flowing inner energy, a naked dance of the spirit uninhibited by diagrammed steps and rigid conventions. Daydreaming, he swayed naked around the shower room. Maybe things hadn't changed so drastically. Maybe today's kids had the same hopes, dreams and aspirations as he did when he was their age.

"Excuse me, sir." The fitness membership salesman stood in the shower entry. "There is no dancing in the locker room."

Amaryllis, meanwhile, had wound her way through Laurel Canyon, down Crescent Heights Boulevard into Fairfax. She parked and followed the scribbled directions to the Hayworth Avenue address. In front of the convalescent home, blue bus benches looked out of place, white rocks covering the parkway were too bright, and aluminum umbrellas offered little shade from the sun. Wearing large orange protective sunglasses, the residents of Shalom Village retreated into the air-conditioned lobby.

"I'm here to see Gita." Amaryllis, a head taller than anyone in sight, greeted the Jamaican receptionist. "Is she in her room?"

"Gita Seltzer?" she responded. "You mean the Shalom Village bingo champion. She's upstairs playing even now."

The elevator stopped at several floors to let on and off the slow paced seniors. As the doors opened on the sixth, the sounds of medicated gaming filled the space. "B-10, B-10."

"What?" screeched a lady seated next to Amaryllis' Grandmother.

Gita was annoyed. "She said '10'. Pay attention."

"B-10?"

"Yes, B-10. The letters don't matter anyway. B-10, P-10, Z-10. What's the difference? Just look for the numbers." Gita's eyes met her granddaughter's and her lips broke into a smile. She wore lavender polyester slacks, a striped blouse, beige stockings and black orthopedic loafers. Her bright red nails and lipstick were too neat to have been applied without help. Her hair was a light magenta color; her eyes, a faded milky green. "Well, you're looking good," she said as Amaryllis sat down beside her.

"Grandma, I missed you. How are you feeling?"

Gita's fingers were busy placing small red chips on a well-worn card. "Fine."

"Are you winning or losing?"

A lady leaned across the table. "You're short, but your granddaughter is tall."

Gita glared at her, then turned back to Amaryllis. "I win some, I lose some. It's just for pennies. Do you have a boyfriend?"

"No."

"You working?"

"Not yet. I got a job as a waitress, but they want me to wear a see-thru blouse." She opened the box and showed Gita the garment.

The old woman felt the material, inspected the seams, then returned to the game. "Do you keep the tips?"

"They said minimum wage minus eighteen per-cent during training plus half of the tips."

"Wear a white leotard underneath. No minus eighteen per-cent. No training period. Not half—all the tips.'"

"I-19, I-19."

"Do they have to turn that up so loud?" asked Amaryllis.

"Some of the ladies don't hear so good. What you gonna do?" She shrugged. "At least you're looking good. You got a boyfriend?"

"I said no. Gita, I need some advice."

"That, I can give you. Advice from what?" She nudged a chip to the exact center of the numbered square.

"Max."

"*Oy Geyvalt!*" Gita's face grimaced as she knocked several chips out of place and onto the floor. Her skin turned red. Her fists clenched. "Mr. Wheelchair Pusher! I raise him to be a doctor. He ends up driving de cranke *mentshen* through the halls of the hospital. *Oy, Mama!*" She looked to the sky and then at her granddaughter as if pleading a case. "I wanted children."

"But that's just it. He retired."

"IQ tested, bona fide legal genius. Piano lessons, violin, tennis, a science tutor, I paid. What didn't the child learn? And what happens, he goes to college and becomes a hippie. Mama, Mama, take me." She opened her arms to the ceiling. "Deserve it I didn't!"

"O-75, O-75."

"He's obsessed with the sixties."

"Sixties, he's only fifty-three."

"No, you don't understand. I mean the nineteen sixties. He just stays inside now, living in the past. I think he's depressed."

"Nah!" The old woman objected with disgust as she put the game markers back in place. "My happy boy wasn't depressed a day in his life. He's rebellious. When he came home from class, I asked him, 'Did you learn math? Did you learn physics? No? Then what?' 'I learned America is run by corporate *hazerim*.' A's all his life. I send him to the best schools, help him with the homework, and what does he do? He curses the police and tells me not to buy fruit. He won't go no more to Clifton's like we did when he was a baby. Four years old, he already asks for a balloon. Big deal? He asks for it in French." She shook her head from side to side. "Mama take me. If I wasn't ready then, I'm ready now." She shrugged and then suddenly smiled. "Well, at least you're looking good. Do you have a boyfriend?"

"Okay, okay, I have a boyfriend. He's in Santa Cruz."

"Ach!" she exclaimed fading away blissfully. "Bring him to visit next time."

"G-54, G-54"

A man with a walker paused behind Gita's chair, "Excuse me, I am trying to decide which one of you young ladies is the most beautiful." Gita grabbed for her cane. He walked away and slurped from the drinking fountain.

"Grandma, Santa Cruz is up north. I probably won't see him for months."

"Santa Cruz? I thought you said Santa Ana. In that case, forget it."

"But that's not what I need advice about. I came to ask you about your son. It's disheartening. He's not his old self. I almost don't recognize him. What should I do?"

"What should you do about Max?" she asked, shaking her head. "Darling, if you want to worry about somebody, you can worry about me instead. Look at all these bruises. I got so many—if only I'd invested."

"But this could be serious."

"A bruise isn't serious? Oooh," she moaned. "Now, you've upset my stomach. Why should you do a thing about Max? That *kleyninker veyner* isn't worth a second thought. I raised him to be a practitioner and instead he puts dead bodies into the freezer. For that, I could have stayed on the East Coast. Listen, you're the daughter, not the doctor. Max takes care of Max. Amaryllis worries from Amaryllis." She looked up to the textured ceiling. "Mama, enough is enough. How much more can a person take." The old woman slouched over, backbone bent and protruding, face inches from the table. "Please, may I soon rest beside you!"

"O-68, O-68."

"Bingo!" shouted Gita jumping up. "*Mazel Tov!* I got a bingo! I GOT A BINGO!"

In the late afternoon, the staff of Chez Bernard were preparing for the dinner crowd. Waiters and waitresses buzzed around the dining room spreading tablecloths, folding napkins, and polishing silverware. With the black-and-white box under her arm, Amaryllis waited for Steve to finish reviewing the day's purchase order and check the reservations book. In command, dressed to a tee, hair and fingernails groomed to perfection, Steve, after ten minutes, found time for the new employee.

"Amaryllis," he said graciously. "I have some forms for you to fill. We're in for a busy night. How would you like to start a day early?"

"I'm sorry, I can't. I came to tell you—"

"Lets talk in my office. You can sign your W-2's and we'll discuss the details of your job there. Follow me." They walked through a short maze of corridors, past several walk-in refrigerators to the back of the house.

In contrast to the dining room, the kitchen was small, grimy and crowded. A half a dozen cooks and dishwashers walked on worn pieces of mat and above, the permanently grease-stained hood grinded out a disturbingly loud hum. The tallest cook was chattering at his lead who was busy seasoning a soup.

"Jimmy, *déjame trabajar de pizzero hoy. El ventilador no sirve y el* grill *esta muy caliente.*"

"But Martin's working pizza."

"*No. El esta enojado contigo porque corristes a Victor.*"

"I didn't fire him, he quit."

"*Sí yo sé, pero él quiere regresar.*"

They simultaneously looked up to see the two strangers to their small realm. The kitchen fell silent, the cooks all ignoring the newcomers and concentrating on their tasks. Steve approached. "This is our new waitress."

Jimmy poured his soup de jour into a double-boiler for service. "Hope she's better than Jeanette."

Flipping chicken on the grill, Martin laughed. "That girl spilled everything. Look up top. We hardly have enough plates left."

Steve persisted. "Amaryllis, meet Jimmy, Martin and Rosario."

Rosario, shorter by a head, stared up and said nothing. Jimmy whipped him with his towel. "*Nunca has visto una ruca asi grande. Que Paso? Te estas enamorando de la Escalera? Para de soñar!* She's too tall for you midget." Rosario blushed and returned to his chopping.

Steve turned and pulled Amaryllis towards the office. "Don't worry, you'll get used to them."

She glanced back to see the cooks laughing and the dishwasher lifting Rosario onto a plastic milk crate. "But that's just it. I've been trying to tell you that I'm really not sure about working here."

Steve gave her a hurt look and turned his key in the door. In contrast to the chaos of the kitchen, his office was immaculate, cool and serene. A contempory art print hung above a leather sofa. A coffee table held a selection of magazines. At his desk a computer, telephone, fax, and printer seemed to make up the control center of the whole operation. "Have a seat and lets talk." They sat. "I like you Amaryllis and am sure you'll make a great waitress. I like to think of all the employees as being part of a family."

Patricia appeared in the doorway. "Steve, we don't have enough napkins for my section." She saw Amaryllis. "Oh, hi. So Steve did hire you. See what I said."

Steve was annoyed by the interruption. "Can't it wait until I'm finished?" He turned back to the new waitress. "Now, what seems to be the problem?"

"I'm uncomfortable about wearing the uniform."

Steve looked concerned. "Oh you're right. I should have explained. The uniform is part of our policy."

Patricia smiled. "Don't worry Amaryllis. Just wear a leotard underneath. When you saw me before, I was hostessing."

Steve grabbed his clipboard from his desk. "And I'll tell you what. Forget about the training period and you can keep all your tips." He handed her a pen. "Now if you would just sign here, here and here..."

On her way out, Amaryllis, still holding the checkered box, passed the kitchen. She tried her best to seem confident and friendly to the busy cooks. "See you guys tomorrow."

Jimmy looked up. "See you tomorrow *Escalera*."

Amaryllis pulled up to her father slouched over on the bench outside Valley Fitness Emporium. She decided to avoid small talk and just let Max ride in silence.

He sat back in the passenger seat wondering if he was the only "Fitness Misfit." What could he do? It was like he had been trapped in a time warp. Walking the halls of St. Sebastian Medical Center day after day for twenty-two years, he'd fallen into a trance. And now, here he was, a thawed mammoth, reawakened yet extinct in the nineties. He stared out the window, his head heavy; his body tired. His intestines growled and he needed to pee. He tried to remember the last time he had smiled or laughed. A hard laugh. The kind of laugh that doesn't—won't—stop. The kind that makes your belly ache. He slumped and ran his hand through his hair. And what of the youngsters, the fitness trainers, the supermarket clerks? They talked, but he didn't hear; they touched, he didn't feel. He closed his eyes and hoped to fall asleep. He missed everyone and no one. He opened his eyes and brushed away a gnat. He closed his eyes again.

His memory drifted back to the days before Patient Transporting. The days of *Free Press* abandon. Summer of '69, the time of his life. Morning walks along the Venice Boardwalk with Melissa. Late-night debates inside those mellow old hotels looking out to the shore. Sitting cross legged, watching long-haired friends roll joints. Everyone in blue jeans. Blue jeans, loose or tight, torn and faded, bulging or creased—like a second skin, blue jeans shouted sexuality. The names of Max's former lovers may have vanished from memory, but the blue jeans they wore remained.

Straining to pull that pair of hip-huggers off a prone arched torso, wriggling and praying for the moment their tight fit would finally give. Tickling knees through a frayed pair of bell-bottoms, the embroidery having long since worn away. Massaging that pair of low riders, waiting for permission to unbutton the waist and lower the zipper. He could remember Levi's so faded they were white—thrown on the floor by the fireplace in a pile with the midriffs, halter tops, sandals and perhaps his own camera case. Naked bodies posing in autoerotic bliss, twisting and turning, contorting, quiet as statues, the silence interrupted only by the sounds of the models breathing and Max's snapping camera.

"Gita said that you were a child prodigy," said Amaryllis.

Max turned away from the window. "She exaggerates. No, I take that back. She lies."

"She says you could have been a doctor."

"I couldn't even have been a journalist."

"And what was Mom's opinion?"

"She was too preoccupied with your grandmother. Oh, how they would fight. My mother called Melissa everything from a 'tramp' to a 'skunk'. But the more she cursed, the more attached I became. By the time you came along, Melissa was determined to leave."

"What happened then?"

"I had to ask my mother for money. I listened to her lectures until I could take no more. Melissa returned to school up north. You stayed with me so she could finish her courses in a hurry, then come back and get you.

"Why did it take her so long?"

"After the Bachelor's came the Masters, after the Master's came the breakdown. Two years turned into four, four into eight. I gave up photography and became a Patient Transporter."

"You gave up photography for me?"

"No, I gave it up because people refused to see what was right before their eyes." Max looked back out at Nordoff Street, its eight-lane width virtually empty of cars. "I covered a major protest march. They said, 'It's not interesting.' I snapped a shot of a CIA hit man. They said, 'He's just the security guard.' I composed a portrait of a great artist deep in thought. They asked, 'Who's the junkie?' Finally, their ignorance wore down my eyes. At the end, I couldn't see any better than they could."

"Well, as Grandma would say, one thing ends and another begins. You retire and I—as soon as I can find a white leotard—start work at Chez Bernard. Then this weekend is the Exiles first summer practice.

That Saturday was a scorcher. The Valley, always ten degrees hotter than the city, reached one hundred. Windows down, Amaryllis felt the temperature drop as she headed over the Cahuenga Pass through Hollywood and into Downtown for the first practice, her destination—Patriotic Hall.

Near the new Convention Center and next to the Freeway, the hall was an old brick and concrete building with a gym on its top floor. Its vaulted lobby contained oversized leather seats and glass showcase displays of each US war. The auditorium sat empty and an elevator operator read a newspaper between trips.

As Amaryllis approached, the man put down his paper and stood up from his bar stool. "New player? I bet you want the tenth."

"Right. Am I late?"

"Even if you are, your coach is later." He shut the door, watched the floors roll by, pulled the control lever and swung the door open. "Watch your step." Sunlight from high windows shone into the large gym and a breeze flowed from the fire escape. A large patch of brick resembling a map of Asia showed through the worn plaster finish. She looked around, took a seat on the concrete bleachers and dropped her bag on the floor between her knees. Flor Ortega chatted with the returning players, exchanging hugs and smiles. She took several minutes for greetings, then regaining an official composure, referred to her clipboard.

"LaRonda Lewis." LaRonda had beautiful long thick braids, perfect orange nails and gold jewelry. She wore loose patterned cotton pants and a silk shirt. Her shoulders were broad; her arms, long and her legs, big. A rebounder, no doubt about it.

"Violet Jaharbian." Violet, skateboard at her side, sat by herself, earphones on her ears. An olive-skinned punk rocker, she had a black buzz cut, a nose ring and silver hoops lining her left ear. She wore black denim thrasher shorts, combat boots and a white ribbed tank undershirt.

"Margaret Mawson." Peggy Mawson was the well-known center from USC. She was tall, husky and dressed in a gray sweatsuit. Her sports bag read MTA—maybe a bus driver.

"Daisy Little." Daisy was the oldest player. Not coordinated enough to be a starter, she fit in well, scratching heads and patting backs—the 'team mother' type—emotionally supportive, maybe be slightly annoying if you weren't in the mood.

"Dahlia Logoromi." Logoromi looked tough. Buff arms popping out of her tight V-neck T-shirt, she was pissed about something. Everything about her—her hair, her face, her walk—seemed tight and tense. Not someone to mess with.

"Iris Williams." Iris liked to dress. Her designer rayon suit probably cost a bundle. Amaryllis already knew that Williams was the last name of the team owner. Maybe this was his daughter.

"Patricia Aguilar." Patty hadn't stopped talking yet. Chubby and chatty, she was showing off her latest ballhandling trick. She acknowleged Flor's second call with a little wave. Apparently, this was her gym.

"Diane Elizabeth Villa." Diane had that unmistakable head-to-toe basketball strut. She seemed happy to be back and was dressed to play in her baggy, black mesh shorts and jade jersey.

"Good, everyone is here on time."

The team snickered.

"Yeah, yeah, I know—almost everyone," Flor conceded. "Terry will be here soon. As you know, she's occasionally—"

"Occasionally?"

"Alright, alright, always—late."

Whispers turned into gym-filling chatter as they awaited their tardy coach. Finally, the elevator whirred, the door swung open and a nervous freckle-faced redhead stepped out and greeted the team.

Amaryllis recognized her signature walk immediately—former All-American Division I co-captain two years running, U.S. Olympic Gold Medalist, former WPBL star guard, mystery athlete of the eighties and current coach of the Exposition Park Exiles—Theresa "Terry the Taxi" Taktikabian.

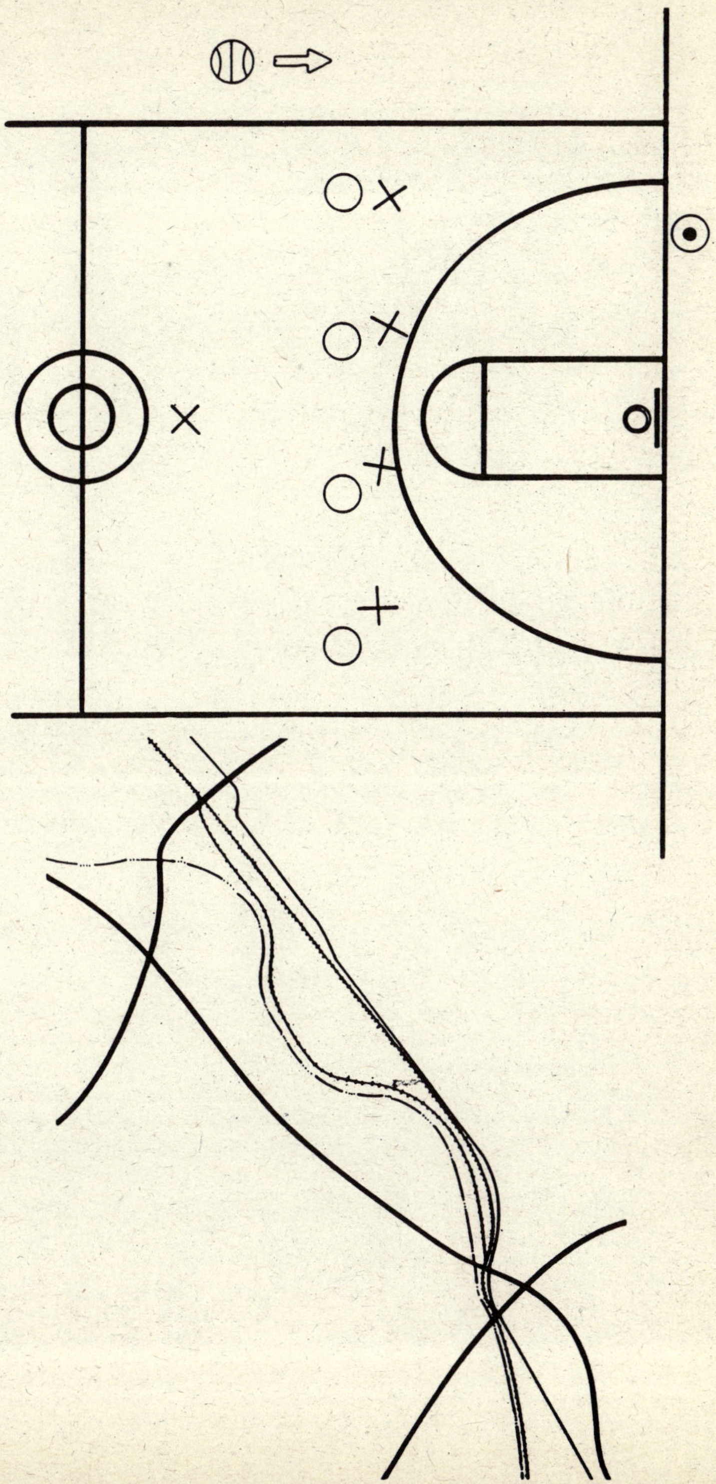

"Hey Shrinkie, why the big sports rivalry between UCLA and USC?"

"Because Finkie, sports rivalries are usually just a reflection of institutional competition. All institutions attempt to survive and enhance themselves. Being in the same geographic location, both colleges naturally are vying for students and faculty."

"But Shrinkie, isn't education the important thing? What's the big difference between the two of them anyway?"

"Finkie, one's private and the other is part of the UC system."

"Is that all?"

"One is a smaller campus in the center of town and the other is a larger commuter school out in Westwood."

"Can't they just be friendly neighbors?"

"Finkie, one's better academically; the other has a larger funding base with superior corporate and business connections."

"But Shrinkie, shouldn't that mean they just work together all the better?"

"Finkie, one wears red and gold; the other wears blue and gold."

"But Shrinkie, why do they taunt the players?"

"They want their team to win, Finkie, of course!"

"Isn't the idea to play your best and have fun?"

"Ah fooey, let's go down to Pinkie and Wes on the sidelines. There happens to be a women's basketball game in progress."

"Uh, hello, this is game announcer Westside Wes along with color commentator Pinkie the Cow. Do you know the letter of the day?"

"Oh yes, Wes. 'E' is the letter of the day, and here inside the Los Angeles Sports Arena, it's very E-X-C-I-T-I-N-G!"

"And why is that, Pinkie?"

"Why, you know, Wes. Because the score is close and there are only E-I-G-H-T seconds left!"

"Pinkie, you're right again. Only eight seconds to decide which Southern California women's basketball team will be going to the 1977 Final Four at Cal State Fullerton. Will it be the UCLA Bruins led by Terry "The Taxi" Taktikabian, or the USC Women of Troy led by 'Sly' Sylvia Logan? The house is packed! The crowd is going wild! I've never seen it get so out of hand!"

"Neither have I, at least not since Crenshaw faced Manual Arts here last weekend. Look, Wes, up in the balcony, how beautiful, they're doing the wave!"

"That's not the wave, Pinkie. That's the mace-toting security staff chasing teenagers through the aisles."

"Wes, why are the UCLA starters doing their homework during time-outs?"

"Between part-time jobs, classes, practice and socializing, it's the

only time they have left to study."

"Wes, why is the Oxford tennis team marching around in search of an automatic teller?"

"Pinkie! That's the USC call leaders warming up the crowd."

"Wes, why is the referee blowing her whistle?"

"That's because the teams are now set for the inbounds. Let's go up to Uh-oh and Thatsnofair for the play-by-play."

"Hello out there. This is Uh-oh up in the broadcast booth. Uh-oh, Terry has the ball with eight seconds left. Uh-oh, her team is behind by one. Uh-oh, she's being guarded by long time rival Sylvia Logan. Uh-oh, Sylvia's reaching in trying to get the ball."

"THAT'S NO FAIR!"

"You're right again Thatsnofair, but don't worry, Terry the Taxi is racing ahead towards the basket. Uh-oh, she shoots with less than a second left. Let's go to Geo and Jazz for the final results."

"Chic designer's assistant Jasmine here with fashion expert extrodinaire Geo Williams. What's with that buzzer? Is it stuck or something? Anyway, Geo says that Terry looks simply smashing in her silk mesh uniform and those porcelain mini-basketball appliqués through the laces add that typical 'Taxi' touch. What's that? Did she make the basket and win the game? I'm not sure. Down to Vampiro on the floor for a mini-cam interview with the victorious team captain—whoever it is."

"Thank you Jazz. My goodness that buzzer is annoying. I'm trying to get close to our hero, but she's covering her E-A-R-S. She's searching for the plug. But unfortunately, pulling it out doesn't do any good and neither does lifting the device above her head and smashing it on the ground. E-X-C-U-S-E me Terry, why are you jumping up and down on the buzzer controls? She's not answering, just snarling, hands held out like claws, teeth E-X-P-O-S-E-D, nostrils flaring. Her face is turning red. Ohhh, this is getting very scary. Take it E-A-S-Y, girlfriend. She's steaming mad and is stalking off in search of the saboteur that rigged the wiring. The referees are disgusted. They've disqualified both teams. No one's going to Fullerton! What a horrible E-N-D to an action-packed season! This is Vampiro saying so long and wake up out there! It's time to wake up! Isn't that right, E-V-E-R-Y-B-O-D-Y?"

"That's right. Wake up! Wake up! Wake up!"

"Wake up! Terry, wake up! You're having a nightmare!" Coach Theresa Taktikabian's eyes flew open. She growled and reached for the throat of the large dark woman by her side. "Terry! It's me—Karin. You're having another nightmare."

Coach Taktikabian leapt from the bed, ran to the bathroom and yanked the clock/radio cord from the wall. "Damb buzzer!"

"Well, good morning to you too. Why don't you just smash it into a hundred pieces?"

"Good idea," grunted Coach. She slammed the clock/radio against the wall. "What a stupid alarm! What happened to the music we always have?"

"Eeek!" screamed Karin. "Someone call County. She's lost her memory. She forgot she told me to set it for 'alarm' last night!"

Coach smiled. "Oh yeah, you're right. But even so, you were awake. Why didn't you get up and turn that off?"

"There goes the memory again. Okay, let's take this one step at a time. You're the coach. You have to go to a meeting today. I'm the girlfriend. I have the day off. I get to sleep in. And all this is beside the point because it wasn't the alarm that woke me, it was you talking in your sleep. You kept on yelling, 'Sly! Sly'!"

"Oh yeah," said Coach standing and bouncing a pretend ball. "I made the shot right at the buzzer and won the game. Sly looked like she was taking it kind of hard, so I went to give her a hug, but I kept on getting distracted by Vampiro who wanted an interview."

"You were dreaming about Sly Logan again? Karin paused and looked perplexed. "Vampiro? Vampiro wanted an interview?"

Coach bit her thumb trying to recall. "Yes, yes, Westside Wes was doing the broadcast. The game was being brought to you by the letter 'E'. Shinkie and Finkie were the team analysts. Vampiro was on the floor. Wes and Pinkie were the color commentators. Uh-oh and Thatsnofair were doing the play-by-play and I think Geo and Jazz were there too for some reason."

"Jasmine? Now you're dreaming of Jasmine? First it's Sly, then it's Jasmine."

"So what. Pinkie was in my dream. Are you going to be jealous of her too?"

"Sly and Jazz are real people. Pinkie is a Luppet."

"Look, let's not argue about a bunch of children's TV show characters who drive around in customized golf carts then fall over and cry when they crash? Just drop it, okay?"

Karin continued teasing. "No, I don't want to drop it. You always try to put off the important stuff. I refuse to—"

Coach approached, lightly kissing her lover's face.

"Yum," sighed Karin as teeth nibbled the left slope of her neck. She reached up to embrace Terry.

Coach jumped up and grabbed her favorite sweater and pants. "Damn it. Why am I always late to these asinine appointments." She delivered one last kiss, then headed for the shower.

Karin flopped back pining. "But we never spend any time together."

"Please, don't start."

"But I'm your girlfriend. The one—"

"Karin, this is getting irritating."

"—who rides her bike to work to avoid polluting the air. The one who protests for animal rights. The one who goes to group counseling sessions like last week's, alone because you were still in a meeting downtown. The one—"

"Karin please."

"—who cooks and cleans and keeps this place looking decent. The one who is nice and upbeat and calm and pleasant and not getting irritated all the time."

"I'm not irritated."

"There goes the memory again. You just said you were irritated and let me guess why it is this time. You're irritated because you have to drive off to some meeting while I ride my bike to my minimum wage shift—"

"You just said you have the day off. And since you transferred to the 'Asia' section, aren't you making one dollar more an hour?"

"Plus all the carbonated soda I can drink."

"Plus all the carbonated soda you can drink. And anyway, I thought you're going to fulfill the academic requirements for 'Assistant Zookeeper' by next fall, and get medical benefits."

"I'm just arguing theoretically."

"You're about as theoretical as a car alarm. I'm glad I smashed your present. At least I don't have to listen to that elevator music you usually switch on."

"I like anesthesia mind control in the morning. And it's not elevator, it's soothing—mellow."

"Soothing? Why do *you* need to be soothed? I pay the bills. I bust my butt. Of course you're mellow, you have nothing but free time on your hands and instead of doing something constructive, you just sit there and hibernate."

"It's meditate, not hibernate. Don't make fun of my exercises!"

"But you don't understand I'm going nuts. I told you how hard I tried to make it to that group counseling session, but you didn't appreciate it. You don't know what I go through. You don't have to jam through rush hour traffic just to listen to poorly dressed company reps talk about the latest 'Scenario'. You don't have to try to fire up an underpaid, overworked basketball team, scout off-season recruits and then come home to some tuned-out—"

"You're rambling again."

"I know. Don't interrupt."

"But, it's a quarter to seven—by last estimates, anyway—and I'm tired of thinking. You're forty years old. Let me go to sleep."

"In a minute. It's a completely different situation now. When I was twenty-six, I practiced with the Olympic team, jogged eighteen miles a week and also had a full-time high school coaching job. You have it easy compared to me. I was less supported, less encouraged—"

"Less boring?" Karin turned over in bed, covered her face with a pillow and snored.

Coach was taken aback. "And you told me I'm bitter. I'm not the bitter one, you are."

"Well, of course not. You keep me up early mornings letting all your bitterness out."

"If you call someone bitter and then ignore them, it becomes a self-fulfilling bitterness—they become bitter from being ignored."

"Hummm."

Coach raised her voice. "Hummm? What's 'Hummm' supposed to mean?"

"Hummm. I think I've lost a clock and gained a cuckoo."

"Don't start that 'I'm neurotic, you're not' business either. When we talk now, you make me feel foolish. When I try to write down my feelings, I feel drained. So that's why I stopped doing either of those things and decided to just let it out whenever it came."

"Whenever what came?" Karin's frustration was beginning to surface.

"A conflict," said Terry slipping on her sweater.

"A conflict?"

"Yes, I've given it a lot of thought and it's very clear to me. You may be younger and emotionally braver. You may have wished someone would love you. But I didn't have that much internal space to do that, and because—I think—you make me laugh, I was beginning to rearrange things so that I might."

"Terry, you're not a living room. What are you talking about? Rearrange what things?"

"Inner things."

"Which inner things?"

"Last year's inner things. You see, I figured it out driving home last night." Coach pressed her fingertips against her sternum and continued. "I was afraid when you went back to school and started meeting new people. I was doubting our relationship even though I have always thought I was fair to you."

Karin scratched her head. "What have you been doing with the money you said you paid the therapist with? There's no way you've been going every Thursday."

"Please just be my friend," begged Coach coming close and rubbing her nose into Karin's neck. She sighed. "I got to get going babe."

"Don't *babe* me. That is, unless you promise that we're going on a bike ride together this weekend."

"Alright, alright babe, I promise."

On her first day of work, Amaryllis set tables, made coffee and poured water for the first customers. It wasn't until the restaurant was full that Patricia led her to the back to show her the order computer. In the busy kitchen, she watched dumbfounded as the cooks tried to keep up.

Jimmy kicked the stove. "Light sucker light!" He punched the pilot button twice, dropped a towel over the range and watched the gas finally turn blue with flame. The orders stretched down the ticket bar and the strip of paper ticking out of the printer was spilling off the table.

"*Jimmy, y que hago con estos tickets?*" Toño the dishwasher was ackwardly assisting on the line. Jimmy took the gum out of his mouth and handed it to him. Toño began sticking the orders on the wall.

Patricia pressed buttons on the computer while instructing the new waitress. "You have to call out the order and they have to answer. Once they acknowledge, then you know they have it. You try."

Amaryllis cleared her throat. "Two Chicken Picattas, a special salad and one Steak medium-well." No one responded.

Patricia poked her head through the window. "Jimmy, call the order back. We've been waiting forever and they're complaining."

Jimmy garnished two baked potatoes with sour cream and butter, then threw chopped parsley on top. "Good."

Patricia caught the manager. "Steve, he said good. He doesn't care. Why should he? What difference does it make to him if people wait. Look at his face on pay day and it's a different story. He's all smiles and 'Hello, how are you?' But when it comes to a busy day when we stand a chance to make our car payments..."

Steve poked his head through the window. "Jimmy I need you to pick up the pace a little. You're way behind."

"Yes, Stevie. I know Stevie. Where's the masking tape I asked you for Stevie. I can't fix the blower without it Stevie." Jimmy held two pans in one hand. He kicked the oven door shut and ladled sauce onto two entrees. He slid six plates onto the window, tore the ticket, rang the bell and went onto the next order. Toño stood in a daze. *"Trae los* steak sauce set-ups*!"*

"Ya no hay."

"¿Te fijaste detras de las lechugas?" Toño ran back to the walk-in while Rosario mixed eight salads in a stainless steel bowl, threw handfuls onto chilled glass plates then stood on a box to slide them through the window. Jimmy barked at him. *"Enano, trae mas platos."*

"Tu buey!"

"Ayudame chaparro."

"¿Y si yo te ayudo, quién me va a ayudar a mi?"

Patricia stood at the window. "He's just standing there Steve. Make him do something."

Jimmy opened the low frig. The red sauce back up was empty. "Damb night shift." He grabbed a can opener and yelled. *"Oscar, un bote de* ketchup."

"Sí, sí, Chef Jimmy." Oscar reached into the pantry and threw him a can.

Jimmy threw it back. *"Abrelo inutil."*

Oscar tried opening it but the can opener jammed and he cut his finger.

Jimmy grabbed the can, threw the opener in the trash and slammed the wide end of his knife through the metal. He dripped ketchup into a pan of boiling cream then added a handful of Parmesean cheese, hot pasta and parsley. "Patricia! Your Diablo's in the window."

"But, I don't need a Diablo."

Jimmy threw the dirty pans into the bus tub and started the next order. "Yes you do. You're trailing on table fourteen. Take it and come back. I'll have your ribs." He threw a rack into the convection oven. Slammed the door and grabbed his tongs. He opened the oven with his foot, pulled out the pan of four chicken breasts and grabbed the bottle of Marsala.

Bridgette appeared in the doorway behind them. "Jimmy, your girlfriend is on line two and Victor is here and wants to see you."

"I'm busy."

"She says she needs a ride home from her mother's and he says he wants his job back."

"Tell her to ask her sister and tell him no."

"But her sister isn't home and Victor's crying. I don't have the heart to tell him no."

"Tell her to take the bus and tell him to come back in a couple hours."

"But he said he can't come back because—"

"Fine! He can have his old job back."

"Okay, I'll tell him. I didn't know you were so cheap Jimmy. If my boyfriend ever told me to take the bus, I'd break up."

Oscar nudged in beside him holding a plastic tray of individually wrapped ramekins. "Steak Sauce, *aquí esta,* Chef Jimmy."

"¿Donde esta Toño?"

"Ayudandome con los platos Chef Jimmy."

"¡Tu lavas los platos! Dile a Toño que regrese aquí."

"El no quiere Chef Jimmy."

Jimmy grimaced. *"Entonces, tú seras el nuevo asistente."*

"Sí, sí, Chef Jimmy."

Steve appeared in the window. "Here's your tape."

Jimmy put on a phoney grin. "Thank you Stevie. Just leave it there, Stevie."

An old man in a gray suit walked into the kitchen smiling. "Well lookie here! Great job fellows. Who made those ribs? They were delicious."

Jimmy didn't turn around. "Sorry sir, you can't stay back here."

"Oh, I know that son. Nevermind me. I just wanted to see how the big boys do it. By the way son, you better take care of that fellow's cut. My kid brother Dennis--we all called him Dennis the Menace--he had a cut get infected when we were just children. And let me tell you..."

Jimmy looked down at Oscar's hand. A gash ran across three fingers. Blood dripped onto his apron. Jimmy reached above him to where he hid his clean towel, grabbed Oscar's fingers, wrapped them and squeezed.

Amaryllis watched shocked as they worked. They desparately needed help. What should she do? "Where's the first aid kit?"

Jimmy ignored her and tried to think.

She tried again. "Jimmy, where is the first aid kit?"

"Below you in the cabinet."

Amaryllis reached below and grabbed the white tin box with the red cross on it. She stuck her arm through the window, but no one paid attention to her.

"Why won't you take it?" she asked.

Jimmy remained silent. Rosario looked at her and gestured for her to open the box and look inside. She opened it—empty except for a tiny band-aid and pieces of trash.

"Chaparro, tirame el oregano," hollered Jimmy

"Pero el oregano no va en Chicken Marsala."

Jimmy stomped his foot. *"DAMELO!"* He poured a handful into his right hand, then gripped the bloody fingers. He wrapped the cut with paper from the printer and the tape Steve had just left. He took a packet from his wallet, tore it open and rolled a condom over Oscar's fingers. He washed his hands, poured four soups and plated the chicken.

Oscar looked at his fingers and grinned. "Chef Jimmy..."

"Callate inutil."

"Sí, sí, Chef Jimmy."

Scanning the off-road billboard ads as she headed south on the 5, Coach was forced to face facts. As slick and efficient a businessman as team owner Warren Williams was, neither his influence nor his funding, could stretch through another season. If her team was going to tour, they needed more money. To get it, they would have to enlist sponsors. Compromise was in order, but Women's Pro Exhibition Basketball would not become Beach Volleyball: bathing suits, boobs, beer and banners. Spandex uniforms were out. Brand names across butts were out. Even trade-name caps with ponytails hanging out were out. But, if sponsors would pay for a rotating sidelines table ad, the Exiles would have to give it to them. Wouldn't life be easier if the games were brought to you by the letter 'E' like in a Westside Wes TV Show dream.

Reaching downtown, she pulled into the subterranean parking garage, took the escalator up to Pershing Square, walked past a homeless man showering in the fountain, entered the old office building lobby, took the elevator to the eighth floor and pushed open the "WilliamsWear of California" front door. She stepped in just as a power struggle transpiring between two family members whose ages differed by sixty-two years, was coming to a head.

Five-year-old Sunny Williams leaned dangerously out the window. "Look, Grandpa. There are the Raisins. They're getting all wet!"

"Come away from that window Sunny," said Warren Williams, a tall, stern faced man with cardboard colored skin and a perfectly tailored wool suit.

"No! Uncle Geo promised to take us to meet them. They live in the purple computer tower." The little girl giggled. "They come downstairs to take a bath."

"Sunny, please come away from that window." There was a trace of sadness in the man's monotone voice. "Look what I have. And you can give one to your brother too!"

"Candy bars!" shouted the little girl quitting the window and grabbing the treat from the huge wrinkled two-toned hand.

With the conflict resolved, the grandfather turned towards his new visitor and pulled out a chair. "Ms. Taktikabian, can you tell me why sisters and brothers can't stay friends after childhood? There is so much to admire—so much to share." His grandson Sonny and granddaughter Sunny stood behind his leather chair. "If young men and women could get along as well as these two, the world would be a lot nicer place. Don't you agree?"

Coach nodded.

"My son Geoffrey and daughter Iris argue like cats and dogs. And over the silliest things—an earring, a hairstyle, a shirt collar. I've given into it, but I still feel sorry for them. The only thing I can think of is that perhaps they miss their mother." He glanced over to a photo of himself and his wife in ballroom attire. "My Rusty passed in 1990. It has been a cold winter for the Williams family since then, even in this climate." He swiveled in his chair. "Sonny, don't put candy in your mouth after it fell onto the carpet."

"But Grandpa, Uncle Geo said that if you hold it up in the air and say, 'God kiss it!', you can still eat it and you won't get worms."

Terry cleared her throat. "Mr. Williams, did you want me to bring the players by for fittings yet?"

"Please, call me Warren. Oh yes, the uniforms. Geoffrey does take his time. Sometimes I worry about that young man. I have to be careful with him. He's very..." Warren hesitated, "...delicate. Iris, as you know, is more hard-working. That's the reason I spoil her. If she wants me to co-sign on a new sedan, my name is on the form before hers. If she wants a new townhouse in Pasadena, I call the movers to pick up her furniture. If she wants new uniforms for her team—"

"Actually, Warren, it's our team, all of us, and I requested the new uniforms. If we are going to start touring, we need to look sharp."

"Of course, but to be perfectly frank, I just wasn't sure the team's budget would allow for it. Attendance has declined again."

"That's just why we need Geo's talent. Could you please ask him if the uniforms will be ready by Santa Barbara?"

"Yes, I can, and will, Ms. Taktikabian. But I'm telling you now, he can't be hurried. He's..." Warren deliberated, "...sensitive. I've talked it over with my family back home, my friends here, my doctor, my pastor, my barber, even my dentist. But I end up back where I started." He suddenly jumped forward. "Sonny! Sunny! What in heaven's name are you two doing?"

"The 'Dog'. It's a dance Uncle Geo taught us."

The man stood and brought several toys from the closet. He set them in front of the children, returned to his chair and continued. "I'm getting older now and I won't lie to you, Ms. Taktikabian—"

"Call me Terry."

"Terry, I won't lie. Ever since you coached Iris in college, I've trusted you. I confess that I have done many things in life my son would have been ashamed to do. I washed dishes for eight years in the Navy. After that, I worked two jobs and did everything and anything to get ahead back then. And now that I'm owner instead of employee, I get more confused by the day. They tell me my son is..." he paused, "...creative. I say, if I behaved like that, they'd have thrown me in jail. He's artistic, and talented. Talented is a scissors split or at least a nice Balboa, not bending over and bow-wowing like a dog while someone scratches a perfectly good record."

"Times have changed, Mr. Williams. Maybe if I can at least see the design, I can pick the right players for first fittings?"

"Yes, Terry, of course." He rubbed his neck, readjusted his lapel, stood and pushed the intercom. "Geoffrey, pick up line one." He spoke briefly in hushed tones. "He'll show you now. Please step this way." He turned to the children. "Come on, you two."

"But Uncle Geo said—"

"Uncle Geo said this, Uncle Geo said that. Who do you think we're going to go see right this very minute? Your beloved Uncle Geo!"

The group walked together past a conglomeration of offices, through an assembly line warehouse and upstairs to the studios. Geo's assistant Jasmine awaited them at the top of the stairs. Three jerseys decorated with fresh flowers lay in a pile on the floor. The sound of television commercials blasted in the background. "Mr. Williams, Geo changed his mind. He said he isn't finished yet. He says—"

Mr. Williams took out his handkerchief and wiped his brow. "What!?"

"Geo says it's not ready. He says it's too 'Rose Paradey'. He says—"

"But I just spoke with him—"

"Geo says come back later. He says everyone will think he got a bargain at the Flower Mart. He says—he says—he says..."

"Geoffrey, will you please come out now!"

The television volume became louder. "Go away," shouted a voice from behind a partition. "GO AWAY AND TAKE THOSE BAD CHILDREN WITH YOU!"

Amaryllis, at the end of the lunch shift, was exhausted. Patricia counted her tips, then used her calculator to divide them among the wait staff. "Depending on how much they help, you have to tip out the bussers and the bar. On a real busy night, you even give some to the hostess. What's the matter?"

Amaryllis said nothing.

"You didn't do too bad. Nobody expects you to be perfect on your first day. So you dropped a tray of entrees and they had to do them over. That's what the cooks get paid for." Patricia counted out thirty-two dollars and put it in Amaryllis' hand.

Steve came over and put his arm around Amaryllis' shoulder.

"Congratulations, you made it through your first day. Pretty soon, we'll give you your own section. Now, why don't you relax and get yourself a bite to eat. Ask them to make you something off the lunch menu, it's on the house."

Amaryllis walked to the back. The cooks were busy cleaning up and replenishing the line for the dinner shift. She poked her head through the window. "Excuse me. I wanted to say I'm sorry about dropping that tray. You guys looked so busy. I wish I could have been some help, but I just ended up making things worse. I can't believe how you manage to keep things together. Well, anyway, Steve said I could get something to eat. All I really want is a small salad. Is that alright?"

Jimmy looked up. "You need a ticket."

Like lightning, Rosario had grabbed salad and dressing, mixed it and slid it through the window. He smiled at the new waitress.

Amaryllis smiled back and reached for the plate. Jimmy frowned, took back the plate and threw it in the trash. "You need a ticket," he repeated.

Later, in another restaurant, in another part of town, Coach and Karin were having an early dinner before practice. Their waiter wore high-waisted pants, a tight knit shirt and suspenders. His hair and body were buffed and styled to statuesque perfection. "What can I get for you tonight?"

Trying to settle down, Coach looked through the dinner menu, then put it aside. "I'll have a Greyhound."

Dining al fresco, Karin faced in and Coach faced out. Across the street, the stout and symmetrical "Emerald City" and the long and sharp-edged "Blue Whale" wings of the Pacific Design Center hovered over Karin's left shoulder. Ironically, the two twosomes—diners and buildings—each added an outrageous touch of humorous competition to their respective environments. The buildings feuded visually while the lovers wrestled verbally, each pair all in all indifferent to their surroundings.

"It's just so frustrating," said Coach pointing her finger. "Santa Barbara is only three weeks away. Our spirits are low enough without having to play in old rags." Coach sipped her drink and gaped at the passing waitress. "Why do we come here? It makes me feel old."

"You're much sexier than her." She put her arm around Terry's shoulder. "Repeat three times: I'm not getting older, I'm getting better, I'm not getting..."

Terry brushed off the instructions, but not the affection. No big deal, thought Coach, feeling the hand kneading her leg beneath the table. As long as these good times lasted, she could deal with her various phobias: corporate rep-o-phobia, meeting-o-phobia, lose-o-phobia. What did it matter, she was in love, and in a professional position she'd worked long and hard for. Strategist, advisor and counselor to nine of the best women's players in L.A., a professional barnstorming exhibition team. So what if she was in no emotional state to keep herself together. She would have to hold out. Take it a day at a time. "How's the new dance routine going?"

"It's okay."

"What's up at the zoo?"

"Just the usual—cramped cages, drugged animals and huge crowds." Karin leaned back and lit a cigarette.

."Hey, don't smoke," whined Coach.

"Why not? We're sitting outside. Or are you Mother Teresa tonight?"

"Oh, get lost."

"Don't be a jerk, Terry."

"I'll be a jerk if I want to, Karin. Don't be so demanding."

"Just wait, next you're going to want me to tell you how important our relationship is."

Coach dropped her napkin and turned red. "I only wanted you to say that when, and only when, you really meant it."

Karin, wanting to trigger, but not detonate, backed off an itsy-bitsy step. "Terry, take it easy. Maybe it's time for that talk we've been planning."

"Maybe it's time to give up."

"If you say that once more, I'm outta here."

"It'll be easier to forget each other than you think."

Karin pushed her chair away from the table. "That's enough. I've had my fill."

"I'm so sick of this." Coach rose, found their waiter, paid the bill and walked out the door.

Karin, dismayed at the real trouble brewing, followed Terry out to the sidewalk and grabbed her arm. "God, it's always the same thing. Nothing ever changes. Another stupid argument about absolutely nothing."

Coach jerked her arm away. "If it's so stupid, why don't you go stay with your mommy tonight?"

"What are you going to do without me, read?" asked Karin.

"I'll go back home is what I'll do. I won't write. I won't return your phone calls."

"You're neurotic!"

"You're overweight!"

"I'm calling a cab and going home," said Karin.

"I'm going to the bar and getting drunk."

"Not without me you don't. Rochelle is probably hanging out there tonight."

"So?"

"So life sucks!" said Karin.

"Life does suck," Coach answered bringing her face inches away from Karin's, "because everyone is so selfish."

"Why should I share with you?" spat Karin, finally losing her temper and throwing two fingers into Terry's sternum. "You don't take me seriously. You treat me like a child."

Terry turned and retreated down the sidewalk. Karin, two steps behind, arrived at the bar entrance. Inside, Rochelle, bending over the pool table, cue in hand, breasts brushing the green felt, took aim at the ten ball by the corner pocket.

"Hi, Rochelle," said Terry.

"Hey, Taxi," said Rochelle, making the cross table shot with a slow soft touch. Karin pouted.

"Something wrong?" asked gel-haired, bank-shooting, mahogany-skinned, paisley-vested Rochelle. She straightened her back and leaned her hip against the table. "I hope it's okay if Taxi and me play a quick game?" Her plum lips slid into a wide smile. Her bright white teeth glistened.

"I just have to talk to Terry alone for a second. Then you can have your game or whatever."

"Go ahead and talk." Rochelle turned towards Coach. "Taxi and me have lots of time." Her handsome thick eyebrows bent in together. She leaned back over the table, her pants tightening over her rear, her honey-colored eyes focusing on the fourteen ball near the side.

"Terry listen," began her shivering lover in a whisper. "So we have trouble communicating. But please don't do this. Just let's go, okay? Don't make me jealous. You know how I get. Anyway, you have to be at Patriotic Hall in an hour."

"There's something in your hair," said Coach, brushing away a piece of lint.

"We're still learning to be together—that's all," continued Karin. "Let's not ruin it. We can work it out."

"So what am I supposed to do?" asked Coach.

"You're supposed to hug me, play one round of pool, drink one more Greyhound and then we'll jam."

Coach smiled satisfied, then felt Karin's big shoulders melt into hers. "I'm sorry. Sometimes I forget you're still a kid." Karin nodded fast. Their eyes met and they made faces like two basketball-happy teenagers. "Well alright! Is Ro-chelle up for some Ro-ta-tion?"

Rochelle thudded the striped ball into the side pocket. "You two are the strangest pair I have ever encountered—period." She chalked her cue and spat. "How much longer can this go on like this? I'd bet a hundred dollars your relationship is over within a month."

Karin stepped up to her. "You've got a bet."

At seven-thirty-five, Amaryllis was five minutes late and nervously riding up the Patriotic Hall elevator. "Anybody up there yet?"

"About half the team. Tenth Floor. Watch your step."

The door swung open and a stray ball bounced at Amaryllis' feet. "Just in time," said Patty. "Three-on-three."

Villa pointed to Amaryllis. "Me, her and Iris."

Patty laughed. "Right. You get all the height."

"Then you make the teams."

"*Me*, her and Iris. Play to eleven. Our ball."

"Fine, just take it out."

Patty liked three-on-three without a ref. She put her shoulder down and drove the baseline, then lobbed it into Iris. "Cut!" she shouted at Amaryllis.

"I'm cutting," panted Amaryllis already out of breath. They all played even better then she'd imagined. Iris, the starting center, moved well for someone six-foot-four inches tall. Once she got the ball inside, she was almost unstoppable. Dahlia, only five-foot-ten, liked to use her muscle, aggressively moving opponents out of the key. She could bank from either side. When double teamed, she would either power up a lay-in or draw a foul. LaRhonda must have run track or played volleyball. She could jump thirty plus inches vertical and outrun anyone. With long arms and fingers, she liked to tip-in misses even if she was boxed out.

"Time-out. Time-out." Patty approached Amaryllis. "You've got to cut off of Iris. Then I can get the ball to you and you give it back. Get it?"

"Will you just play?" said Villa. "It's only three-on-three."

"In a minute. I have to explain things to her."

Amaryllis listened like a school kid, feeling too inadequate to object. Yeah, even Patty was superb. As point guard, she moved well, shouting instructions all the while. A good ball handler, she was hard to catch and could weave through the holes in the defense. She was a decent shooter, but choosey, selecting only her favorite spots.

Then there was shooting guard Diane Villa. Now she had real skills. Her mastery both made you want to be on her side and challenged you to stop her if you weren't. She seldom missed and had a force that seemed to carry you with her. A smart player, she'd circle under the basket to get free always on alert for the coming pass. Her jump shot was a river, liquid and flowing. She dribbled the ball like it was just another part of her. She had the strength to back into anyone for a lay-up and her fakes left you in the dust. But even as good as she was, Villa remained friendly and considerate.

"Take your shots. Clear out," shouted Patty. For the time being, Amaryllis followed the instructions. But just when she was going to say something—anything—back to Patty, Flor and the rest of the players stepped out of the elevator.

"Okay everyone stretch out and warm up. Terry will be here soon." The game broke up and the players layed on the floor stretching, then individually began running sprints, steps and squats.

Amaryllis leaned over to Daisy. "You mean we each do our own warm-up?" Daisy nodded. That was new. Everywhere else she'd played, the team warmed up together. Maybe things are different with a barnstorming team..

After stretching and running, they shot around. Amaryllis was nervous and missed more then she made.

Villa walked up. "Don't mind Patty. She's really nice once you get to know her."

"I was actually more worried about you. You play a nice game. I just hope I can keep up with you."

"Thanks. Flor told me about you too. You're our new 'Defensive Specialist'."

"I *am* beginning to feel defensive being around you pros."

"Don't sweat it. Relax."

Flor clapped her hands, then pointed to Villa, Violet, Daisy and Peggy. Iris, Patty, LaRhonda and Dahlia waited their turn behind. Amaryllis watched on the side as the Exiles executed their show drill. Weaving, cross-cutting, precision passing—they looked perfect. How could anyone ever get all that down?

After the show drill, they began to run their option plays. Minutes later, the elevator door swung open. Coach strode over to the bench, threw down her bags and wriggled out of her blazer. "Fall back!" she yelled to LaRhonda. "I said Fall back! No, not that side. Okay—stop." She took the ball to demonstrate. "Center brings the ball in. She pivots out of the key. Shooter turns and fakes the pic. Violet goes high. Center pins the cover. Pass is out to shooter unless the switch is made. If they make the switch, just start the weave. Otherwise wing makes contact leaving the shooter open for the pass. Daisy falls back. Everyone else in for the rebound." Coach then turned to Iris. "And Ms. Williams, remember to box out!" The five women had to practice the play four more times before Coach was satisfied.

Maybe Terry was always late, but when she got there, she sure knew what she was doing. "Enough offense. We've got to get the Inbounds Denial drill right in time for Santa Barbara. I don't want to see the bumping, finger pointing and blaming each other like last time. They can play a strong second half and do most of the damage in the last three minutes, so we have to deny them the ball as much as possible. You know they're going to set pics, so coordinate the switch. Now every 'A' Squad take a 'B' and line up along the free throw." Coached looked at the new player. "You play with the offense." Flor you throw it in. I'm going to blow the whistle and count to five. 'B' Squad, vary your strategies; we've got to be prepared for anything." Coach waited for Amaryllis to take her place then blew her whistle. The ball was in-bounded immediately. "Try it again!" Coach frowned. "Again!"

That Thursday was the long awaited showing of the new uniforms. As soon as Terry arrived at the WilliamsWear office, she was introduced to several coropate reps who began right in with a pitch for "Spandex". "Believe me, Terry," said the Whitney Ale Brewers rep. "I'm on your side. Its just that the committee chairs are all insisting. They say I should be telling you, 'We demand Spandex Uniforms,' not asking you for them. I'm really just trying to help you out."

The LadyLocker/Teen-Hair-All Cosemetics rep jumped in. "Face it

Terry, ninety-per-cent of the sports viewers are male, and you know what they want to see. You have to compromise a little. Spandex is part of the action. It has sex appeal."

"Males do not make up ninety-per-cent of the viewers," retorted Coach. "And can't you believe that people might just want to watch a good game?"

"Of course we can. We really believe in what you're trying to do. But our polls show that Spandex is what sells."

Coach was approaching her boiling point. Little bubbles were breaking the surface of her patience. The deal-makers sensed her uneasiness and closed in for the kill. "Get with the program Terry. When our company got the call from Warren, we considered his proposal and said, 'Hey! If we can help him out on this one, it'll be great all around.' This is a 'Win-Win' situation. The 'Spandex Phase One Scenario' is good for everyone. Don't be the odd man—" The rep hesitated for a solicitous moment and then continued. "—I mean odd girl out."

Coach had had enough. "The Exiles are professional athletes, not Go-Go Dancers. You're not going to turn my league into a strip show. We've done just fine by ourselves so far. I've been through this many times and—"

"Our companies are not sexist!" insisted the Go-Get-Em Natural Drink rep with a sly teasing smile.

"Then when will you be satisfied? When #16 is a centerfold and #4 fixes your breakfast and #12 does your laundry? You show us some respect before you start in with—" Just as Coach was falling right into the standard corporate ruse, the lights went out. Geoffrey, microphone in hand, appeared spot lit from above. He stood on his toes, rested back on his heels, bowed to no one in particular, adjusted his shirt and began the presentation.

"You will see four alternatives. The first is the circle. The second is the stripe The third is the triangle. The fourth is Spandex." His tone was smoothly pedantic; his voice, deep and theatrical with a slight English Accent. "The circle mimics the shape of the ball and the rim. It is symbolic of the team together as in a huddle. Keiko!" A girl, her long black hair wrapped in a Princess Lea bun, tossed a ball against a prop backboard. Her uniform of bright colored circles and fine black lines glinted under the spotlight. Geoffrey continued. "The stripe is a study in verticality—the height of the players, the forces of gravity, the goal of the basket. Mimi!" A thin woman with angular features and dark eyes jumped for an imaginary rebound. She slipped off her jacket to reveal striped shorts and jersey. Geoffrey, stepped back into the light to introduce his third flashing alternative. "The triangle is a stable shape that can take on a personality of it's own. It can be hills, a skyline, a direction—"

"Come on Geo." The Whitney Ale Brewers rep stood up. "Where are the Spandex cheerleaders you promised us?"

"I'm saving them for last." Geoffrey, stepped aside for the next model. "Esther!"

Coach's eyes were suddenly captured by an alluring sight; a happy, hyper, Sade look-alike cart-wheeling to the center of the platform. She layed on the floor then did a half-kip to a standing position. Her uniform was a field of triangles, loud and extraverted. Coach instantly loved it. Something so "In Your Face" that you finally forgot all that bouncy bouncy stuff and let someone finally play some hoops. Triangles was the choice. "That's it!" shouted Terry. "Geo, you've done it again!"

"But what about the Spandex cheerleaders?" asked the Go-Get-Em Natural Drink rep.

Geo smiled. "And without further ado—Precious... Todi...Alex...John—lets see the Spandex design."

"John, who's John?" Jaws dropped as four male body builders danced onto the stage, flexing, posing and thrusting.

That weekend, as agreed, Karin and Terry went on their bike ride. They followed the L.A. River on their way to Patriotic Hall, downtown. As they made their turn south, Karin took a breather by a bus stop that looked out towards the stratified face of the hills of Elysian Park.

Terry was growing impatient. "How long are we going to stay here?"

"Long enough for you to learn a little about time. Do you realize that if the earth's life span were condensed into a single year, then only hours ago, these mountains weren't even formed yet and this whole area was underwater."

"Oh yeah?"

"Only seconds ago, the Indians maintained the forests and a fraction of a second ago, the L.A. river ran freely and the first Freeway was built."

"Wow, that's weird, but what's the point?" asked Terry.

"My point is that I love you and I'm glad we're getting a chance to spend some *time* together."

Coach fell silent and remained so as Karin continued her lecture. Signs of the geological past where all around. Within yards were volcanic rocks from when nearby volcanoes spewed out their hot lava. Below, was the L.A. River, a rare antecedant stream that cut through the hills along Elysian Park as they rose over time. And on the other end of the park, was Fern Dell, a natural grotto that used to be a Gabrielino Village.

Terry got back on her bike. "We got to get going."

"But you're alway rushing everything."

"Don't start again."

A hunched over homeless lady sitting on the bus bench lifted her head. Her eyes were bloodshot and layers of blankets covered her shoulders. "Why are you two fighting?" she asked aloud.

"She's always in a hurry."

The lady thought a moment. "That's good. Be in a hurry. A hurry towards kindness and understanding. Could you please spare a quarter?"

Terry gave her a few bucks. "It's not that I'm too fast. It's that she's too slow."

"That's good. Be slow. Slow to anger."

Karin opened her wallet and also gave. "But how can two people who are so different, find a way to be together?"

The homeless woman looked out at the concrete lined river bed. "Follow your heart. It will know the right path."

As they rode on, Terry thought. Sometimes she felt it really would be better it her and her young partner went their separate ways. But other times, she felt strong hope and promise for both of their futures. Spending time together was healthy, but it took away from her life's work. Terry looked out at the mountain ridges, the river banks and the foothill roads and recalled Karin's words about time. Which was the right path? Hadn't people been following the same paths for thousands of years? As Karin had explained, people had always used trails that followed natural contours. The Indians developed them; the Spanish followed them to connect their pueblos, presidios and missions; the Mexicans supplied their ranchos and drove their cattle to market on them; the Americans built their railroads and water distribution system on them, and, as the city grew, highways, power cables, telephone lines, trolley car routes, flood control channels, roads and freeways all stretched along their elegant curves. Everyday, as Coach sped or chugged down the Golden State Freeway, she paid little attention to the River and Mountains on either side of her. Maybe, if she slowed down, she might be able to communicate more naturally, whether it be with lover, her team, her sponsers or a homeless person on a bus bench.

At Patriotic Hall Gym, Coach felt revitalized. "Okay, lets practice the Inbounds Denial Drill."

"Not again." groaned Patty.

"Yes again. And just for that winning attitude, you get to be the in-bounder." Coach looked to the others. "Remember, block the passing lane, switch on the pics." She blew her whistle and watched as the ball was easily in-bounded.

"You see," said Patty. "Let's just scrimmage instead."

"Later Patty. First we have to get this right. Again." Coach retreated only to watch the same defensive play fail twice more.

"It's hopeless Coach. What's the point?" said Patty. "They'll never get it."

Coach took a deep breath. "I hear you Patty. What is the point? In fact, this whole game is a waste of time. Years go by and nothing changes. No one appreciates us. Our pay is low. The fans are cruel. There are too many injuries; too much arguing. We try to prove ourselves, but, whatever we excel at never seems to count." Terry bounced a ball. "Take a break. Everyone go outside, stretch, look out at the view, then come back inside, because we're going to have some fun."

When the players returned, Coach began from square one. "If you think of this play as a steal, then what we're doing is really rather mean. So lets think of it another way. The ball belongs to you. It's yours. The referee told Patty here that she can only borrow the ball for five seconds, then she has to give it back." Terry spun the ball on her finger. "Have you ever had something you really wanted and someone took it and wouldn't give it back. Well, here is an opportunity to make sure you do get it back. Sometimes it's fun to take something back. You have to work as a team and communicate with each other to get your ball back and that makes it even more fun. Villa is floater. She has to look after the four of you. The rest have to deny the passing lane and switch when you're blocked out. Remember, it's your ball. Patty must give it back. You all are just making sure she does."

Coach put on her high tops, joined the players on the floor, then blew her whistle. Amaryllis, on offense, bolted down court as instructed. Everybody began to push and race. This time however, there were no holes in the defense, no openings, no unseen opportunities. With one of the five seconds left, Patty tried to lob the ball to Amaryllis at half court.

Floating down into the group of players, just as Coach had planned, the ball fell right into Villa's waiting and eager hands. There was nothing Patty or Amaryllis could have done. The inbounds was denied. Villa got her ball back.

Exiles *1996 Summer Roster*

#	Player	Ht.	Position	College/Hometown
4	Daisy Little	5-9	Guard	Ventura/Venice
10	Margaret Mawson	6-2	Center	USC/Baldwin Hills
14	Violet Jaharbian	5-10	For/Guard	USC/Hollywood
22	Dahlia Logoromi	5-11	Forward	CSDH/Long Beach
24	Amaryllis Seltzer	6-0	Forward	UCB/Santa Cruz
28	Patricia Aguilar	5-9	Guard	CSLA/City Terrace
33	LaRhonda Lewis	6-0	For/Cen	LACC/Los Angeles
36	Diane Villa	5-9	Guard	UCLA/Boyle Heights
44	Iris Williams	6-3	Center	Stanford/Pasadena

Head Coach: Theresa Taktikabian

Assistant Coach and Head Athletic Trainer: Flor Ortega

Team Sponsor: WilliamsWear of California

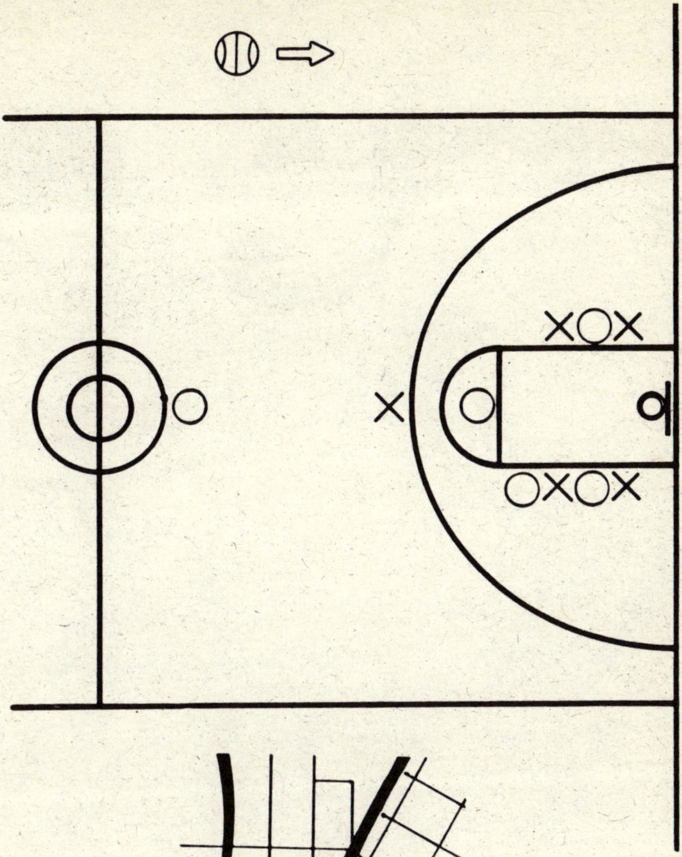

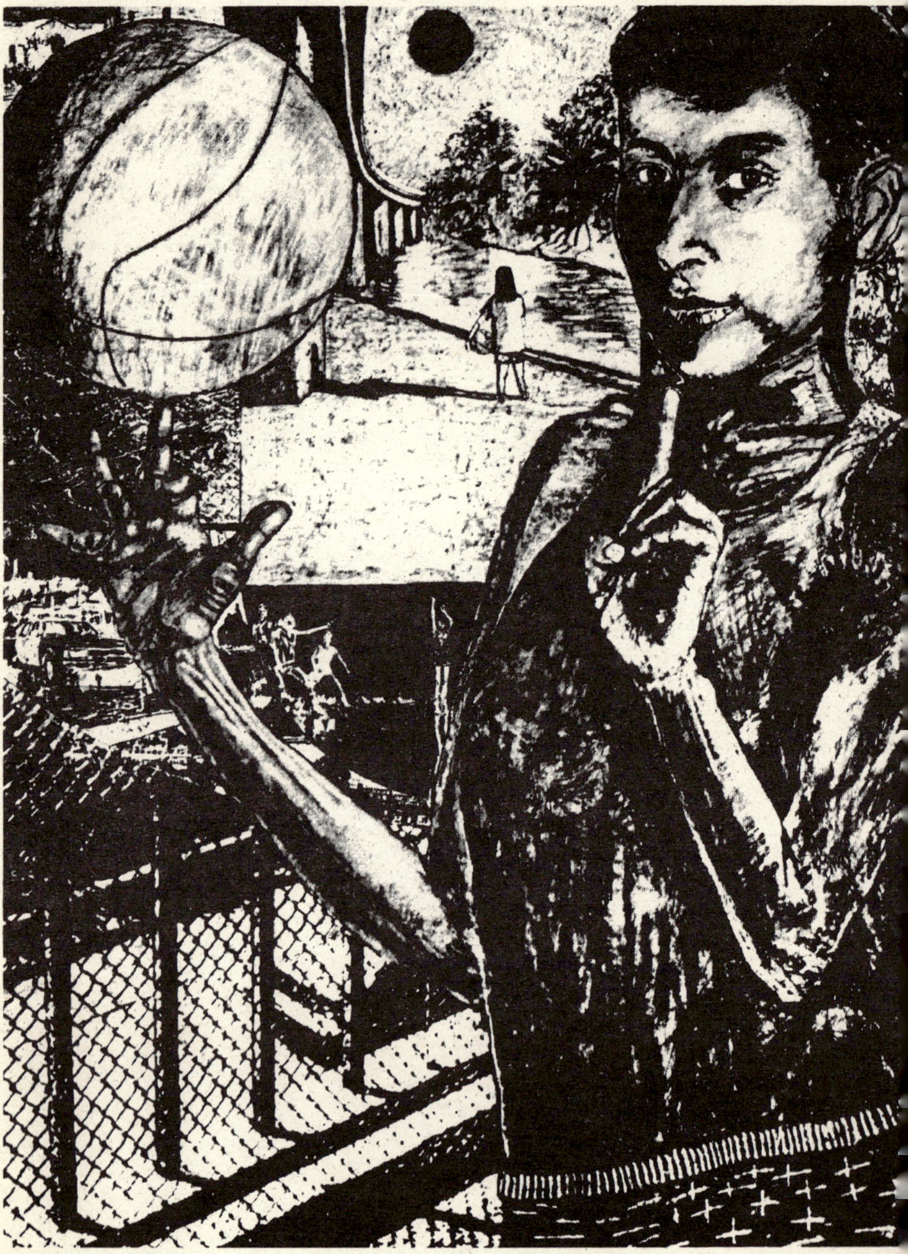

Duckie Bridge 4

She was twenty-seven and still didn't know how to drive. So what. It didn't matter much. She could get around. In any case, she was not about to try to learn now. Especially after that last disaster. But that was already four years ago—forget it. Diane Elizabeth Villa sat chewing potato chips and fidgeting on the dusty bus ad bench. She looked down the street to see if the #68 was coming, then took out a brown folder from her bag. Flor had given everyone a travel itinerary stapled to tickets and a slick shiny brochure.

"We'll be staying at the San Miguel Residence Hall. It's perfectly nice, but for those of you who want to pay a little extra, you can try the UCSB Faculty Club next to the Events Center."

"Yeah right, Terry! On our salary? You must be kidding."

"Patty, some of us save our money so we can treat ourselves well."

"That's really getting old."

"I thought you just became a Sales Associate at Home Center Depot. What about all those dividends?"

"What about them?"

"It's only twenty dollars, Patty."

"Then you're treating?"

Villa stared down at the photo of the round wading pool and the girl in the bikini. Coach and Karin will stay there. Glamour Girl Iris and her boyfriend will be there too. Maybe Peggy and Daisy. No, Daisy was trying to save money. What about that new girl? What will she do? Villa smoothed the folds of the pamphlet. She looked down the street, glanced at her watch and sighed.

Away games had their pluses and minuses. Villa loved hotels, cafes, bars and gourmet restaurants. Bus seats, train station waiting rooms, crowded taxies and tight schedules, however, were less than thrilling. On the road, just when you were beginning to have fun, it was time to come back. She shuffled through the folder and removed an old paper that she always brought for luck—the do's and don'ts of girls' basketball:

"Of course, girls like to play basketball. They play in elementary schools, high schools and colleges. To play a good game, girls should be healthy and strong. For good health, obey these simple rules:

1. Help yourself to a nice, clear complexion by washing and bathing regularly. Use plenty of soap and water to make you look and feel fresh and clean all the time. Eat good, nourishing food. Cokes and potato chips do not make a well-rounded meal.

In other words, take care of your face so that a wild elbow can slash open your eyebrow and leave you looking like Frankenstein.

2. Get plenty of sleep. Movies and parties are not for weekdays when you have to get up the next morning to go to school. Play outdoors and don't be afraid to walk. Go to the store and help your mother with the shopping. Walk to school and to the library.

Translation: Don't have fun. Stress out and be high-strung twenty-four hours a day.

3. Don't rush the high heels. Girls who begin to wear high heels when they are too young will find that these shoes may affect the posture. High heels may also cause back aches and other discomforts. So wear shoes with comfortable heels.

Try telling that to Iris.

4. For practice and everyday outdoor play, wear a playsuit or slacks and a blouse.

Diane smiled. She could still remember the first time she'd read the pamphlet in third grade and the subsequent conversation with her mother.

"Mama, when are we going to the library?"

"Mija no te molestes. Hay muchos libros aquí. No iremos a la biblioteca. Por favor deja de botar esa pelota!"

"Can we go shopping?"

"Shopping...*y para que?*"

"Anything, *pero no tacones.*"

"Niña, no hagas mensadas. Ya te dije que dejes de botar esa pelota. No has parado desde las seis de la mañana. Anda, ya!"

"But I had to see *si servia.*"

"¿De que estas hablando?"

"The paper."

"¿Cual papel? No seas traviesa. Vas a llegar tarde a la escuela. ¡Ya vete!"

"But I'm not afraid to walk to school."

"Y porque tendrias que tener miedo de caminar a la escuela si no mas esta en la otra esquina?"

"Mother, why can't school be farther away, then I could really get good."

"Por favor, Mija, ya vete y trata de meterte cosas buenas en tu coquito."

"Esta bien, pero no compres chucherias."

"¿Chucherias? ¿Come se te ocurre?"

Diane's mother, Guillermina Luz Villa, was a wonderful cook and would never serve junk food. Unfortunately, her daughter was always too busy playing ball to be taught anything about a kitchen. Villa's calloused fingers searched for the last potato chip before tossing the bag into the center of the wire-mesh trash can. If the #68 didn't come in ten minutes, she'd miss the train. Running late made her nervous. Her mother had fixated three "good" habits permanently in her mind. *"Hay tres reglas: lavarse las manos, nunca llegar tarde, y no botar la pelota dentro de la casa."*

Villa unzipped her sports bag and took out her basketball. She spun it on her fingers like a toy, let it fall down on the wood slats, then dribbled to a rhythm blasting out of the liquor store. Dribbling calmed her nerves, and this was her favorite pet ball—*La Bola*. Four basketballs she owned (actually three and one soccer ball that thought it was a basketball): La Bola, Tiny, Humberto and *La Pelota*. La Bola was new, all leather and was only allowed to touch wood. She came with Villa on road games and was placed in the trophy display cabinet when not in use. Humberto was rough and tough, worn and torn. As she bounced him between the cracks of the sidewalk, he'd be like her sixth sense, rebounding with a quick thump off asphalt and concrete, splattering slowly off gooey melted sidewalk gum, splashing with a kerplop in puddles, pattering down the gutter. Humberto was *bien cochino*—a real slob, not at all like Tiny—an oversized stuffed orange sphere given to Villa on her birthday by a fan. Tiny was soft, round, orange, lazy, and faithfully stayed on the bed with the dolls and stuffed animals until Diane's return. Finally there was La Pelota, the deluded soccerball. La Pelota had been with her since she was a skinny and long-limbed hyperactive nine-year-old. Villa, at that age, was difficult to control: always getting into trouble, messing things up in the garage, pushing her baby sister full speed in the toy car, spitting her blue jawbreaker down the steep hill road. But the day Tio Dani gave her La Pelota, all that mischief came to an end.

La Pelota wasn't new; she was old, torn, dirty with patches. Villa didn't know it then, but she wasn't even using her right. *"Corazón, kick it. Don't* bounce it, es soccer." Tio Dani said lots of funny things like that. He took a marker and drew eyes, nose, mouth and ears, then said, *"Recuerdate que quizas en esta vida, esta pelota sea tu mejor compañera."* Tongue out, fascinated, she threw her new buddy down again and again. She kept a ball with her always, wrestling it away from older sisters, stashing it under the desk during class.

The bus bench grew hot from the summer sun shining through the layer of Eastside haze. Villa wore a loose white button-down men's shirt, plaid Bermuda shorts, expensive jogging shoes and matching ankle socks. Her style of dress carried a certain sporty conservatism stemming from her three years in Catholic School. Orange brick, scholastic achievement, discipline, uniforms; she would never forget it.

At Sisters of Serenity, Villa, a thin, flat-chested late bloomer, easily buzzed past the J.V. girls, forcing Coach MacDormatt (Sister "Door Mat" behind her back, the only real nun on campus) to place a seventh grader on the Varsity Squad for the first time in Serenity History. But off the court, Villa did not fit in as easily. Her inability to cope with the cliques, catty chatting, cautious reprimands, whispered secrets and castigating looks restrained her usually hyper behavior, leaving her to sit by herself (ball at her side) through recess and lunch.

One afternoon, she felt herself pushed from her spot. She toppled back, her green-and-blue tartan-plaid book sack flying through the air and landing on her face. Laughter rang out as she got up from the muddy grass by the curb where the jock girls sat during break. "Hey!"

"Damn, you're light. Sorry, I didn't think you'd fall so easily." Tammy nodded to the other girls. "But after all, you are in my place." Villa got to her feet and glared at her assailant. She remembered Tammy's silhouette from the shower room, being almost entranced by its graceful movements. Why was this popular pretty girl becoming hostile? "And while we're on the subject," Tammy showboated. "Just because you can play doesn't mean you can sit wherever you want. So why don't you take your bony butt over to the other curb." Villa was caught off guard by the challenge, but still, it was nothing new. She let Tammy mouth off, then at the right moment tripped her over the trash can. "You got some guts! You think you're bad?" Tammy's head bobbed back and forth. She brushed off the trash staining her clothes. "You better watch your back, Skinny."

In the locker room after practice, Tammy tried to twist Villa's arm behind her back. Villa wriggled free. "Why are you doing this?" she asked, moving towards the older girl.

"You're a snob. Don't tell me you're not." Tammy threw a dirty towel. "You think you're better than everyone just because you can play. Everyone hates you."

Villa smelled mop bucket fumes and felt her stomach sink. "Listen, Tammy, please." Diane Elizabeth Villa was beginning to waver, fearfully worried of being branded an outsider.

Tammy stuffed her clothes in her locker, slammed the door and headed out across the playing field.

Villa quickly gathered her things and followed the older girl. "Hey Tammy, what's going on here?"

Tammy took a swing, just missing Villa's jaw. She grabbed handfuls of hair, scratched and tackled. Villa ground Tammy's face into the grass and pinned down her arms.

"Get off me!" grunted Tammy.

Villa held fast.

"Get off!" Tammy struggled, then suddenly relaxed. She looked up and grinned. "Dyke!" she spat. "I saw you watch me in the shower. Everyone knows you are, so don't try and hide it." Where were the other girls so they could hear too? "Get off Dyke! Get off before you get off!"

In front of the bus bench, a taxi slowed down and the driver looked at Villa. She opened her wallet and counted her money. Keys, attached to her billfold, jangled as she sorted through her cards and photos and brought out her bus pass. The sun beat down on her black hair, making beads of sweat gather on her scalp. She ran a comb across her head and glanced down at the old junior high photo. The long ponytail dated the picture precisely; that was the semester she had it all cut off.

Before the haircut, though, came the fight—the showdown with Mama. Villa had decided that one way or another, she must return to public school. At the bottom of the pecking order, no amount of bargaining, joking, playacting, compromising or trickery could seem to get her head above water. There was another reason Villa wanted to escape to public school. She craved the lively crowds. She wanted to play against Garfield and Crenshaw and Manual Arts and Bell and Jordan and Wilson; enter a gym packed with rowdy teenagers yelling, screaming, taunting, turning their backs at bad calls, lighting lighters, throwing trash out onto the floor, shouting at the top of their lungs. And then there was the pagentry: the drill team chanting, the bass drum pounding, the band roaring and the sparkling dance squad performing another thrilling routine. Villa knew she deserved to be at the center of all that, proudly jogging out to circle the floor, the fruit of the community, its hope of excellence, its belief in the future—the star women athletes.

In her first year at Roosevelt, Villa made the athletics program suddenly seem like a good investment. She had filled out by the tenth grade; her body graced with well-defined abdominals, a slightly high rear, muscular thighs, long fingers, sturdy ankles and beautifully tapered calves. Guys would hang out whenever she played. Girls too, including beautiful Catalina. Like her mom had said, "Men only want one thing," but what did baggy-pantsed, gangsta-zipper-shirted, long-haired Catalina want? When coach closed the doors to practices, Villa would ask Catalina to stay and sit down with her allies, filling the bench with a wonderful warm and confident cross-legged presence. And during the dozens, Catalina made sure everyone knew that Villa was better.

"Who's going to handle Garfield's Ms. Slick Point Guard?"

"Villa."

"But that's her fourth three-pointer in a row."

"Villa will take care of it."

"She's too tall."

"Villa will use that up. She'll shut her down. She's the best. She's better than anyone."

Villa *was* better—consistently, noticeably, obviously, unforgettably better. She shot and scored from up top and on the side. She backed in with authority and powered up the lay-in. She'd run the play and understand it first time out. She'd just smile at unfair calls, bouncing up and down on the balls of her feet, anxious to get back to play. When she did get angry, all that fuel and fire would go straight to her legs as she dribbled around, through, over and under the sixteen and seventeen-year-olds.

"Cheryl Miller?"

"Villa's better."

"Teresa Edwards?"

"Villa's better."

"Carol Blazejowski, Lynette Woodard and Anne Meyers?"

"Villa's better! Better, better, better!"

She was Roosevelt's sure placement in the Pac 10, and the Rough Rider Yearbook displayed her full-page action photo in the Girls' Basketball section. Diane Elizabeth Villa would surely have been listed as "Most Likely to Succeed," if it weren't for one thoroughly disseminated piece of gossip— "*Es marimacha.* She hangs around with Catalina. Villa is a lesbian."

Finally the bus showed up. The #68 rolled under the freeway, over the channel and past the jail. From the Union Station stop, Villa had to race up from the street, heading towards the walls of the side-entrance courtyard. Heaving a sigh of relief at the sight of Sunny and Sonny attempting to climb one of the huge courtyard trees, she slowed down.

"Hey, where's your mom?"

"In line."

"What are you doing?"

"She doesn't want us to get dirty sliding on the floor inside. So we're here."

"But you're covered with grass."

Villa led them to the gift shop, bought them candy, then took them by the hand to Iris waiting inside the cavernous station.

Iris waved. "Hey, we were beginning to worry about you."

"The bus was late."

"Where did you find them?"

"Climbing the tree."

Iris stared down at her children blankly. "I thought I told you two not to get dirty."

"But Uncle Geo said if you can touch the top of the tree, you go to heaven."

"Uncle Geo will be going to heaven when I get my hands on him." Iris looked at Villa. "Are you going to stay in the halls or at the Faculty Club?"

"Faculty Club. I don't like dorms."

No, she did not like the dorms—she hated them. At Cal State Fullerton, she spent as much time away as possible. Sure, during the day she'd drop by the tiny room to pick up her books and change clothes, but at night she stayed with Liz. The dorms were cramped, noisy, sterile, cold and impersonal. Liz's bungalow was cute, cozy, warm and full of antiques. Liz wined and dined her young athletic girlfriend and after two years of her doting, Villa had become spoiled—a "M.A.P." (Mexican American Princess), the Eastside Katharine Hepburn.

"Where to tonight, Diane? Drinks at the Polo Lounge? Dinner at Spago?"

"But Liz, the hostess was so rude. A table away from the window—really! Their little vista is so overrated anyway. And who can converse in all that chatter. Why my ears are ringing at the very thought—"

"Say no more, darling. You're so right. But where to then, L'Orangerie, Citrus, Rex?"

"Liz, do you think we could just do the Golden Chopstick once more? I know we were there already this week, but—"

"Of course, my dear, whatever your heart desires. After all that ball bouncing, you must be so exhausted."

The intercom echoed the first call for the San Diegan north to Santa Barbara. An electric luggage car buzzed by the team in the long, wide tunnel. As they fed through, the new girl solemnly walked apart from the others. That didn't seem right. Why, when Patty came on the team, her Friendship Campaign was like a fresh Twinkie: ninety-per-cent sugar and a shelf life of twenty years. Villa brushed shoulders with the pensive six-footer and spotted an unusual label on her travel bag.

"Hey Amaryllis, is your bag really recycled?"

"The clerk told me it's made of hemp."

"Do you save money buying recycled things?"

"No, actually they cost twice as much."

Villa laughed. So she does have a sense of humor. "Excited about your first trip?"

"Sure," said Amaryllis shrugging, "but I don't think I'll be playing."

"Oh yeah, you're right. I forgot about that. But don't worry, that's Terry's routine for all the players. Everyone watches on their first time out."

"I'm not worried."

"Nervous?"

"No, I just feel out of place. I'm not sure I know why I'm here."

"Ah come on, you did pretty good at practice."

Amaryllis looked at her crossways and followed the others up ahead. Clanging noise and wind blew in as the team climbed the stairs to platform C and waited for the coach car. Ribbons of rocks, rails, bumpy rubber paving, corrugated aluminum and late afternoon sky stretched into the distance as the locomotive huffed out its loud breath and the dangerous steel wheels came to a stop on the shiny track. Villa grabbed a seat by herself keeping her bag at her side. It felt good to get away from it all. A row of lights marched along the ceiling to the next car. Down the aisle, the cars creaked and groaned, shifting in line as the train pulled out of the station. Where was that new girl sitting? Villa spotted Amaryllis' arm four seats in front of her. New Girl was kind of strange—self-conscious, smart, a little goofy, naive, inexperienced—doesn't know what she likes yet. At least, she hustled. She was green and fresh and still enthusiastic about practice, unlike the rest of those stubborn, jaded, opinionated vets. God, was she ever getting tired of their stupid old jokes.

"Check it out, fresh meat for Princess!"

"How was the Palms last night? Get a real workout?"

"Move it, this isn't Dinah Shore Weekend."

She stared at her reflection in the train window. After all she had been through, her face still looked trusting. Trusting? Gullible is more like it. Oh, don't get on that again. It was four years ago, forget it. Villa suddenly sat up, grabbed her wallet and walked over to where New Girl sat.

"Hey, want something from the snack bar?"

"Oh, no thanks. I'm not hungry."

"A cup of coffee?"

"I don't drink it."

"Oh well, how about tea?"

"I drink tea, but not out of a Styrofoam cup."

Doesn't drink out of a Styrofoam cup? "Oh well," said Villa, moving on. She walked along the train aisle, shifting and balancing, looking down at the staring faces on the way to the club car. The display was standard: candy bars, cookies, packaged pastries, microwave pizza, all-beef hot dogs.

"What can I get for you, senorita?"

Great, here we go again. "Two cans of orange juice, a candy bar, a sandwich and peanuts."

"You sure look healthy. Why all the junk food?"

Villa stared and handed over the money.

"Where are you from anyway?"

"I'm from East L.A." Here it comes. Are you in a gang? Duck any stray bullets lately? *¿Cómo está usted?*

"Duck any stray bullets lately?"

"No."

"From East L.A.. And where are you going?"

"Back to my seat." She returned to her place, unwrapped her sandwich and candy bar, poured her drink, cracked a few peanuts and found that she'd completely lost her appetite. Unfortunately, processed packaged food always brought back those same memories.

After Liz, transfering to UCLA was a little difficult. UCLA: impressive, prestigious, beautiful campus, expensive cars, intelligent people...cafeteria food. Maybe she could have put up with the boredom of the dorms—everyone so straight, no bars, no dancing, just study and practice—but those dinners? How could everyone keep eating them? Villa's face contorted at the mere thought of Salisbury steaks in lumpy floured gravy or watery macaroni and cheese with bean and beet salad—yuck!

Of course on the weekends, instinct would lead her back home to do her laundry, gobble down enchiladas (sauce made from scratch, just the right amount of onion inside), slurp up buckets of sopa de albondigas (with just the right touch of mint and cumin) and munch on crispy taquitos de pollo by the dozen. By Sunday, Villa's stomach would be extended over her belt about to burst. Unfortunately though, a person does get hungry during the week too, especially when that person runs twenty-eight miles and practices four times.

One week, strolling through the Village, Villa overdid it, splurging on tapes for her morning jogs and leaving herself with nothing but her meal card until her grant payment came in the following Friday. She was too ashamed and friendless to confide to anyone that she was completely broke and had actually borrowed some of her (bad) roommate's shampoo. All those tall bottles and cosmetics displayed on the common dresser dwarfed Villa's sparse arrangement of bargain-brand soap and discount items. Shampoo. Shampoo to wash a head of hair that had long since outgrown its normal layered styling.

At least her other roommate, Rachel, was funny, a left-wing clown to balance out the nightmare-inspiring Miss Religious Right— born-again Whitney. Maybe it hadn't been the best idea to "come out" to both of them during their first meeting.

But what was worse than that, what made Villa cringe (and hate herself even after four years of obsessing), was the thought of Stewart. Sure, everyone makes mistakes, but this was so obvious. What was it that had dragged her in when even a naive freshman would have known better? Was it his place; so nice and clean? Was it the shimmering fountain or the tall tropical drinks? Maybe it was the promise of a job waiting after college or the impressive big names whose money he handled. Deep down, Villa knew it was none of those. No, she knew what it really was. After Liz, it was bound to happen. It was the food. How could anyone resist white wine and pasta primavera when the alternative was boiled wienies and grease-filled pork-and-beans casserole? A childhood of sweet tamales canarios does not prepare one for eggshell omelets, one-hundred-percent ground-fat burgers and stir-fry slop.

If she could only go back in time, she would have seen it coming? Climbing the Ackerman Union "Book Zone" stairs to that wonderfully loud video arcade, there he'd be, stuffing quarters into her favorite killer video game so that the only way she could play was against him. A few weeks went by and she said okay to a small salad at the bar (alright, alright, so it was more like a mountain of marinated mushrooms, artichoke hearts, sunflower seeds—she hadn't eaten all day). Then of course, it was, "Try the new Italian place in the Village?" And from there, try the fancy restaurant, try the exotic lounge, try the trendy coffee house. Try it, try it. Tipsy from champagne and attention, her stomach had done it:, convinced her to trust. "Try it."

"I thought you already knew, Stewart. I'm gay."

"You mean you've never had sex."

"Of course I have, just with girls, not guys."

"You mean only with girls?"

"Only with girls. What's wrong?"

"I just wish you liked guys too. Do you want me to take you home?"

"Don't be like that. Anyway, Whitney's probably there now. She's really been driving me nuts. I asked her if it was okay that I borrowed some of her shampoo. I mean like a palmful. She got all upset and gave me this long lecture. I just sat and stared at her. Hey, I thought we were going to play your home video games."

"Well, if you're staying, you might as well stay in style. I'll open another bottle. Try it, okay?

"Okay, okay, I'll try," she agreed later that same night. She heard her own words spill out in the air like mushy TV *novela* dialogue. She felt her control fade and her misgivings swell. Her mother's words echoed in her ears. "Men can protect you."

Champagne, nice car, nice place, nice food, became a tongue filling her mouth. An elegant fantasy of light scents and smooth skin became the weight of him suffocating her, pressing closer than the most savage of court competitors. Where was Liz's attention, Catalina's admiration? She turned her mouth away and gasped. That lie of a maid-serviced, unpaid for condo. That prop of a leased sports car. There was no job waiting for her. The smell of his breath filled her nose. He groaned loud; his eyes bulging. Then, when the pounding against her finally subsided, when she had pushed his body off, gathered her clothing and gotten him to take her back, where was she? At the driveway of that dorm, bittersweetly relieved to be back, grateful for a chance to shower with her discount soap and humble to borrow a palm full of Whitney's shampoo.

Factories and blank industrial yards passed by as the train cranked forward through the Valley. Villa spread out her things and began to draw with a pen and paper. Dusk had fallen and the orange opal lights of the suburbs danced like fireflies. It became pitch-black outside as the train passed through the last and longest of the Simi Valley tunnels before winding down into Oxnard. The darkness just focused her mind back on that obsession.

"I'll call you."

"I don't know."

"You're mad. You didn't like it. I didn't do anything you didn't want. You have to grow up. You can start working part-time in the office pretty soon. I've told my mother about you. I have some time off next week. We can go stay at my friend's place in Vegas. You'll like him. You can practice your driving on the desert roads. A few more lessons and you'll have it."

In her dorm room, Villa showered and lay in bed until dawn. She got up, showered again and walked to the campus chapel to wait until it opened.

"Hello. Oh my, it is you, isn't it? You're Diane Villa. You play for the varsity squad."

"Yes, Father."

"I'm a big fan. I saw you play last week against Rutgers. You're the best."

"Thank you, Father."

"Remember in the last ten seconds when you drove to the basket, were you planning to pass or try to draw a foul?"

She didn't sleep that night or the next and went back home to do her laundry on the weekend as usual. Once inside that protective environment, her shell cracked. Kneeling at her mother's feet, her face turned to lava, a contorted landscape of molten tears.

"¿Pero que es lo que te pasa? ¿Porque te comportas tan extraña?"

"He promised he'd teach me to drive."

"¿Quien te prometio? ¿Y por eso lloras tanto?"

"He said after I graduated he'd get me a good job."

"¿Loca, de que estas hablando? ¿Cual trabajo?"

"Madre, yo no aguanto a los hombres. No me gustan."

"¿Y a quien le gusta los hombres?"

Try and try again, the promising new Bruin found that she had been away from home too long and no longer seemed able to make her mother understand. So, desperately, her arms holding tight around Guillermina's waist, she became, for passing minutes, a girl her mother could understand—not a superstar, not an athlete, not the force behind the team. "*Yo pensaba que él era mi amigo, pero me mintió,*" uttered Villa between sobs, "*Me mintió.*"

She walked like a zombie from class to class for days. She was lethargic at practice and the coach gave her lectures and warnings.

"What is wrong with you? You've been missing all week."

"I'm sorry."

"You don't talk to anyone. You're not working on your drive. You still haven't got the 'Four Fake' drill down. What is it?"

"I don't know."

"I told you to start varying your moves. Suppose Washington State puts their specialists on you and you can't get open to shoot. Suppose they press or trap. You rely too heavily on your set shot. You have to learn to crash the boards."

"I'm trying."

"Try harder. You're supposed to be a team leader and you haven't even as much as smiled at anyone since last weekend. I won't take the silent treatment from my starting players. You better get with it. Get with it or you won't be starting next game. Understand?"

"Yes, Coach. I understand."

"I'm giving you the rest of the week off. Take care of it. Whatever it is, you take care of it."

After changing, Villa sat on the locker room bench, lost, head between knees. If she went home, she'd just be misunderstood. If she went to her room, she might have to face Whitney. She swung her bag around her shoulder, grabbed Humberto and bounced him to the library staying there until it closed. Later, tired and without anywhere else to go, she crossed her fingers pushed open the door to her room and breathed a sigh of relief that it was Rachel, not Whitney, sitting watching TV.

"Hey, Smiley, how you doing?"

"Not too good, I guess."

"Tell me about it. I've got two midterms coming up and all I've done is watch the Late Late Show."

"Where's Whitney?"

"She went to her Fellowship. She asked me to go with her."

"You too?"

"She asked you? Let me guess. She wanted to change your lifestyle."

"No, she said I've been too depressed lately."

"You don't say. I wonder what would make her say a thing like that? You just stopped talking to either of us. I was beginning to think you had laryngitis."

"I'm sorry."

"Why are you sorry? Maybe you didn't have anything to say. Want some popcorn? It's a little burnt. I'm the only person I know who burns microwave popcorn. I mean, you put it in, you set the timer and press 'Start'. Open the door. Burnt."

"What movie is it?"

"Who knows? It's an oldie but a baddie. I've seen it twice and I still don't know what it's called. I hope I never find out."

"Can I sit down?"

"Sure. You're just in time for my favorite part. See the guy who looks constipated? He's the heavy. The sweet old man with the cane is just about to get thrown off the side of the building...here it comes. Going down! Basement floor! Linens, towels, lingerieeeee! Pretty neat, don't you think? Wow, look everybody, Villa remembered how to smile. I thought I was losing my touch. Now that you're smiling, would you mind going down the hall and buying a new bag of popcorn? This stuff is worse than the movie."

The train passed a lumber yard fence holding back piles of rusty pipes and broken wood pallets. Streets appeared, intersections, cars waiting behind flashing ringing signal arms. A grove of trees brushed by and then the view opened up to the ocean—big and dark. The immense emptiness drew her out; out along its expansive surface, out where waves chopped and winds howled for attention.

"It's pretty at night." It was New Girl sitting on the opposite arm rest.

Villa took La Bola in her hands and sighed. "Yeah."

Boulders held back the crashing waves along the shore and in the distance floated huge oil derricks, their lights reflecting on the waters. "The whales go through there each Spring. They're an endangered species. Every year, they migrate up and down the coast."

In the distance up ahead shimmered the harbor lights of Santa Barbara. It felt good to get away. In less than an hour, Villa would be settling into her fancy room for a long night's sleep. "Well, I hope they make it." I hope guys like Stewart don't harpoon them or spill oil in the channel or—stop it Diane—stop worrying about him. It was four years ago. Forget it. She smiled up at her new team mate. "Yeah, I really hope they make it."

At the Faculty Club the next morning, Villa opened her curtains and looked out over a sunny swimming pool and Frisbee-tossing students speckling the grassy slope by the water. The pool area was filled with visiting faculty, each wearing sunglasses and resting their elbows as they chatted over iced tea.

She drew a bath and in its steaming waters went over the new bruises: the welt over the rib cage where she took the charge, the swelling in the ankle where she came down wrong, the black charley where someone's knee crashed into the side of her leg. After putting on her uniform, she sat massaging her feet and ankles and wrapping them. Socks went over the bandages; protectors over knees. She stood, laced her high-tops and wiggled her feet inside her shoes. The hard fighting energy surged up her legs and filled her body. She slipped on her starter's jacket, looked in the mirror and smiled.

Villa met the team on the cedar chip path to the Events Center rear entrance. And inside, warming up under the huge concrete pillars, Villa began forming her strategy. How would she play them this time? On the court during play, it's not like you can stand there saying to yourself, "Well, I suppose I could run there, but then again, I could always go over there." No, it's more of a thirsty crunching stampede, a dry-mouthed gasping race to water. Sometimes she had to feel things out. But after sizing up this team, Villa knew right off what she'd do. After jump ball, she'd just keep it simple, retain possession and crash right down the middle.

In the first few minutes, having made three lay-ups and drawn two fouls, her teammates awaited the setup. Villa barreled down on the UCSB zone that had already shifted to try and prevent this "ball hog" from penetrating. She stopped short and passed to her left wing. The ball came back to her immediately. She yelled to her right, dubiously jerked her arms and shoulders, then snapped an overhand pass to Patty underneath for the lay-in. What fun would it be if you didn't throw down a few fakes?

Patty pointed to Villa. "Saw it coming."

Peggy slapped Patty's hand. "They didn't."

Villa still wasn't satisfied. The next few times down she lobbed the ball into Iris. When the defense had compensated, she faked the drive and stopped short for her favorite twelve-foot jumper.

"All day," said Patty.

"Time-out," said the USCB Coach.

Seeing that their opponents had switched to man-to-man, Villa held up two fingers, fed the ball into LaRhonda and began the weave. LaRhonda bounced it to Patty, Patty to Dahlia, Dahlia to Iris. Iris faked it to Villa, then instead dropped it back to a well-positioned Dahlia for an easy four-foot bank. Simple.

A nervous foreboding overcame the UCSB team. They were faced by a smart, crafty, dominating opponent. An opponent that read their minds. What would they do? They would run, shout, become frustrated, disillusioned, then they would lose. It was over before it began. By halftime, the Exiles were already discussing what they would do in town after the game.

Santa Barbara is a clean, quiet coastal city. Chaparral mountain forests surround its mission-style homes and well-kept streets. Downtown, the upscale restaurants and retail shops along State Street bustle with tourists and locals. Out on the sidewalk, Peggy, LaRhonda, Villa and Amaryllis occupied a set of green chairs in front of a popular bookstore and cafe.

"You were in there forever. What did you get?" asked Villa.

Amaryllis set down her plate. "I just browse. I'm a bookstore addict."

Villa chomped her oversized chocolate chip cookie. "No, I mean to eat."

"Herbal tea and an organic salad."

Peggy chuckled, "You're with us—on a diet. Unlike Princess here."

"Our star eats nothing but junk—cookies, cake, potato chips," said LaRhonda. "Does she gain an ounce? No."

Peggy poked at her plate. "I signed up for a low-sodium, high-carbo diet. Two hundred dollars and eighty chicken breasts later, I still weigh the same."

Villa rolled her eyes and looked at Amaryllis. "How did you like the game?"

"Game? That was a slaughter—a splatter film."

"Just a taste. We didn't murder them as bad as some of the teams we played last winter."

"You don't really even seem to need me."

Peggy shook her head. "Terry has a surprise in store. I think she's lined up some tough teams."

"All the more reason for me to stay on the bench."

LaRhonda changed the subject. "Get this. Violet practiced her drumming until two last night. The dorm manager had to come up to her room to tell her to stop. Her band must have an upcoming gig. How is the place you two are staying at? It looks fancy."

Peggy answered. "My room is like a condo, but with some paneling stolen off a boat."

"Did you go in those little pools. They're *bad.*"

"What about the 'Continental Breakfast'?—a bowl of cereal."

Villa sipped her soda. "The view is nice. It looks right out on the pond."

"Pond? You mean lagoon."

"Fine, lagoon."

"Who else is staying there?" asked Amaryllis.

"Coach, Karin, Glamour Girl."

"Who's Glamour Girl?"

"Iris—you know, our center—Miss Fashion Plate."

"She put the team together. Her dad is WilliamsWear. He's the owner."

LaRhonda put down her iced coffee. "Iris was a top college player, but had nowhere to go after she graduated. Most get discouraged. Not her. She picked up eight of us to go out barnstorming. When she called me, I wasn't sure I should take her seriously."

Peggy looked at LaRhonda. "Not me. I was like, 'Okay, when do we start?'"

"I started crying," said Villa. "Here I was, in my prime, adding up a line of numbers and writing reports downtown. Then, Iris called me to do lunch. It was sad. I broke down right in the middle of the restaurant. All those execs and secretaries must have thought I was mental, but I didn't care. I switched to part-time that afternoon."

"Tell New Girl—I mean, Amaryllis—about Coach."

"Oh yeah. It was a nightmare at first. Nobody could get along with Iris. There was always a dispute."

"Dispute? You mean fistfight."

"Don't exaggerate, Peggy. So she shoved Patty once. After that, Mr. Williams hired Terry."

"She was reluctant at first. But once she got to know us and got Flor as her assistant, she got into it."

LaRhonda opened her eyes wide. "And the rest is herstory!"

"We're not that famous," Villa denied with a humble look that instantly changed into an ambitious glare, "but we will be!"

LaRhonda laughed. "It was pathetic at first. You wouldn't believe who we played—community colleges, local industrial leagues, intramural teams. Little by little, Terry worked us into Division I and foreign pro team exhibitions."

"Maybe one day we'll go against the National Team or even the U.S. pros."

"We'll take on anyone," said Peggy.

Villa looked at Amaryllis. "She drives for the MTA."

Amaryllis recalled her ride. "That's a tough job. You must have some guts."

"It's not that bad. How about you? Have you managed to get a job down here yet?"

"Yeah, in a restaurant. But it's kind of depressing. I have to wear a see-thru blouse."

Villa choked and spit out her soda. LaRhonda gave her a napkin. "I can't stand that. It's so typical."

"So far it's no big deal." Amaryllis shrugged. "So what's everyone doing now? We don't go back until tonight."

Peggy slumped forward. "I'm going back to my room. I'm tired."

"Me too," said LaRhonda.

"I thought I'd go down to the beach," said Villa.

Amaryllis smiled. "Going to check out the Santa Barbara dudes?"

Peggy and LaRhonda looked at each other. "No, Amaryllis, Princess here is going to go check out the Santa Barbara babes."

Late that night, the San Diegan pulled into Union Station. The night was warm and the team quietly carried their bags through the station to the parking lot. Amaryllis caught Villa's eye outside. "Where's your car?"

"I took the bus."

"Where do you live? I can drop you off."

They drove east down Cesar Chavez and took a right on Saint Louis. Even late on a Sunday, radios blasted ranchero music and shouts filled the air on Villa's street. People sat out on their porches while children played out front. Amaryllis was charmed by Villa's little cottage, if not envious of her independence, She inspected the garden, the cute living room and small kitchen.

"I love it. You remind me of my grandmother in a way. She had a place like this too—pillows and afghans and old plates and pictures. I bet your bed is full of dolls and stuffed animals and knit spreads. You probably collect antique dessert glass."

"You're right about the bed. You're wrong about the Carnivalware. I wish...too expensive. But I do collect stuffed dolls."

"It's funny. I think my father once told me he grew up somewhere near here. He said it was once a Jewish neighborhood."

"Yeah. I heard that too. There are those little boxes on all the doors."

"It seems so nice now. I wonder if he was sad to move." Amaryllis paused. "Can I use your phone? I should tell him I'm back anyway." She dialed and talked with her dad.

"Was I sad to move from Boyle Heights?" asked Max. "Well, no, not exactly..."

Actually, in 1959, Max was overjoyed to leave behind the Eastside Jewish community and move to Fairfax to finish his senior year of high school.

Max's joy was not without reason. The old days. The Old Days. THE OLD DAYS. Mother's friends continually recounted how things used to be. By age seventeen, Max had earned a Ph.D. in "The Neighborhood Is Changing."

"Max, the neighborhood is changing. In the old days, you didn't drive so much like today."

"The trolley ran down this very street. All you had to do was hop on."

"Not no more. Nowadays, everybody gotta have their own car. I guess this is what they call a modern city."

Most had moved out already, but the ones who'd hung on used but one tense—past. No, Max was not there during the thirties. No, he didn't speak Jewish. No, he'd never met Minnie or Mendel, Sarah or Sam, Lottie or Les."

"Max, the neighborhood is changing. In the old days, I used to meet your mother by the cupola in the park. We'd walk around the lake two times."

"All the parks had lakes back then—Echo Park, Lincoln Park, Westlake Park. Our park was the fanciest of them all. People said it had real style."

"Westlake Park and Lincoln Park were more wider, but Echo Park and Hollenbeck Park were long like."

"Nowadays they call Westlake Park 'MacArthur' and they call Central Park 'Pershing Square'. They're always changing things."

"That's right Max, in the old days your mother used to like to feed the ducks. They'd come swimming from both ends of the lake and follow us all around. Every time they saw her, oh how they'd quack. Quack! Quack! Quack! But, that part of the lake isn't there no more."

"They're always changing things."

During Max's teenage years, Boyle Heights was indeed changing, its residential fabric being torn to pieces. Industry cut into a large section, public housing patched another, and transportation tore through the whole quilt itself. The new freeways were brutal. One-hundred-and-fifty-foot-wide barriers plowed through neighborhoods, dead-ending streets and uprooting homes. They interupted foot traffic, divided families and friends and put an end to the streetcars. They dissected parks and even cut off ends of lakes.

"Hey, tell Max about the bread crumbs."

"That's right. She'd bring a bag with her from the day before. We'd sit under the bridge at Sixth Street where the boys fished. We used to call it 'Duckie Bridge'. That was her favorite spot. But the bridge isn't there no more. Quack! Quack! Quack! Oh how those ducks would quack."

"Max, your mother's house used to be on Brittania below Brooklyn. My house was in the flats with the Russians. On Wednesdays, on my way to my music lesson, I'd get off the trolley car, walk down Boyle Avenue and stop near the bridge just to see if she was there."

"That's right. See, I lived across the street and I was jealous. So if I heard the ducks, I'd look out the window to see if she was there with him. Us two squabbled so much, she went and married your father. Quack! Quack! Quack! Oh how those ducks would quack. You couldn't make 'em stop quacking."

Now Duckie Bridge, as the old-timers used to say, "...isn't there no more." Instead, on the south end of the lake, a mess of urban and pastoral elements entwine where the Golden State Freeway chopped off the park's western half. Concrete pylons emerge from still waters. Two curves of concrete ramp rumble overhead, a sliver of sun shining through. A row of trash dumpsters borders a picturesque grassy hill. This cavernous space now substitutes for the missing other half of a hundred-year-old public promenade. In search of bread crumbs or a fish, "Quack! Quack! Quack!" say the ducks as they swim past a CalTrans sign that reads, "Hollenbeck Lake Bridge #153-1359."

Amaryllis put down the phone and Villa brought out her antique tea set. She poured a cup.

"How was the beach?" asked Amaryllis. "Did you meet anyone?"

"I met this volleyball player, but she lives two hours away. Long distance relationships are too difficult."

"Tell me about it. I have a boyfriend in Santa Cruz."

"Well that's not good. You should try and meet someone down here."

"Wow, you really are like my grandmother. If it were up to her, George Hamilton and I would be honeymooning this minute.

"At least for you, it's the right sex. My mom wants to fix me up too and believe me, it's not with other girls." They drank tea and chatted, then Villa escorted her new teammate out to the curb. "Well, I'll see you at practice."

Amaryllis stepped into her Dodge. "That's going to be quite a day. I have to work the lunch shift, then afterwards, Terry told me to go for my fitting downtown, then later on, it's practice. Jimmy in the morning, Geo in the afternoon and the Exiles at night."

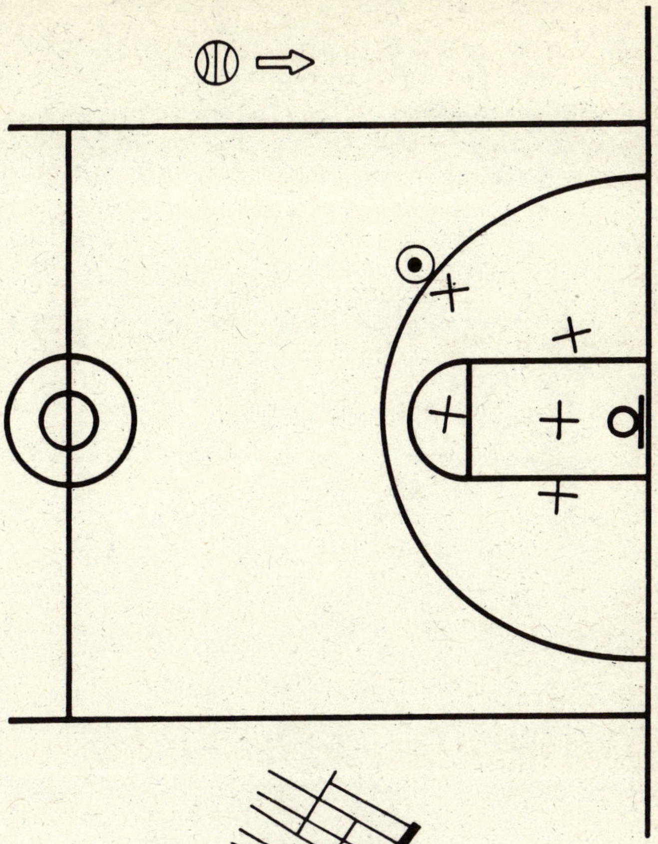

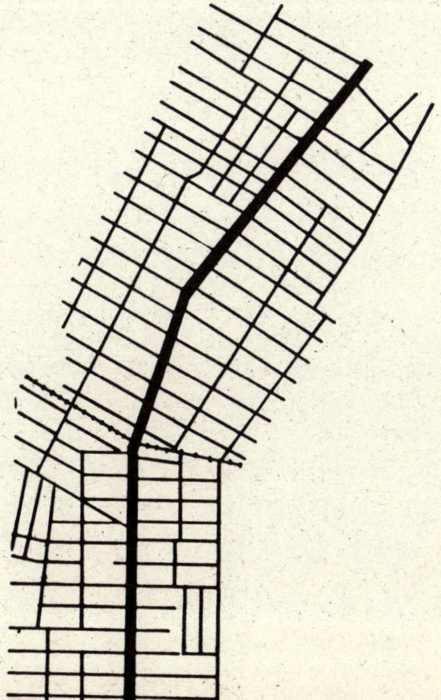

Williams Wear of California
CENTRAL AVENUE

"You're on fire babe," shouted Peggy. "On fire!"

Amaryllis couldn't help but smile. Four set shots and a three-pointer in the first half and then that offensive rebound and another jumper in the second. She hadn't missed yet. How was it possible? Her cover was at least six-one with arms that reached high into the air. Somehow Amaryllis had even gotten off against their best player—that too slick wiry natural who was born on the court.

Maybe they weren't invincible. That's right. She was just as good as any of them. And more important, she was good enough to be on the team; good enough to be an Exile. Amaryllis caught the pass, stepped up and sunk another one.

"On fire babe! Someone call the trucks. The New Girl's bursting flames." Amaryllis heard a siren and saw flashing lights. "Here they come babe. Coming to put you out."

Something was wrong. It was all too literal. She looked at her arm engulfed in flame and closed her eyes. "Villa help! What's happening to me?"

Villa spun around. "Open your eyes and find out."

Amaryllis opened her eyes. It was eight-thirty. She had to be at work by ten. She jumped out of bed, showered, ate granola with apple juice and opened the rear sliding glass door. "Max, I'll be back tonight."

Max turned away from trimming his herb garden. "Okay, good luck," he said, then turned back and continued his meticulous clipping.

After two weeks of training, Amaryllis had finally been given her own section, yet still, each day, something seemed to go wrong. At noon, the restaurant filled and plate after plate slid through the kitchen window. Amaryllis picked up a steaming quarter rack of ribs. Veal, Pork, Beef—can't anyone get steamed vegetables? Nevermind, just concentrate. Okay, it's ribs for the Grannies, salads for the secretaries and more ice tea for the love birds. Amaryllis filled the two glasses and surveyed her section. Two men waved at her from the corner table. What do those two want? They got their lunch. She waved back, put down the pitcher and went to their table.

"Do you see any mayonnaise on this sandwich?" asked the small bald man.

Okay, don't freak out. You can handle this. "Would you like me to take it back and add mayonnaise?"

"No, I want you to answer my question." He looked across the table, "You can't get decent service anymore. Remember, I said smother this sandwich in mayonnaise and bring a plate of it on the side." He scowled. "Do you see any mayonnaise on this sandwich?"

"You're right. I remember." She looked into his glaring eyes then down at the plate. "Let me take it back for you right away."

"First, I want a simple answer to a simple question. Do you see any mayonnaise on this sandwich?"

Yesterday it was not fast enough. The day before it was, 'You spilled my soup!', today, no mayonnaise. Maybe Max is right about this world. Uhm, try apologizing. "Sir, I have a full load of tables today. I'm sorry there was a mistake. May I—"

"DO YOU SEE ANY MAYONNAISE ON THIS SANDWICH!?!" People from other tables began staring. Steven walked over from across the room.

Okay, just let Steve handle it. "I'll be right back." She could hear Jimmy's bell sounding. What does he want?

"Hey *Escalera*, what are you going to drop today?"

Rosario frowned, but Martin's face lit up. "That was a good one Jimmy." He laughed and spun the salad dryer. "It's a long drop from way up there."

Amaryllis sighed, shook her head, grabbed two plates and returned to the dining room. Watching Steven and Mr. Mayo out of the corner of her eye, she delivered the new orders, filled two more glasses of Iced Tea, sent Gustavo out to pour coffee, then returned to the kitchen.

Jimmy rang the bell. "Right on time. Three New York Steaks all well done. Watch it, the plates are hot." She grabbed a plate and dropped it. Jimmy laughed. "I told you they were hot. Get a napkin or you'll drop this order too."

"Will you please lay off!"

"What's the matter? Someone giving you a hard time?"

"It is hard when I have to take dishes back. Why didn't you put mayonnaise on that guy's sandwich?"

"Why didn't Jimmy put mayonnaise on the sandwich? Jimmy didn't put mayonnaise on the sandwich because Amaryllis didn't ask Jimmy to put mayonnaise on the sandwich." He handed her the ticket. "Jimmy has been at Chez Bernard for four years because Jimmy never gets an order wrong. Jimmy is overdue for a raise because Jimmy is a soft touch and a sucker. Jimmy..." Amaryllis retreated back out towards the dining room, but bumped into Steven, plate in hand.

Steven looked annoyed. "Jimmy, put mayonnaise on this sandwich and give me a plate of it on the side." He turned to Amaryllis. "Why didn't you answer that guy's question?"

"I told him I'd take it back for him. He wouldn't let me."

"Look Amaryllis, first you got to get the order right. Second, you give good service. Now, why didn't you answer his question?"

"About the mayonnaise? It wasn't appropriate."

"Appropriate? You're their waitress."

"I know, but it was rhetorical."

Jimmy popped his head through the window. "Rhethorical?"

"A rhetorical question is just for effect. It doesn't require a response. That means...you don't answer it."

Jimmy made a face.

Martin laughed again.

Steven grimaced. "Jimmy, don't you have any work to do?"

"Is that a rhetorical question?" asked Jimmy. "Hum—now let me see. Do I have any work to do? I have to drain the stock pot, make pesto, cook the pasta, peel four tubs of potatoes, clean out the reach-in and trim the quarter round, but I don't care, because I would much rather listen to this little drama right here."

Steven put his arm around Amaryllis' shoulder "I know customers can be demanding, but, its better just to give in. All the waitresses do it."

"But—"

"You don't think you're better then they are, do you?" Amaryllis looked down. "Now, go out there and give him back his plate, and if he asks if you see mayonnaise on the sandwich, just answer him." She grabbed the sandwich and returned to the dining room.

"Thank you, waitress. Now, do you see any mayonnaise on this sandwich?"

"Yes, I see mayonnaise on the sandwich." The two men burst out laughing, spitting their food on each other and waving their napkins. Amaryllis bit her lip and headed for the bathroom. She locked the door and was alone—alone with the cheap wall paper, plastic flowers and stupid smell of pine air freshener. A ceramic swan hand towel holder stared up at her sorrowfully and she swept it off the toilet shattering it against the wall. She sat down, her head in her hands and closed her eyes. Why aren't things going right? She looked at the mess on the floor. What's happening to me? The weeks passed before her eyes "I'm not good enough to play for that team! I'm not good enough!" She stared blankly, shook her head, then began picking up the broken pieces. She hid them at the bottom of the waste basket, took a few deep breaths, rinsed her face, unlocked the door and returned to her section.

Later that day, at the WilliamsWear office, Amaryllis waited forty minutes for her uniform fitting before Jasmine came down from the studio.

"Geo says, you may have your fitting now."

Iris was irritated. "What took you so long?"

Jasmine flipped back her hair. "Geo's recovering from a root canal. He's in pain and would prefer that you didn't leave your purse out where he can see it."

Iris hesitated. "Why doesn't he want to see my purse?"

"Geo says, it isn't a purse. It's a lens case with stainless steel rivets, a strap and appliqués."

Iris stared at her. "Jasmine, do I look like I'm in the mood for fashion tips?"

"Geo says, this isn't about fashion. It's about English vocabulary. Geo doesn't want you to call that lens case a purse, because it isn't one."

"Look, you tell Geo that if they can make a dress out of credit cards, a cap out of aluminum cans and edible underware out of candy, I can have a purse that used to be a lens case. I put things in it. I use it. It works. It's a purse." Iris turned to her father. "Why do you put up with this?"

Warren Williams stood. Why did he put up with it? The arguing never seemed to end. Ever since he'd moved his business downtown, he'd tolerated his son's extravagance and his daughter's expensive tastes. Why, he'd even bought her a basketball team. He went to the window and looked out towards Pershing Square—the place where he used to meet with Rusty.

One humid autumn day in 1949, Warren spotted his steady girl wearing polka dots amist the ferns, palms and soapbox fanatics. Warren snuck up behind the pretty shipyards assistant bookkeeper.

"Excuse me Miss. Do you believe in love at first sight?"

Rusty smiled without turning. She stared out at the flirting cross-dressers and seniors dozing on wood slat benches. "Of course, it happens everyday."

Warren sat beside her and began unwrapping the deli lunch he'd just bought. "I better be quiet so my good girl can hear the sermon." Rusty elbowed Warren's ribs and chewed her pastrami.

A fundamentalist preacher shouted from his crate. "Beware my friends! They have evil plans for this little park. They're going to dig it all up and put a parking lot below."

"Best way to get rid of the Commies, Fairies and Hopheads," responded his entire audience, a single heckler. "You said so yourself."

"Now hold on there a minute. Maybe I said this place needs a little cleanin' up. But any fool could see that. I don't like it anymore than you do, but does that mean they gotta go changing everything? My goodness, in just eighty years, they done this square over four times. Over and over, they done it—now it's overdone. Why, they do this square anymore, it might as well be my Aunt Winnie's brisket on Labor Day."

"Hey, how you know so much?"

"Seen it with my own eyes. Going way way back, the old Zanja ran through here."

"Zanja?"

"An aqueduct Sonny. They filled it in, planted trees and laid out curvy roads. After the turn of the century, they trimmed those trees and built a grandstand in the center. Maybe that stand wasn't so grand, because about fifteen years ago, they replaced it with a fountain and straightened the roads out."

"But, why you care what they do?"

"Why? Because it's the Devil's work! Brothers and Sisters, pray the Lord grant mercy on this poor place. In other cities, they know to leave well enough alone. Why don't we? Who ever heard of a parking lot down below the Town Square! Why next, they'll be painting the whole thing yellow, purple and pink"

Finishing their lunch, the couple strolled the park until Rusty had to go. "Meet me at Twelfth and Central at 11:00 tonight," she said. "Swing shift for me." A warm wave tingled Warren's belly and a low whistle escaped his lips as the small girl ran off.

The "B" Car ride south from that famous corner featured a club on every block: Jack's Basket, Ritz, Glenn's Backroom, Memo, Bird in the Basket, Nickel Spot, Sweet Dreams and down by the Dunbar, Club Alabam and The Down Beat.

They stepped off at LK Ward so Rusty could grab a 78 for her sister Betsy before closing time. Set for a lively evening, Warren slipped his satiny girl two crisp new dollars. He waited on the sidewalk by the building's patio entrance and kept a watchful eye peeled on the store's plate glass window.

"Sh...Sh...Shine Sailor? World's Finest." Four wood red-cushioned thrones sat empty. Warren couldn't say no to anything that night, not even a stuttering skin and bones bootblack. "That's a cute one you got there, S...S..Sailor. Where'd you make that c...catch?"

Warren stepped up. "Pershing Square," he said repressing a smile. His feet were ticklish, "and it's Seaman, not Sailor."

"Righto Seaman. Gonna take her to see D...D...Dizzy?"

"Who's he?"

"Hey Seaman, the navy done put you in shape—the square shape. D...D...Dizzy blows the horn. D...Dizzy Gillespie.

"Is he the best?"

"D...Dizzy, Hawk or Bird. C...C...Can't go wrong on Central this weekend."

A husky ball of talk in green pants sat down next to Warren, laid his tan fedora on the next seat over and put his light brown boots in the stirrups. "Hey there World's Finest. Talk to me, baby. Life still a bitch, but what you gonna do?" Two cops, their polished shoulder straps glistening, walked by on their beat.

World's Finest sprayed his bottle and sponged. "All that you can do."

"I said talk to me. My ship come in?" Green Pants snorted. "What's the news."

"Only news is bad."

"What you talking about? We won the war."

"Ain't changed nothing over here, right Seaman?"

Warren mulled it over. "Still can't buy my date a drink at the Biltmore."

"Even so, there's still plenty of opportunity," said Green Pants slapping his arm rest. "Now then, gimme a cigarette."

World's Finest arm brushed away like a windshield wiper. "What kind you want?"

"Oh, so my ship did come in. I'll take the Columbian kind, if you got it."

"I got it," he said slipping out a concealed tray in between brushings. Seaman Williams looked down at a neat arrangement of prophylactics, hemp and heroin. "I got the hay, the horse, and the gloves to go r...r...ridin'. Like I said. C...C...Can't go wrong on Central this weekend."

Green Pants traded three dollars from his clip for a penny matchbox and a pack of Zig-Zag wheatstraw. "See here! Things *are* looking up." He leaned back against the cushion. "You hear the game today. Pasadena's own hit another two homeruns in one game."

"Who Robinson?"

"Of course! The greatest of them all."

Warren was getting a little annoyed. "There's plenty out there good as Jackie. There's just still no room for more than one."

"How do you know? Did you ever try?"

"Played two years in the Negro Leagues. Tried out three times for the majors—White Sox, Dodgers and Cubs."

Green Pants balked and leaned forward as he if was about to call Warren a liar. Williams had had enough and began to get up. World's Finest blocked his way and snapped his rag loud. "Few hits off that and you won't w...w...worry about no White Sox, Dodgers or Cubs. I got some other stuff that'll make you forget about baseball altogether." World's Finest winked at Warren as he applied a coat of neutral to the issue patent-leathers, smoothed them with the clean brush and snapped them shiny.

Rusty back on his arm, Warren resumed his walk down Central. Corner after corner, small round table to standing room only, club after club, it wasn't until after one, that the couple finally stepped off of Forty Second and into the lobby of the famed Dunbar Hotel. Tall sultry women, Gardenias pinned to their chest, pressed themselves close to their dance partners. Spanish wagon wheel chandoliers hung amid tapestries and murals. Terrazzo steps led to a mezzanine and atrium dancing featured the best of the bands. Warren led Rusty to the floor.

"I can't stay out much longer," she said resting her head against his chest.

Warrren's arms tightened. "Your mother?"

"No, my boss. I'm behind. He told me to balance the accounts for the last four billing periods or else."

"What about tommorow morning?"

She leaned back to look up into his eyes. "No time. I was going to do it before I went to sleep tonight."

"Maybe I can help you?"

"Are you good with numbers?"

"I'll get good."

Rusty smiled. "Where would we go? I can't take you home and the library doesn't open until ten."

Warren petted her head. "Come home with me."

She closed her eyes. "You know I can't do that."

He lifted his eyebrows. "Then we'll do it right here. I'l get us a room."

"Warren, No!"

"Don't worry, we'll just do the books. Business before pleasure."

Warren separated from her then took a look into his billfold as he approached the Front Desk.

"So sorry sailor. All filled up tonight. Not a thing I can do. Let me place a call over—" The clerk's eyes became teary as a folded twenty dollar bill slipped between his ring and pinkie. Silently, he slid the guest book over the counter and took a key from box number 202.

202 was the VIP room. For Cozy, Cab, Duke, Lena and Joe, it was always room 202. But tonight, it was for Rusty Whitaker. For her elegant arms and small round face, sturdy bosom and regal posture, dark brown eyes and inviting plum lips.

Alone in the room together, away from the blinking neon flashes, horns and clanging trolleys, their eyes shone with the delight of having found a companion in this hot and hostile overgrown cowtown. Warren reached out eagerly to embrace warm perfumed flesh. The touch of soft skin enveloped; her breath entranced. They sat on the edge of the bed. Warren carressed her thigh and began to slowly slide a black slip up smooth silk stockings.

Rusty shoved him. "The books, Popeye. Remember? Business before pleasure." She pushed him with her feet, twisted his ears, placed a ledger from her purse in one of his hands and a pencil in the other. They sat on the floor adding rows of numbers, erasing arithmetic errors and cross-checking sums for hours. Finally at daybreak, Warren came to the last line.

"Cargo compartment twenty-eight: four thousand eight-hundred and eighty-seven." He yawned.

"That's right Popeye."

"Cargo compartment twenty-nine: three thousand nine hundred seventy-six."

"Um-huh."

He stretched and yawned again. "Compartment Thirty: four thousand six hundred—"

"Say Cargo compartment Popeye."

He took a deep breath and shook himself awake. "Cargo compartment thirty: four thousand six hundred and twenty-two."

"Hurrah, we did it! Here's that kiss I promised." Warren smiled at the teasing; not only were his feet ticklish. She took his head onto her lap and stroked his hair.

He closed his eyes. "You work too hard."

"Business before pleasure."

"The Navy was never this rough."

"Maybe it's time for you to get out of the Navy."

"And do what?"

"Whatever you do, you'll do well."

He looked into her eyes. "All I want is for our children to have it better than this."

She nodded.

"I want us to have a house and a yard and a boy and a girl. He'll grow up to play in the majors and she'll be a great artist and..."

The ackward silence inside the WilliamsWear office was broken by the sound of Jasmine popping her gum. "Geo says, just because you put your compact, keys and address book into something, doesn't make it a purse. He says, if your Granny accidently put her hair brush in the refrigerator, it doesn't magically turn it into a purse. He says, a purse must be designed. It must—"

Iris gave a worried look towards her father still staring out the window then put her hand on her forehead. "Jasmine, just take her up for her fitting."

Jasmine turned and beckoned Amaryllis to follow her upstairs to the studio. "Now remember Geo is only trying to make you look good. So if he asks you to do something—do it. He likes to listen to music, but he doesn't like it when his models dance. And is that your backpack?"

"Yes, do you like it?"

"Fabulous—but don't let him see it." They arrived at the dressing rooms. "Now put on your uniform and take off your shoes." Beautiful thin models buzzed around Amaryllis as she changed clothes. Jasmine pulled her over to the full length mirror. "Wonderful, fantastic, marvelous. Now just relax." She stuck her head through a pair of drapes. "Geo, she's ready!"

Tape measure, squeeze bottles, pins and material in hand, Geo approached. He squirted glitter glue on the back of Amaryllis' starter jacket, then slapped on two pieces of material. He turned her around and adjusted the collar.

"Fresh!" exclaimed Jasmine. "Geo wants you to reach into the air." Amaryllis reached. Geo smoothed the fabric, squirted, pulled and pinned.

Jasmine squealed. "Work it Geo! Work it! He wants you to bend over and touch your toes."

Amaryllis bent.

Jasmine turned up the music. "Now stand up straight."

Amaryllis stood.

"Hop up and down on one foot." Amaryllis hopped.

"Good, great, excellent."

"Can I switch to the other foot? I'm getting tired."

"Fine, but not to the music. Geo doesn't like it when models try to dance." Jasmine held Amaryllis' jerking shoulders while Geo worked fast. "You're too much Geo. Too much."

Geo halted abruptly and stepped back. "Spell my name!"

"G.O!" Jasmine cheered.

"And should I stop?"

"Stop? Oh no! You GO GEO! You GO!" Jasmine fell to her knees. "Yes, yes, beautiful. I love it. I love it." She breathed deep and wiggled. "Twirl Amaryllis. Twirl! Spin around so Geo can see!"

The music blasted. Lights flashed. Amaryllis imagined photographers snapping pictures and the crowd oohing and ahhing from the sides of the runway. She soon found herself spinning in place to the rhythm.

Geo raised his hand. "Stop!" he commanded before turning and leaving the room.

Amaryllis came to a stop. Jasmine took her by the hand and led her back to the dressing room. "You can change back now. Don't feel bad."

"But what did I do?"

"I told you not to dance," said Jasmine. "Now you've made him depressed."

Later, Amaryllis nervously drove to Patriotic Hall. Evening practices were especially rigorous. Flor insisted that the players stretch for a full half hour. Amaryllis, distracted, anxious and tense, just wanted to get up and start playing already. Seated around center court, fingers to toes, nose to knees, the athletes prepared their bodies for the main scrimmage. Pattern drills had loosened up Amaryllis' legs, but tightened her shoulders and when the five-on-five began, she kept missing. Playing the left wing on the three-two zone, she read Patty's signal and planned a defensive fake. She backed away from the line of the coming pass, waited, bent low, bounced back, bounded forward and reached in to steal. She threw the ball down court to Violet, only to have it intercepted by Villa.

Setting up once again, Villa lobbed the ball into Iris. Amaryllis held her hands up, jumped and got a couple fingers on the ball. Iris faked a second shot, then handed the ball off to Dahlia instead, leaving Amaryllis in the popcorn machine.

The next time down, Villa held out the ball defiantly. Face to face, Amaryllis immediately tried to jab it loose. Villa pulled away, leaving Amaryllis with a wild swing. "Strike one," Villa joked after she'd popped the twelve-foot jumper.

"Now was that nice?" shouted Peggy.

Patty was mad. "Come on Amaryllis. Get serious."

Exasperated, Amaryllis watched Villa's unconventional two-hand fall-away go in from all angles. To make matters worse, the all-star was calling tickie-tack fouls and feigning injury to nearly every portion of her body.

LaRhonda laughed. "Get up faker."

"Lover girl crashed again?"

"Come on, this isn't Dinah Shore Weekend."

Amaryllis was relieved when the practice was over. She'd had it with Villa's joking around while she was struggling just to keep up. But on the other hand, the two hours of intense concentration had cleared her mind and brought her deeper emotions to the surface. Amaryllis knew she felt lonely and needed someone to talk to. She missed Harold and longed for his willingness to listen. Staring into her open locker, she finally rose and stepped into the shower next to Villa. "You sure you're okay," she said. "I was going to call the ambulance for you."

"What can I say? I have a low pain threshold," replied Villa. "But, while you are on the phone, you might call the hotline for yourself. Why were you getting so pissed? You didn't even like stretching out. That's my favorite. Don't you know basketball is supposed to be fun. You looked like you were about to scream."

"Nobody would have heard a thing over your whining. What a show." The shower valve closed. Amaryllis tilted her head back and wrung the water from her hair; the droplets falling and splashing. Sure, Villa can afford to clown, she's the best out there. "I don't even know what I'm doing on this team?"

Villa sang as she dried and got dressed. "Just hurry up. Terry's going to give us the summer schedule.

Dressed, Amaryllis returned to the floor of the gym. She found Daisy still shooting free-throws. "I'm getting old," said Daisy. "It's the only way I can keep up with you guys." She bounced the ball to Amaryllis and headed into the showers.

"You mean, keep up with *those* guys," mumbled Amaryllis picking up the ball.

One by one, the team assembled on the concrete bleachers for their meeting. Flor took notes. Terry began. "Okay, I know everyone has been waiting for the summer schedule, so here goes. We didn't do as well as we wanted in Santa Barbara, but it was still better than most of our home games. How many showed Flor?"

"Almost two thousand."

"So it wasn't like the disaster at the Sports Arena. But that was my fault and it won't happen again."

"Come on Terry, everyone thought that we could at least fill a quarter of the seats with all the publicity over the Final Four and the Olympics."

"Still, I take responsibility. We're the Exposition Park Exiles, but we might not be having a home game for a while."

"So where are we playing?"

"That's the good news. Mr. Williams came up with the idea. We're going on tour just like he did back in the forties and fifties. First stop: Venice Beach. It's a publicity stunt."

"Terry, you're crazy. I wasn't sure before, but—"

"It's volunteer only Patty. Just those who want to."

"I don't mind playing against guys, but—"

"We're not playing the guys. We're playing the Old Timers, a thirty and over club. But don't get hung up on that because the same week we have a photo shoot."

"Photo shoot?"

"Handle it Patty. From there we're away. We play UNLV, than the Mexican National team in Tijuana"

"We can't take on UNLV. We'll get our butts kicked. Terry, you've gone off the deep end."

"You think so Patty? Both teams are over rated this year. All we have to do is run Tijuana and box out UNLV. You've been begging for competition. Now you've got it. We can't keep playing Occidental, Santa Barbara and Santa Cruz forever. Anyway, we're much better off playing those two then USC."

"USC?"

"We're not ready yet. But next season we're taking on anyone and everyone—USC, Tennesee, Virginia, Italy, Cuba, Russia, Brazil, the US National Team—whoever, wherever, whenever. So get used to it!"

When Amaryllis finally arrived back at Lasaine, black silhouettes of full grown trees swayed in the wind. A light from the backyard threw a glow over the roof. The front door was unlocked and inside, the recliner was empty. "Max, are you home?" She turned off the television, heard the wind whistle through the trees and felt a breeze blow in from the sliding glass door. "Max?" She slid the door open wider and smelled sweet smoke.

Max sat with his legs dangling over the fountain. "Hey Amaryllis." He toked hard on the joint in his hand, then coughed loud. "Oooh, home grown is raspy."

"What are you doing?"

He inhaled again. "You've lived in Santa Cruz since you were twelve and you don't know."

She plopped down on a lawn chair. "So that's the kind of herb garden you planted." An orange from a high branch dropped and thudded on the ground. She looked up to see a squirrel scurrying across the buzzing power wire. "What a day!" In a way, she didn't blame Max. On the outside, he was middle-aged, but inside, he was still just a kid. And what was her dad like when stoned? Pretty much the same.

"Want some?"

"I can't. Remember? I'm on the team."

"Oh yeah. I hope you don't mind. I'm just taking the edge off."

"Mind? Max, I'm a guest in your house."

Max let out a strange laugh. "Amaryllis, this is your house."

She smiled. "Thanks Max."

"How are you doing on the team?"

"Not too good."

"No more H.O.R.S.E. like the old days huh?"

"I guess not."

He inhaled. "Yeah, that was fun. The good ol' days."

She looked up and saw a plane descending into Burbank. The sky, blue and gray, was dotted with enormous clouds. "Yeah, ten years ago I would have never guessed things would turn out this way. Funny how things change."

"They change only to stay the same."

She watched the water dripping into the fountain. "What's that mean?"

"Well, it's like this garden. If you try to force it to be something it is not—something it could never be, eventually it will go back to the way it was."

Amaryllis watched a lizard rustle through a layer of pine needles. "Yeah, I know what you mean. At first, I was so excited to come down here and play. Now, I'm homesick and want to go back."

"Well, that's life. It doesn't always turn out the way you plan."

She sat silent a while then got up from the chair. "Excuse me Max, I'm sorry, but I've got to get some sleep. I'm getting up early to visit Grandma tommorow."

A black crow cawed from a telephone pole. Max took a last toke and threw the roach down to the dark soil. "Good Night, Amy." It was the old name. The name before everyone went their own directions.

The night suddenly seemed too quiet. "Good Night, Daddy."

Leaving behind the traffic and high rise offices of Wilshire, Terry and Karin ascended a flight of granite stairs up into the trendy new vaulted entrance of the Los Angeles County Musuem of Art. With two new wings, it held three of the six main buildings crowding Hancock Park (more commonly known as the La Brea Tar Pits).

Since the laying of the first museum foundation in the early 1960's, the grounds have seemed to resist intrusion. Tar seeped up forming puddles, the main lake overflowed and the old moat leaked into the adjacent buildings.

Now on weekdays, schoolchildren on field trips, unconcerned with this battle between man and nature, play stoop tag on the lawns and stick twigs and trash into the black pitch. Yellow buses line the parks perimeter, their diesel fumes mixing with the ancient smell of tar everywhere. Touring every building, Terry and Karin finally walked outside and chose a tar-free bench. "I liked the Japanese Pavilion best," said Karin. "It was so tasteful."

"Eh."

Humid and gray, it was the first overcast afternoon in a month. Life size statues of Pleistocene Epoch animals stood at the edge of the lake and large methane bubbles rumbled to the surface. "If I got stuck, would you save me?" Karin smiled. "Can I ask you something?"

Terry twisted a twig and threw it on the asphalt walkway. "No, I wouldn't. Can we go? I've had enough of 'Ugly Building Park'? What do you want to ask?"

"No, we can't go. I'm having fun." They heard a banjo playing. "How's that new girl doing?"

"How can you be having fun? This is the eeriest place I've ever been to. You mean Amaryllis?"

Karin opened her eyes wide then crossed them. "So lets be eerie for a while. Yeah Amaryllis. Why did you recruit her?"

"What do you care?"

"She just seems so lost. You thought she would improve, right?"

"She improving. She shows promise—real potential."

"She stinks, huh?"

Terry grew serious. "These things take time."

"You only have the summer."

"Then, I guess it'll be up to her."

"I guess so."

Terry yawned. "This is boring."

"Oh no, not that!" said Karin in mock alarm. "Why is it boring? Because we're sitting still for five minutes?"

"But why do you want to stay here?"

"So I can be with you." Karin's finger poked Terry's ear. "I'm so proud of you. You did it for the future of women's sports. You gave a young girl a chance to be around positive influences."

Terry moved away to the end of the bench. "That's a laugh. She's not that young and we're not that positive. When I was Amaryllis' age, I was already getting thrown out of the WPBL. And what's she going to learn from us? How to lose money?"

"So then why?"

Terry shook her head. "That's what I like about you. You act entirely irrational all afternoon, then force me to walk through some ephemeral-detached-who knows what museum, then stick your finger in my ear when a tar bubble pops, then expect me to give you a simple solution to a complex situation.

Karin looked over her shoulder. A street banjo player was teaching children the Virginia Reel. "*Promenade, forward and back, double swing, sashee, here we go! Old Joe Clark was the meanest man I ever knew before.*"

"Can we?"

Terry balked. "No way."

"He slept on a feather bed, I slept on the floor..."

Plantiff and innocent, the banjo sounds, to Karin, we're near irresistable. "Come on Old Joe. Please."

"But we're too old. It's for kids." Terry shook her head. "Sheesh. Oh alright, but then we're leaving." Towering over the children, they got in line across from each other and awaited their turn to be lead couple.

"*Swing your partner,*" hollered Banjo Man.

"Actually," called Terry across to her partner. "It seemed like the right thing to do. I don't know, maybe I didn't want to negate Flor's decision, even if it was rushed."

"Do-si-do!"

"So you made a mistake, right?"

Terry circled Karin. "Not a mistake. We needed someone right away. Amaryllis is sincere and tries hard. Also, maybe the team could use someone they could give pointers to and encourage instead of compete against all the time. And Cheryl asked me to."

"Cheryl?"

"The Assistant Coach at Cal. Cheryl said she had a good forward with the potential of a defensive specialist."

"Promenade!"

"Cheryl wanted to surprise Head Coach Paroni and recommend her as co-captain in her next season. She said Amaryllis showed leadership potential and needed some hard work to develop it."

"So you're doing a colleague a favor."

A fourth grader wearing glasses looked up at them. "Are you teachers? "You don't act like it. Where's your class?"

Terry looked at the pit in mock alarm. "Oh no, they were playing over there just a minute ago!" She turned back to Karin. "No, not that either. When I finally met her, I understood what Cheryl had in mind. Amaryllis could be a defensive specialist if she works hard enough."

"Doesn't she deserve to know about this?"

"Sashay!"

"Cheryl wanted to find out if she'll hang in there when things get rough. It will be hard on her, but she'll be stronger next season."

"How tall are you?" asked a girl in a uniform skirt.

"Ten foot-five," said Terry.

Karin bent down to the girl. "She's five-ten and I'm six foot-two." She then formed a cup with her hands and yelled across to her partner. "I'd let her know if I were you. It's only fair."

"Reel on down!"

"You worry too much. She'll make it just fine."

They took the lead and formed an arch. Pairs of children passed easily underneath. Terry broke away, dropped two dollars into the banjo case, grabbed Karin's wrist and dragged. "We're leaving."

"One more song."

"No. No more songs. No more dancing. No more sitting, talking and poking. No more bathrobe museums. Quality Time is over. We're going home."

"Very funny."

"Come on." Terry pulled.

Karin stuck out her lower lip. "But I wanted to tell you something."

"Tell me later."

"Yeah, sure," said Karin. She was silent a minute then spoke. "How do you think the rest of them will do tomorrow in Venice?"

"What could go wrong? We're going to pick up the permit right now."

Sunlight filled the curtains of Gita's room. A spoon in a glass dish in front of her, a car chase on TV, she mixed a deck of cards. "So maybe you'll play a game Gin Rummy with your Grandmother? No, I can't shuffle like I used to," she said, rice pudding sticking to the corners of her mouth, "but I can still deal 'em out."

"But I need more advice."

"More advice? Listen, we'll play a game. Maybe we finish, maybe not. In the meantime you tell me your troubles. But please, no more about Max. And turn up the sound." Gita nodded at the screen. "Look.

Robert Wagner, *hahnishe, no?"*

"He's okay, I guess", said Amaryllis glancing. "I don't know where to start. Everything is happening so fast. I'm blowing it at work. I'm uncomfortable at home. And I can't keep up at practice. I'm not playing well."

"I give away the Four of Hearts," Gita sang. "Now you discard." Amaryllis picked up the four and threw down a Queen of Clubs. *"Ach, maine fraind* the Queen of Clubs. *Es iz azoy gut aich tzu zehn.* You give me the Queen of Clubs. I give you a Jack. Now you discard." Amaryllis looked at her Grandmother. She picked from the deck and threw down. "Darling," said Gita rearranging her hand. "Life is a game of gin rummy. You want something, you gotta give up something, then you wait. If you play smart, maybe you get what you want." She brought the spoon from the bowl to her mouth. "What a delicious pudding!" she exclaimed, her mouth full. "Meet a nice person and go to nice places. Enjoy yourself. Don't worry. Discard."

"I met a nice person. She's the best on our team. She's fantastic. She did this turn around jumper that two people got a hand on and it still went in. If I could play like that..." Amaryllis sighed. "But I can't. And next week we have a publicity game in Venice Beach. I know I'll blow it. I'm the worst one on the team."

"Please God, strike me down with such worries. Maybe I'll go to Venice Beach instead. What next? You find a million dollars, but you don't know how to spend the money." The old woman wiped her mouth. "Speaking of money. Did you get your first paycheck?"

Amaryllis watched a Camaro fly off a cliff and burst into flames. "No. Not yet. So far, all I've gotten is teasing from the cooks."

"*Kliene kinder, kleine freyden. Groysse kinder, groysse zorgn.* You do your job. They do theirs."

"But why do they have to act like that?"

"But why do they have to act like that?" the old woman mocked. "*Meydl* wants a reason for everything. You thought it was easy to make a living. Now, you know. *No, mein yungeh tsatske, shver tzu machen a leben.*" Gita shook her head at her off springs naiveté.

"But I don't want to be teased."

"Does he pinch you?"

"No."

"When I worked in New York City, every man felt he deserved to give you a free grab whenever he wanted. Nowadays, at least, you gotta name for men who bother women at work. Discard. Discard!"

"You mean a Sexual Harasser?"

"A Sexual Harasser, they call him now. Discard. Back then, we called him 'Boss'." Tormented, Gita finally shrugged and brought another spoonful to her mouth.

Amaryllis looked around the room. "May I please tell you just one thing about Max?"

"Ooooh," Gita grimaced, choking on the desert. "Now, Max." She coughed into a napkin. "I have a son who just complains about the Government. I have a Granddaughter who just complains about the son. Mama, is there no mercy in this life? DISCARD!"

"I came home one night and he was smoking pot."

Gita took in a deep breath and let it out slowly. "*Men ken keyn mentshn nit der kenen...* Now you know that too. Sonny boy does what he pleases." She stared at the screen as two men shot at each other, one falling off a building. "*Oy vays mir,* the stunt men," she waxed. "You think you got it rough? How would you like to make your money flying through the air twenty stories? Yes, you land on a cushion mattress. But still, what it does to the nerves." She paused a moment. "He didn't offer you none, did he?"

"Yes he did."

"*A shanda!*" She opened her eyes wide. "Listen, when I was a little girl they used to give me wine to drink too. Don't worry *min* six-footer. Go to Venice Beach. Play Basketball. Enjoy life. Dis...card."

"But I don't know what to do?"

Gita closed her eyes in frustration. "Do? Do?" She threw up her arms without exposing her hand. "How should I know what a twenty-three year old should do? You're gonna do what you want to do. I tell you what to do so you be can be sure to do something else. What do you want from an old lady? You think after a life of patted on the head and *knipt* on the *tuches*, I know how to make a cook act nice? You think, after fifty years of wishing my son would be a *mentch*, I should know how to stop him from smoking if he wants to. No, no, you don't want advice. What you want is a horse and a cart." She rearranged her hand. "Even the old gray mare gets put to pasture. *Mine taiere*, light as a feather or heavy as an anvil, your burden is yours to carry." She layed out three queens, the eight, nine and ten of clubs, and the Ace, two and three of hearts. "Gin Rummy," she said without pleasure.

Amaryllis looked at her grandmother staring into the television. "I have to go now," she said gathering her things. She leaned over to kiss Gita's spotted unmoving cheek. "Good-bye Grandma."

"Goodbye. And on your way out, please change the channel." Spoon and bowl in hand, she fell back into her chair as the door closed. Dropping the spoon onto the table, Gita licked the last traces of pudding from the bottom of the glass dish. "Venice Beach," she mumbled drifting off. "Venice Beach."

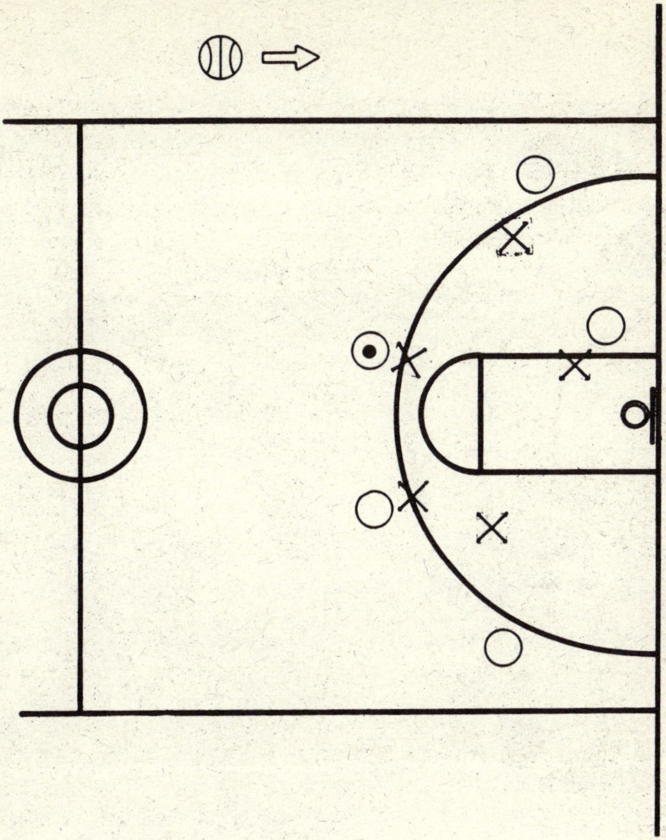

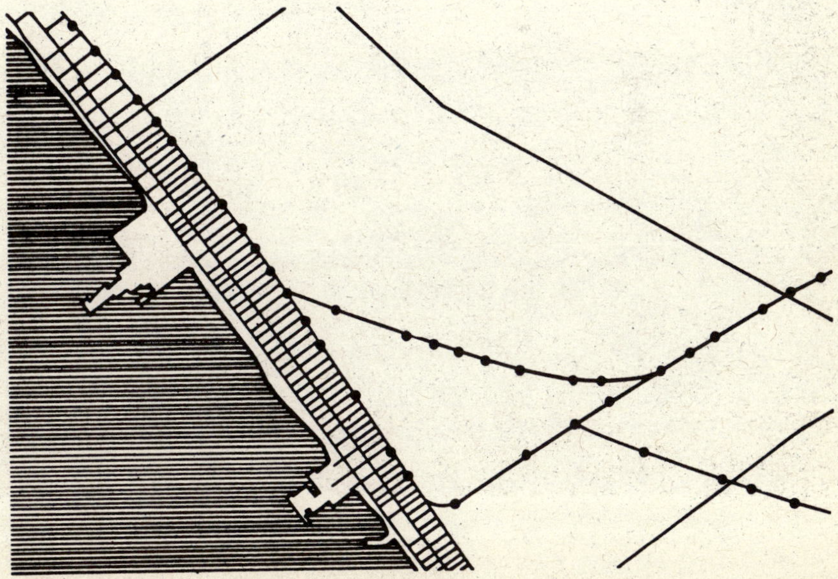

HOLLYWOOD

Boardwalk Rennaisannce 6

Everywhere in Venice were remnants of the recent and distant past: streets that were once canals, a circular drive-formerly a lagoon, arcaded facades that were once old theaters. Remnants of enormous amusement piers—wood posts and piles of rocks—dotted the shore. Along the Boardwalk were storefronts and apartments that had been there since the twenties. Amaryllis, having spent the first six years of her life here, felt vaguely at home as she walked along the covered sidewalks of Windward Avenue towards the outdoor basketball courts.

Each generation of Seltzers held a different impression of Venice. For Amaryllis, it was the setting for her earliest memories. For Max, it was a venue of freedom and expression. And for Gita, it was a vacation of bright sun and cool shade. Decades ago, for a week every summer, she'd take several Eastside children on the Red Car Balloon route to stay at Mrs. Schneider's Boarding House. After releasing them to roam the streets and romp the piers, she would stand in front of the antique gold leaf mirror and slip on her beach apparel piece by piece. Then, she'd apply cream to her forearms, shins and face. Umbrella on her shoulder, she'd step out into the carnival of crowded indoor pools, packed grand ballrooms and jammed packed paths. She'd soak in the sandy optimism of the full beaches, reflect on the beauty of the canals and relax to the roar of the ocean. Even the raucous piers with their men that grabbed and women that kissed for a dollar, provided impious distraction.

Over the years, the hot Venice sun and cool Venice shade became like beloved distant cousins; the Venice attractions, like mischievious uncles who never seemed to loose their momentum. So when the piers burnt down, it seemed natural that they just built them up the next year even bigger. When the lagoon and half of the canals were comdemned, what else, they were changed into streets. Gambling raids, prohibition, bankruptcy, World War, nothing seemed to slow the wheels of Venice from reving their steady carousel moan. And even as late as the nineteen fifties, Gita still enjoyed the excursions with sixteen-year-old Mama's boy Max to newly opened P.O.P (Pacific Ocean Park), the last and worst of the Great Venice Piers.

Amaryllis came to the end of the arcade and looked up at the different hues of summer sky: hazy denim, navy, deep dark blue. Beyond, the wide beach, the Ocean was choppy with voluptuous white waves. To the North, the Santa Monica Mountains were light brown, a layer of smog clinging like a dragon as they stretched out into the bay. Parallel to the Boardwalk ran both a bike path and recreation areas. Amaryllis continued on and reached the concrete bleachers, concrete body building arena, concrete handball walls and the three concrete basketball courts: "A", "B" and "C". Rows of players sat bantering and bleacher refereeing, waiting their turn, to run, jump, shout, holler, fall and get all scraped up.

A court rookie called a foul. "Charging!"

The crowd laughed. "Charging? That's no call. That's not charging. That's backing in."

The newcomer pled his case. "He weighs fifty pounds more than me. What am I supposed to do?"

"Move."

"But he's pushing me."

"Then get out of his way. You can't call a charge,"

"Then, why do they have a charging call if you can't use it."

"Not for that. We're in Venice. No charge."

"Thanks a lot."

"No charge."

Amaryllis leaned on the wall with the laughing spectators. "Why are they playing on the 'C' court?"

"They're making a T.V. show on the 'A' court and two crazy ladies are on the 'B' court." The man pointed at Terry and Flor fumbling through their clipboards.

"Action," hollered the director, a white haired man in casual slacks and a red plaid shirt. Extras: slender full chested rollerskating twenty-year-olds in string bikinis, bleach blond men carrying surfboards back and forth, and shirtless bikers in bathing suits and sunglasses circled round and round. A large stunt man fell over a table, an actor in a police uniform jumped over a fence and an actress screamed.

Amaryllis spotted Villa and walked over. "What's going on?"

"Terry can't find the permit."

Just then, Coach jumped up waving a paper.

"Cut," yelled the director from his chair. Everyone stopped. A woman holding a walkie-talkie and an aluminium clipboard approached.

She stared at Terry. "You just ruined that take. Why are you disrupting our shoot?"

"It's our court. We have a game here in twenty minutes. Here's our permit." She held the paper in the woman's face. "Now get off." The woman reached for the paper, but Terry pulled back. "Ah, ah, ah, don't touch, just read."

"Jerry, they have a permit," said the woman into her walkie-talkie. Jerry shook his head and held up two fingers. The woman continued. "We only need four more shots."

"Too bad."

"But that's only about two hours. Don't you think you can put off your game until then?"

"No I don't. And tell the extras to get lost."

Her antenna almost poked Terry's eye. "Jerry, we've got another blackmailer. Can you come over here please?"

The actors, crew, caterers and off-duty on-site LAPD all gathered around Terry. Disgusted, the director got up from his seat and approached, a stunt man and a security guard flanking him on each side.

"What's the problem here?"

"No problem," replied Terry. "We have a game. We have a permit. Get off!"

"A game? You mean a girl's basketball game? We're going to waste time and money so you can play a girl's basketball game?" He turned to the security guard. "First it's volleyball, now basketball."

"That's right." Terry lifted up her sunglasses. "And now it's move."

"You want us to pack everything so a bunch of overgrown—"

"We're a professional team."

"Now I've heard everything. A women's professional basketball team. That's cute, but those uniforms are ugly. Have you made a big name for yourselves yet? What do you call your professional team anyway?"

"The Exiles."

"And you must be the coach. How adorable," joked the director. A girl in a bikini giggled and the stunt man laughed. "Let's take care of this fast. Lisa, give me the standard form. How much Ms. Exile?" He scratched a few lines than handed the paper to Terry. "How about five hundred?"

"No."

"Fine, one thousand. If you like, we can even work you into the background. Alright?"

Lisa looked up. "Being on *Beach Watch* will give you more free publicity than you've ever dreamed of."

"Don't want it."

"Two thousand and that's our final—"

"We have the court. We don't want to be on your show."

"But—"

"No buts. Scram!"

The director turned in a huff and huddled with his crew. Flor tapped Terry's shoulder. "Terry..."

"Finally he got the message. Okay, lets see who showed up. There's Peggy..."

"Terry..."

"...Villa..."

"Terry..."

"...Dahlia and Amaryllis. That should be enough to start with. Are the Old Timers here yet?"

"Terry!" Flor turned Terry's shoulders around so she faced the other way. "Look!"

Terry gasped when she saw that the 'A' court she'd just fought so hard to get had been taken over by the Venice regulars. "No, not you guys," she said storming over. "I'm sorry but you'll all have to move. We have a game here."

"But we're not finished yet," said the man taking out the ball.

"Yes you are. Here's our permit. We have a game in ten minutes. We have to warm up."

"You're as bad as they are," the man said pointing at the crew. "Where's the respect?"

The man on the other team chimed in. "It's a public court."

The whole crowd was getting fed up. "Why don't you wait in line like everyone else? We want to play just like you."

Terry turned around. The Old Timers had arrived and were sitting on the bleachers waiting. On the sidelines, the movie extras had resumed circling, the stunt men had resumed falling over tables and the director had resumed filming. She looked at the crowds, the players, the crew, the cops and the kids. "You know what. You're right, it's a public court."

Flor gasped. "What do I tell the Old Timers?"

"Tell them I'm pissed."

"They know that. What do I tell them about the game?"

"Tell them I've got next."

The crowd laughed at Terry. "You can't have next. He's got it—then him—then me."

"You don't have next. I watched you and him play last game over there. I've got it."

"No, I do," said a six-foot-six inch man in the top row. "I've been waiting since that film crew showed up."

"Then pick us up." Terry pointed to Lily, Dahlia, Villa, and herself. "Us four and you. You play post. We'll do the rest." The man nodded and the crowd exploded with whoops and whistles.

Amaryllis couldn't believe her ears. "What is she doing?"

"Taking the court," replied Villa.

The winners' forward in-bounded to his guard wno showboat dribbled between his legs then alley-ooped to the team's big man who missed but got his own rebound and laid it in. On the Exiles' first possession, Terry brought the ball up court and fed it into their big man who returned the favor and banked it in. On the winners'second time down, Terry stole the ball, and fast breaked two-on-one. Avoiding a collision, she dropped the ball off to her trailer—Villa—who stopped short for an easy six-footer. From then on, it was more of the same. Working it in to their post, screening their covers and sinking outside shots, the Exiles established an early lead. The regulars were irritated at first, but then resigned to the fact that the Exiles didn't miss. In top shape, the women outran their opponents, fed it to the inside, set their picks and waited for it to be kicked back out. Then, they made their set shots and fast breaked when they could. Flor, Amaryllis and the Old Timers watched Terry's squad take and hold the court until it was the their turn to play.

Villa sat down on the bleachers. "Hey, you play this round," she hollered up to Amaryllis.

Nervously, Amaryllis walked out onto the asphalt. It was just a publicity game, but still, the crowd was big and growing bigger. She joined Terry and the Exiles against the Old Timers. It was an easy game with lots of running and lots of fresh ocean air. She sunk a few shots, made an easy steal, and grabbed a few rebounds. Their squad was taking it easy and leaving the Old Timers to take on whoever was next. By then, the edge had been smoothed over and it was just basketball by the beach, no longer a *Beach Watch* battle of the sexes.

Sitting down again, Terry looked over the team. "Good work. Who wants sodas?" She looked around. "Where'd Villa go?"

Amaryllis looked over her shoulder. "I think she headed out. I'll go look for her and get drinks." Amaryllis headed down the Boardwalk, her mind overflowing. Everything looked so familiar, yet she couldn't stop and explore at her usual pace. Get sodas. Find Villa. That shouldn't be too hard. Just look for the rooting section following her around including that redhead with the puffy cap making all that noise and running out to high-five everyone. Who was she anyway? Ah, here's the soda line.

"Do you have recycled cups?"

"No, just Styrafoam."

"Do you know where Jim Morrison's house was?"

"Who's that?"

Amaryllis walked further. On the east side of the crowd were the pastel painted storefronts—fast food places and souvenir shops. On the west were the Free-zone entrenpenours—psychic eye palm readers and holistic tarot card fortune tellers, sunglasses solicitors and Rasta inscense vendors, massage therapists and portrait artists. Amaryllis finally found one place that at least had paper instead of Styrafoam.

"Two orange, two diet colas, two lemon limes and two Root Beers. Do you happen to know which building Jim Morrison lived in?"

"Ask him." The vendor pointed out a long haired man sculpting a sand mermaid on the sidewalk. Amaryllis squatted down beside him.

"Why do want to know?" asked the sculptor.

"I'm trying to find my old house. My dad always said we used to live near Jim Morrison's apartment."

"So, you're a Venice baby in search of her roots. In that case, come with me. It's right over here." The man pointed up a street. "See that apartment. That's the Morrison. That's where he used to sleep on the roof. Now, look down there. You see where there's a blue mural of him on the wall. That's were he lived." Amaryllis walked up the steps and read the metal plaque. She tried to imagine Max's Venice: lively, smaller crowds, fewer police, an expressive place; hippies, freaks, musicians and further back—the brunt of so many of Max's jokes—Pacific Ocean Park.

Yes, Max's first encounters with Venice were on that eerie pier with its giant Neptune statue, octopus building and deep sea diving tank ride. He felt sick during the family excursions there and praised its 1967 financial collapse. When this left-over movie set, nautically-themed amusement Pier closed up, a quiet sigh of relief fell over the area. Like a moth to a flame, all that frenetic Twentieth Century energy had burned itself out. And for Max, Venice's subsequent rennaissance of the early seventies was a hallowed invitation to freedom.

Hippies (including Max and Melissa), musicians and artists joined the locals in the discarded district, liberating it for some good willed low end enterprise. Bongo Players, Bubble Blowers, Ragtime Pianists, and Jazz Flutists made a living next to bookstores, roller-skate rental booths, paddle tennis enthusiasts and professional body builders. But all these were minor attractions compared to the more idyllic Venice Beach pastime (Max's favorite), unofficially sanctioned sunbathing sans suit. Nudity, became the main attraction on the shore. From then, the Venice Boardwalk expanded its popularity until in the nineties two hundred thousand per weekend visit Venice Beach making it Southern California's favorite attraction. An important transformation: oppresive and depressing P.O.P. had become vital Venice Beach.

Amaryllis was tempted to stop at a bookstore cafe, but she still hadn't found Villa and the sodas were spilling. She turned down one of the narrow lanes. What a contrast to the noisy Boardwalk. It was so quiet and peaceful. She heard chimes tinkling in the breeze. She couldn't be too far from it now. The house with too many windows decorated with beads and tapestries. She remembered walks with her father past gardens and pointy white picket fences. They'd cross the canal bridges and stare down at their reflections. Nearer to her house was Ocean Avenue unto which Amaryllis had conjured a childish association to the shore. They were both long, roaring and forbidden.

"Daddy, can we go swimming on Ocean Avenue?"

That was Venice, loose associations of warm funky, freaky colorful people, sand, thorns, broken glass not to be stepped on, dogs, narrow lanes and fog. All of a sudden, she stopped. Ahh, there was her house. There was the big window and the garden and the chimmney. It looked so small and abandoned. She opened the gate and knocked on the door. The house was quiet and the chimes made her feel peaceful. She stood still a while then turned and headed back, but a few houses down, she stopped again. There was Villa...with that girl. And they were kissing in the shade. So naturally too. Were they new acquaintances or long time lovers? Villa tenderly held the plump red head with the puffy cap, talked to her, smiled, then tilted her head and kissed her again. The girl, with her back against the vine-covered fence stretched up on her tippie-toes to meet Villa's smiling lips. What a kiss. Why hadn't anybody ever kissed her like that?

Early the next morning, the Valley sun had already turned Amaryllis' room into a sauna. "Hello," she said answering the phone sleepily.

"It's Steven at Chez Bernard. I need you to come in today."

She glanced at the clock through half closed eyes. "But I have to practice."

"You can practice on the job. You'll get better slowly."

"No, I have to go to practice. My team."

"What about Thursday lunch? We could really use you."

"Okay, okay. Thursday lunch."

Amaryllis hung up the phone and wandered into the kitchen. Passing the living room sliding glass door, she noticed Max in the back yard sunbathing on a chaise lounge. She searched the frig for something to eat and walked back towards her room. Looking out to the yard, she could see Max reading a book, the hot sun beating down on his body. Oh no, he was entirely nude. The phone rang.

"Jasmine here. Coming to the photo shoot? Our pianist will be there. Wear a baseball cap and bring combat boots. You did so well last time that—"

"Pianist? Combat Boots?"

"Exactly."

"But I don't have—" She heard a click. She hung up the phone and it fell on the floor. Reaching down to pick it up, she knocked over her training bag spilling wraps, towels, shoes and socks. She kicked the bag, stubbed her toe, hopped around, sat on the floor whimpering, then picked up the phone and dialed a long distance number.

"Mom, I want to come home. This team is way too good for me. Yesterday, we played the guys in Venice! My team worked the ball in and out and won, but all I did was go buy sodas for everyone. I felt so useless. I told the Coach, 'I'm a defensive player'. So she says, 'You can learn the offensive drills too.' I told her 'Don't expect me to score.' So she says, 'Take your shots. Don't be afraid.' You don't know how much I want to please her. There is this one really good player on the team named Villa. You remember when you took me to that Stanford/Virginia game and we saw that girl who didn't miss and no one could catch. Well, that's who she plays like. How can I ever hope to play that well? I'm really sorry to bother you. I just didn't have anybody else I could talk—"

"Beeeeep, Your message has been received. Press one to save your message. Press two to hear ..."

Amaryllis stuffed her bag quickly and headed out to Patriotic Hall for weekend practice. On the way, she was cut off twice, honked at and cursed for going too slow. Max's car overheated on the freeway and she was given a ticket.

"Late again!" announced Flor, in charge for the day. "You already missed warm up. You don't like to stretch, do you?"

"But—"

"But what? Why can't anyone arrive on time?"

LaRhonda leaned close to Amaryllis. "She's in a bad mood."

"Her and everyone else on this team," added Peggy.

Villa shot the ball. "So what else is new? Lets just play."

Practice went down hill from there. Amaryllis was not an option on either fast break drill. She sat out the first scrimmage and on the second one, was assigned to Villa who kept passing her up left and right. Flor was getting pissed. "What's wrong with you guys today?"

"What's wrong with us?" replied Peggy. "What's wrong with you?"

"All of you are being lazy. Lets move it," said Flor.

"What's it look like were doing?" replied Patty.

"How about you Ms. Berkeley, you're late and then get blown away by Villa." Flor was peppering the new girl, the only one who would not yet answer back to her. "You must like Villa. You give her the base-line enough. L.A. too fast for you? I'll call Coach Paroni to come get you and take you back home early."

Amaryllis became distracted. Suddenly, a passed ball hit her in the face. She covered her nose and walked off the court towards the bathroom. Villa followed.

"Are you okay?"

"Just fine, but I quit."

"Villa turned around to see if anyone had been within earshot. Flor would be there any second. "I hear you, but don't say that to Coach right now. Okay? Just wait. Just say it to me, understand? I hear you. You said you're going to quit and you will."

Amaryllis didn't move. "I want to go home," she said dazed.

"Rinse your face with water. You'll feel better in a minute." Villa escorted her over towards the men's bathroom,the only one available on this floor of the old building. Urine covered the tile floor. Dry crimson splatter from someone's bloody nose stained the sink. Amaryllis gagged. Villa guided her out to the fire escape. "Try taking a few deep breaths, then come back."

"She's pushing me too hard."

"You're right, she is, but you can't just walk off the floor. Just stick out the rest of the practice."

"I told Terry I couldn't play with this team. I'm not that good. Villa, I can't go on."

"No you can't go on."

"There's no use. I'm going home."

"There's no use. You're going home."

"Stop repeating everything I say."

"Stop repeating every...Just kidding, come on Amaryllis, I know it hurts, but if you walk out now, she may not want you to come back. You're not in college."

"I am too in college. I'm on my summer break from college. Why would I be on summer break, if I wasn't in college. When you're not in college it's just plain summer, not summer break."

"What upset you? Is it Geoffrey? Is it work? Is it your father?"

"Yes, and Terry and Flor and them..." She pointed her chin to the team, "and you."

"Me? What did I do?"

"You already know you're so much better than me. Why do you have to blow me away every practice?"

"I like to play hard. You don't want me to go easy on you. I respect you too much. It would be an insult."

"You can play hard, but you don't have to elbow me twice in the chest and scratch me all up. You can see Flor's pissed at me—"

"But she's pissed at everybody."

"But I'm new. Why don't you just ease off until I get the hang of the drill."

Just then, Terry arrived. Villa looked over her shoulder. "I'm sorry. I'll ease off. Now just come back. A few more minutes and she'll replace you. It'll look bad. Please."

The new girl took in a deep breath. "Alright, alright." She threw up her hands. "I'll try. But just stop scratching me up. You might even let me score a basket. I'd like that."

Flor approached and gave them both a severe look. "Did someone get hurt? We're waiting for you two. What's taking so long?

"We're coming."

"What's up?" snapped Flor. "Terry's here and can't take this kind of added stress."

"It's nothing," said Villa. "We'll be right there."

"Nothing, huh? I think Paroni warned me about this 'Nothing'."

"Flor, please. I said its okay."

"You ready to come back now or what?"

Amaryllis became dispondant. "No," she said shaking her lowered head. "I changed my mind. I can't continue."

"Okay, it's your decision." She turned, walked over to Terry, shook her head and hollered, "Daisy's in. You coming Villa?"

Villa gave Flor a hard look then returned to the drill with Daisy. Amaryllis watched and waited for Terry by the fire escape. "What's up New Girl?"

"I can't continue."

"Are you hurt?" asked Terry. Amaryllis shook her head. A soft expression of sympathy momentarily occupied Terry's face. She bit her lip. "Okay, Amaryllis, just wait here. Practice is almost over. We'll talk tommorow at the photo shoot." She put her hand on the girl's shoulder, streams of cars rolling down the 10 Freeway below. "Just relax for now."

At home, Max sat in a steel patio chair studying a clicking sprinkler. Beside him, on the table, a pine cone held a burning stick of incense and an old telescope pointed towards the full moon. Amaryllis wanted to go outside and tell him what had happen. Confess her failure and list her shortcomings, but something inside held her back. It would feel good to be comforted, hear him say that everything would be alright, that there would be other teams, other opportunities. Yes, she knew Max still held that paternal power, but she also knew that it was her who had quit.

Silently, she watched him adjust the springs and water pressure and repair the shifting gears. The sky above was clear and the tall trees, rough edged black shapes, surrounded him like an audience of giants. A power wire drew a line through the sky. A hose was left to water a patch of succulents. Traffic sounded in the distance. It was a beautiful, still, serene Valley night. Her mind filled with questions.

Why was she staying here? How much longer could she take it? Did she have any other choices? A cricket chirped. Max got up and put the hose into a flower pot. Can I just pack up and leave? Where would I go? A black crow swooped down. During the technicolor day, the birds seemed so irritable, attacking the sparrows, driving the pigeons and doves off their territory, fighting for a slurp of a fallen orange. During the cooler evenings though, they seemed slightly mellower, hopping from fountain to gravel patch, guarding their Northridge crowdom, silently searching for crumbs. Perhaps they were tired of trying to communicate, tired of the endless caw-cawing debate over the rules of crow society. Could she in any of her relationships—her father, her job, her team—honestly say she was any different than that bird?

She shrugged, drew her curtain and fell into bed. Well, it looked like she wouldn't be going to Las Vegas after all. She hadn't been there since Harold had taken her along on a protest. Amaryllis remembered a time, underage, they'd snuck into a casino. Overweight gamblers with dyed hair fed coins from plastic containers into slot machines and hoped for a jackpot. Dropping clanking coins, swooping cawing crows. She closed her eyes; crows and coins swirling through the emptiness of her mind. The phone rang. She answered. "Amaryllis, it's Harold. We need to talk."

Amaryllis gritted her teeth and walked into Chez Bernard to set her tables before lunch. The repetitive tasks—folding napkins, polishing silverware, straightening chairs—calmed her frayed nerves. Yes, she was losing hope, but if all her other plans failed, then at least she could be a waitress. A party of ten came in at 11:30 and soon her section was full.

"I think we've got this straight," said the prim office manager at the head of the table. "Three Chef's salad specials, one seafood fettucine, one gourmet burger and cole slaw, two chicken breast in sherry sauce, one with wild rice and the other with salad. It says we get a choice of stuffed potato or steamed vegetables, have you made up your mind yet Sally?"

"The steamed vegetables."

"Steamed vegetables," repeated Amaryllis.

"No, no, the baked potato."

"Baked potato," said Amaryllis.

"No, no, I better stick with the vegetables."

It was turning into one of those days. Patricia was in a bad mood and in the kitchen, the power had gone off.

"I'm putting the order by the flashlight," said Amaryllis.

Rosario slid four salads through the window. Amaryllis looked at Jimmy and saw that he had a sign taped to his back that read, "*Pateame.*"

"Jimmy, did you know you have a sign taped to your back."

Jimmy reached behind his back but couldn't find the paper. Amaryllis stuck her arm through the window, removed the paper and handed it to him. He crumpled it up and threw it at Oscar, then went back to work. Rosario smiled at her. She smiled back. "Jimmy, I'm putting my order by the flashlight."

"Alright, alright, I heard you."

Steve appeared beside her. He cleared his throat. "Ah—um—*tene-mos luz pron-to.*"

The kitchen came to a halt and applauded. Jimmy put on an expression of awe. "Wow, Stevie, your *Español* is really improving."

Steve ignored them and turned to Amaryllis. "Speaking of improvement. You've been doing much better."

Amaryllis smiled slightly. In her present state, even the smallest compliment was appreciated. The reality was that she needed someone to talk to. "I wish I could say that for the rest of my life."

"Why, what's wrong?"

"Everything."

"Oh, is that so? We'll come to my office after your shift. I have something that might cheer you up."

After the lunch crowd had left, Amaryllis placed the ticket for her own lunch in the window.

Rosario smiled at her and gave her the plate. She sat, ate, changed clothes and finally went to Steve's office.

"Here Amaryllis," said Steve handing over an envelope. "This is your share of the tips from last week's banquet."

"Thanks."

"Now, tell me what's wrong. Is it the cooks? If they're giving you trouble, I can take care of it."

"Oh no, it's nothing to do with work."

"Well, tell me anyway. That's what I'm here for."

"It's my team. I quit."

"What else?"

She had to tell someone. "I'm worried about my father"

"And..."

"My boyfriend broke up with me."

"Sounds pretty tough." He stood and opened his arms. His cologne smelled nice and he looked so neat and clean. How could anyone work through a lunch like that one and stay so perfect looking. "You look like you could use a hug," he said warmly.

She could use a hug. People hugged each other in Santa Cruz all the time. Maybe, there were a few sensitive people down here too. They hugged.

His arms squeezed her tight and it felt good. He let go after a few seconds and sat on the couch. "Rest your feet a minute. We should talk." She sat down. He gripped the back of her shoulders and massged them. After being on her feet all day, it felt wonderful—the blood finally circulating after being so tight. "I like you Amaryllis," he said. "You're a nice person."

She closed her eyes and relaxed a minute. It's so nice making new friends. He's so nice and he really cares about his employees. She opened them and saw that Steve had moved closer and was leaning over to kiss her. The door was closed and they were alone. She stood up. "I'll see you tommorow Steve," she said as she walked to the door.

He stared at her from the couch. "Goodbye Amaryllis."

The next day was another scorcher. Amaryllis could feel the one hundred degree heat let up as she wound along Laurel Canyon through the Hollywood Hills. She parked and walked down Hollywood Boulevard, its five lanes of traffic brushing by. On both sides, earthquake damaged stuccoed brick buildings were held together by steel plates and cables. Some larger structures were condemned, chain link and planks of wood keeping loose brick from falling on pedestrians below. It looked kind of raunchy: old broadcasting spires, dusty planters, out of date billboards and glaring signs. Yet, the sidewalk also held new metal benches, trash containers and freshly transplanted palms from the last renovation.

The main attraction of the Boulevard was something about forty years old—the sidewalk. Local residents hung out everyday on that wide walkway. Tourists searching for some incarnate reference to the grand myth settled for this—a list of names in brass at their feet.

Making her way down the "Walk of Fame", Amaryllis spotted then followed Iris through a corrugated aluminum door. The air in the photo studio was cool, bright and dusty. Horseflies buzzed around the high space. There were ferns, bricks, trusses, a cappachino machine and at the bar, Geo played checkers by himself while Jasmine stood to make an announcement. "Attention everyone. Geo says, stand on the stage."

"Terry, what are they doing here?" asked Iris.

"Geo's going to take the team picture," replied Jasmine.

"But he's not a photographer."

"Geo took several courses in photography—Fashion Photography. He's a genius. He says they're his uniforms so he should document them."

"But we need a real photographer and they're not his uniforms."

"Thank God, you're not public relations coordinator," said Jasmine. "Your team would still be looking for the right color high tops."

Iris turned and faced her Father sitting with Terry, "You mean he's going to make everyone pose in a hundred different weird positions. Who does he think he is, Ansel Adams?"

Jasmine was getting snippy. "No he's not Ansel Adams and you're not Yosemite."

Geo looked up. "Try Gordon Parks or James Van der Ver or Coreen Simpson."

"Word!" exclaimed Jasmine.

Iris picked up a ball. "We're Pro athletes, not modeling school freshman."

Geo changed his accent from English to the Bronx. "Sis, whether you're a bunch of jocks or a bunch of bananas, you still have to pose, if you want a picture."

"We deserve a real photographer."

"She's crazy Geo," said Jasmine from the bar. "Take the picture without her."

Villa turned to Amaryllis. "Uh-oh."

Peggy got up. "Iris, tell Jasmine to be quiet."

"Jasmine, stay out of this," said Iris

"What an attitude. Were only trying to help."

Peggy stepped forward. "Iris, tell Jasmine to be quiet."

"Jasmine, stay out of this."

"Look, you're the athlete, Geo's the artist. It's nothing to get upset over."

"Be quiet," said Peggy gritting her teeth.

"Sis, you had your chance," said Geo. "What did you come up with? That same ball in the center composition you stole from your first year design text book.

"Word!" exclaimed Jasmine.

"Shut up!" said Peggy getting up and walking towards her.

Jasmine ran behind the bar. "I won't be quiet. Geo's designs are fresh. Here he is trying to help you and all you can do is threaten people's lives."

"This is geting out of hand," said Flor. Terry sighed.

Jasmine broke down crying. "Geo is a genius and probably the most loving person you'll ever meet."

Villa nudged Amaryllis. "Isn't this fun?" she said sarcastically.

"No."

"They're expressing themselves in their own wonderful way," said LaRhonda

"It's frustrating," said Amaryllis. "Seriously, this could all be resolved so easily."

Terry walked over to Flor. "I'll be right back." She then signaled Amaryllis and together they left the room and climbed the stairs to the roof. Terry took a moment to regain her concentration then spoke. "Now, what's going on? Why do you want to quit?"

Amaryllis looked out at the Hollywood Hills. "It's not that I want to quit Terry. I just couldn't keep going. A lot happened that day. I was overwhelmed."

"I know how you feel. All the players are under a lot of pressure. Then with family and work, it can be hard to hang in there, but you've got to keep trying." On the sidewalk below, a man held out his hand as throngs of tourists passed by. Eventually, one stopped and dropped him a quarter.

"I'm trying as hard as I can and I'm still not making it."

"Think positive. Keep prepared. Put yourself in a position safely away from where you feel like quiting. We're not doing something easy. If everyone doesn't give their all, it won't hold. We're relying on you."

"But I'm not good enough to be on this team. What can I do?"

"Every player can contribute something."

"But, I'm already doing all I can."

"Are you sure?"

"What more can I do?"

"For one, you can take the lead. Cheryl said you were a natural."

"A leader? Me?"

"One aspect of leardership is dealing with new problems when they arise. I heard you talking with Villa."

Amaryllis looked down to the corner where a group of runaway teenagers were dividing a sandwich. "So."

"You said that the argument downstairs could be resolved. How?"

"A number of ways. Maybe start by going around the room and asking each person to say what they thought about the situation. Let everyone vent their feelings. After that, it might be a bit easier to reach a consensus."

"Right. And why didn't you suggest it?"

Amaryllis thought, then shrugged. "I'm too shy."

"Shy? That's not what I heard. Stop making excuses. For the summer, you're as much a part of the team as anyone else. If you have something to contribute, you should speak up."

"But, I'm new."

"Does that mean that you should sit back and watch your teammates make asses of themselves. There are lots of ways to handle new situations."

"But—"

"Suppose yesterday when your car overheated, instead of continuing on to practice, you just waited until it cooled down. You could have gone to a used book store. Villa tells me you're practically addicted."

Amaryllis watched a tourist bus pass by, its passengers staring out fearfully. "But what about practice?"

"You're allowed to miss a practice. Call us. Tell us you can't make it. Then, take it easy. Instead, not only your car broke down, you did too."

She stared down at a street performer, a mime dancing like a robot. "But, its not my fault."

"No, its not entirely your fault. But sometimes it's not important whose fault it is. Relax. Don't push so hard. Take walks. Go with the flow."

Amaryllis felt slightly sick. "But, I'm not sure I can keep this up."

Wearily, Terry looked at her watch, then up to the sky. She tapped her foot and reached into her pocket taking out a coin. "Amaryllis, have you ever seen a mint 1981 dollar? They're rather rare. Back when I played for the WPBL, a fan gave it to me for luck. I'd rub it when I was stressed. No it didn't summon up the ghost of Susan B. Anthony to tell those guys to stop writing us bad checks, breaking our contracts and humiliating us with Spandex uniforms and charm school, but it did help me make it through the day sometimes." She paused. "Look, I know its hard. I dropped out of it myself. But you've got to keep focused. Concentrate and do your best. Maybe you can't see it, but you're only getting better."

Amaryllis swallowed. "Oh," she said softly.

Terry surveyed the hills and flats of Los Angeles' most famous district, then looked into her new player's eyes. "Now for the difficult news. Coaching a women's barnstorming team is not for the squeamish. What we are doing now, talking one-on-one is rare for me—very rare. I don't have a lot of time left over to give. You're an adult and you are going to have to look out for yourself." Terry handed Amaryllis her coin. "Hold onto that. Think things over and come to a decision. Whatever it is, let me know and it'll be okay," Terry raised both index fingers in a gesture of warning, "this time."

Exiles *1996 Summer Schedule*

Location	*Opponent*
Santa Barbara Events Center	UCSB
Venice Boardwalk Public Courts	Old Timers Basketball Club
UNLV Gymnasium	UNLV
Tijuana Fausto Gutierrez Moreno Auditorium	M.N.T., Tijuana
Sports Arena, Exposition Park	Div. I Western Conference Champions

Exiles Away Game Travel Itinerary

Santa Barbara
Meet at Union Station at 4:00pm
Stay at the San Miguel Residence Hall or the UCSB Faculty Club

Las Vegas
Meet at Union Station at 9:30am
Stay at the Desert Rose Motel

Tijuana
Meet at Union Station at 11:00am
Come back the same day.

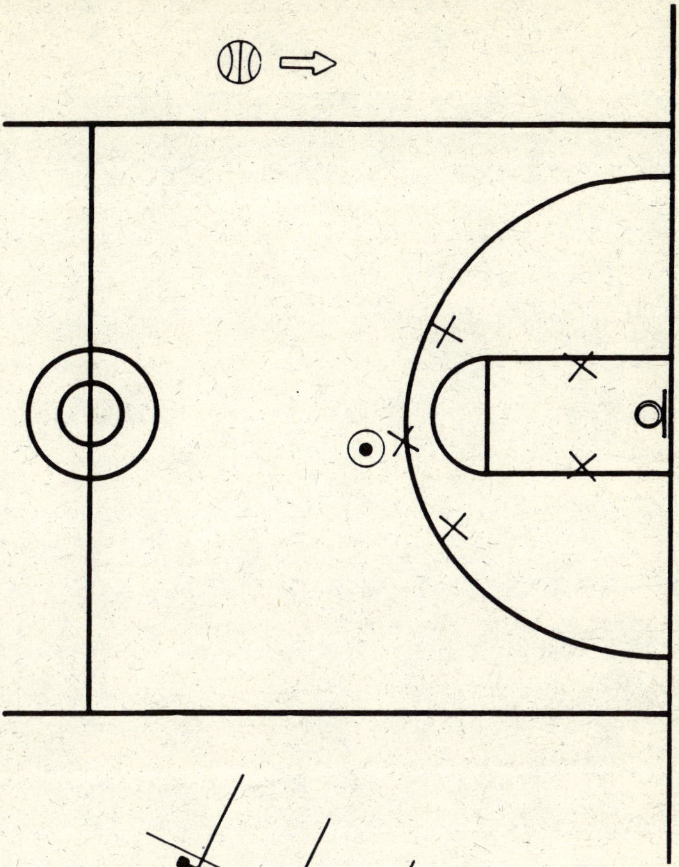

PRIME RIB
CHUCK
USDA PRIME CHOICE
RIB
LOIN
ROUND
STEAK DINNER
SHANK
J i m Y
NV
m

High Desert One Liners 7

Inside UNLV gymnasium, Amaryllis felt herself falling. Somewhere, the skin of a distant knee scraped a polished wood floor. It was quiet. Far off sounds popped in and out like flash bulbs. Layered splashes of color blossomed like bouqets of flowers. Something felt funny on her chin. Oh, forget it. After all, it was nice taking a rest in the middle of a game. Games were hard—running, jumping, diving—resting was easier. And she was feeling oh so tired, you know. But, wait, what's that oohing and ahhing? Oh yeah, that's the way the crowd moans when there's an injury. Who got hurt this time? Amaryllis opened her eyes and squinted up into a web of tinker toy steel bars and irritating bright lights. Damb, couldn't someone just climb up there and turn them off? She closed one eye and tried to touch her lip. Ouch! Something smarts. Why is everyone crowding around? Shouldn't time-out be over by now? And why hadn't her hand ever made it to her mouth?

"Hi Coach," said Amaryllis.

"Stay still," said Terry restraining her player's arm. "Don't move. Don't talk."

Sure Coach. Whatever you say. Poor Terry, she looked so old and worried from this odd angle. And all those wrinkles. Stress can really age a person.

"Looks okay," said Flor feeling Amaryllis' mandible with two fingers. "Nothing's broken." She looked in Amaryllis mouth. "No loose teeth. Caught it right on the button. She'll be all right. Headache tomorrow though, big time."

Terry leaned over and put her hand under Amaryllis neck. "Can you get up by yourself?

What a silly question. Damn, Terry, did you use enough cologne today? Amaryllis saw the stadium come into focus. On one knee, she began seeing stars. On her feet, the blood pumped painfully in her head. "Is my lip still there?" She couldn't feel it.

"Yes, still there," said Flor walking her off the court. "The locker room is this way. You'll feel better after you lay down for a while." They opened the door and found a table. Flor searched her bag. "Bandages, alcohol, antiseptic. Here's the aspirin. At the bottom, of course. Take these." Amaryllis swallowed four and took a sip of water. Flor wrapped an ice bag in a towel and positioned it against her player's jaw. "Wow babe you got hit. You were doing real sweet there for a while. She didn't score once."

"She didn't?"

"No. That's why she was getting so wild. How are you feeling?"

"I'm okay. It's tender, that's all. No big deal really. I'm sure you want to see the end of the game." Amaryllis layed back. "I'll be out there in a few minutes."

"You sure?"

"Yeah, I'm fine." Amaryllis closed her eyes as Flor left. Dull pain reached up into her temples, throbbing her entire skull; buzzing like a beard of bees. Funny images kept passing through her mind and she began hearing voices.

"*Escalera*, got hurt." It was Jimmy talking to the cooks. They were gathered around, staring down at her worried.

"*¿Va estar bien?*" Martin looked over to Oscar.

Oscar stared back. "*No se.*"

Jimmy was annoyed. "Back off you two. Let her alone. Can't you see she needs to be off by herself." Rosario bashfully laid his small hand on her forehead then left a glass of water.

Water. Come to think of it she was rather thirsty. "Thanks..." she said as she opened her eyes and found herself alone. She quit the table and found a basin and a mirror. Cold water seemed to relieve the ache, if only for an instant. She wet her hair, drank and kept splashing. She layed down again, but felt restless. The crowd was growing loud and something else was concerning her. She felt strange—different. Not wanting to be alone, she got up and returned to the gym.

Villa was icing her ankle when Amaryllis sat beside her. "You all right?" asked Villa taking her eyes off the game momentartily.

"I think so." Out on the floor, Peggy backed into "Blade" Becker, the UNLV center. "What happened to you?"

"Came down wrong." Villa turned back to the game. Becker's really throwing them. You got plastered."

"How many fouls does she have?"

"Four. They didn't call that last one. You're laying on the floor and it's still no foul." Villa shook her head. "She's getting away with murder tonight." Peggy's fall away missed. Becker rebounded, searched for her cherry-picker and fired a football pass down court.

"Are you going to go back in?"

Villa looked bereaved. "I twisted it pretty bad." Patty weaved through the UNLV back court press, faked a drive down the middle and bounced passed out to Daisy for a three pointer on the side. "But that's not going to keep me from seeing Vegas. We're hitting all the big casinos." The Exiles were up by one but Becker's spin around move was unstoppable. Grabbing a lob pass, Becker scored the last basket at the buzzer, winning the game by a single point.

In the locker room, most of the team skipped showers, pulled on their sweat suits and traded insults. "Why didn't you cover your own man. Nobody asked you to double team," whined Patty.

"My man was down court. I was free."

"You just got in the way."

"Yeah, blame it on me. She ate you up and it's all my fault."

"Chill out! So we lost one. We're in Las Vegas for the night. Let's enjoy ourselves."

"That's right. Hurry up! We have to check into our fancy hotel rooms, then hit the town."

The team loaded inside a van and drove through town until they stopped at their accomodations.

Looking disappointed, Patty stood in front of the hotel sign. "Desert Rose? Terry, that's a sad name."

"Don't start Patty."

"Desert—I can understand—we're in the middle of it. But Rose? There isn't a rose within miles of here."

Coach ignored her.

Peggy was just as disappointed. "Terry, you're supposed to enjoy you hotel, not feel sorry for it."

"Villa paced the gravel parking lot. "What happened to Excalibur and Luxor and the MGM?"

"Too expensive." Terry searched her bag for the reservation receipts. "No group discounts."

Patty took out change for the phone. "I don't want to stay here. I'm getting a room in town."

"We're in town."

"Which one?"

I'm sorry," said Terry. "That won't work. We'll lose track if everyone stays in different places."

Patty grabbed her bags and started walking across the street towards another motel. "I'm going over there then. At least, their pool has a slide."

Terry unloaded the rest of the bags and equipment. "Fine Patty. Go across the street. Just call us when you have your room. Anyone else want to stay at the 'Glass Pool'?"

"Villa nudged Amaryllis who hadn't spoken the entire trip. "Where are you going to stay?"

"I don't care."

Villa and Amaryllis, and Patty and Peggy, all crossed the street and got two rooms side by side. Villa layed on the bed to rest her ankle. "This sucks. Terry blew it. We could be at the Palace Station or the Stardust or the Mirage right now." Villa looked at Amaryllis sitting dazed on the bed. "You okay?"

"I'm just thinking."

"About what?"

"Everything. Nothing. Everything and Nothing."

Villa reached over and touched Amaryllis cheek bone. "The bruise is beginning to show."

Patty knocked on the door. "Terry's going to take the team to a fancy buffet to make up for the disappointment. Come on."

"Woah, great," exclaimed Villa jumping up.

As the three left, they passed a hippie van parked in front of their room. Amaryllis stood and stared.

"What's with her? asked Patty. "I thought she was feeling better."

Villa took Amaryllis' arm. "Come on number twenty-four. You

need to have some fun tonight."

Located in the middle of the casino, the Circus Circus Buffet was long, yet predictable. Each of the three aisles contained a smorgasbord of salads, meats, seafood, chicken and vegetables. There were egg rolls and mash potatoes with gravy. There was a fish salad as well as carved roast beef. In the dining area most of the formica seats and tables looked out onto aisles of slot machines and a loud clanging casino whir filled the space.

"You sure you got enough there Peggy," joked Daisy.

"Just eat your meatballs, Meatball."

Patty arrived with a mountain of food on her plate. Daisy laughed. "And I thought Peggy was hungry. Patty, it's falling off the sides. Don't put it down, the table will collapse."

Patty nudged in between Daisy and Iris. "I was trying to sample a little of everything."

"You pig. There must be a hundred things on that line."

Iris was dieting. She picked at her salad. "Hey Terry, thanks for the five-star cuisine."

"Sorry everyone. We're on a budget. This is the best we could do."

Dahlia poked at her plate. "Culinary excellence—a treat for the tastebuds—gourmet dining at its best."

Peggy put down her fork and knife and pushed her tray aside. "Well, I know what I'm going to do." She walked into the casino and began feeding a dollar slot machine.

"Hey, why did she leave before your pep talk?" asked Violet. Terry shrugged her shoulders. "Well if she won't wait, neither will I." Violet pushed aside her tray and walked out to join Peggy. Dahlia followed.

LaRhonda jumped up, "Don't play those ones," she shrieked. "You can play longer on the quarter ones."

Dahlia pushed her away. "You just want to take it over," she snapped. "It's about to hit any second."

Leaving Terry with all their trays and trash, the team broke into groups and argued their way out the hotel and down the strip.

"Let's go see the volcano."

"Shut up. Lets go to the top of the needle."

"This is Vegas. You're supposed to gamble. Lets hit the casinoes."

Villa and Amaryllis broke away from the others and walked through several of the hotels. In spite of her ankle, Villa walked briskly, not waiting for traffic signals or stopping to rest. Finally after arriving at the largest and newest hotel, they took a seat at the bar next to a well-dressed woman with long ringlets drooping down across her face.

"Well we're finally here," said Villa.

"Yeah," replied Amaryllis.

"How do you like Vegas?"

"It's okay."

"Just okay? It's fantastic. That elbow must have really knocked you senseless."

"Maybe."

"How do you think the rest of the team is doing?"

"I don't know."

"The last I saw, Peggy, Iris and Daisy got free tickets to a magic act. LaRhonda, Dahlia and Patty lost half their money at roulette and are probably losing the rest of it now playing poker. And Violet is playing the computer slots. Flor and Terry are probably on their fourth round of tropical drinks—"

"I'm on my fifth," said the woman next to them. "I collect the little umbrellas. They're so delicate. When I was a little girl, I always wanted to have a real one, but my mother would never buy it for me." She sipped deeply from the end of a long straw and spilt chips and salsa down her green silk blouse "What happened to your face?"

Villa stared at the girl then nudged her spaced-out team mate. "Amaryllis..."

"Huh? Oh, I got elbowed."

"Elbowed? Boyfriends! Who needs them?"

Amaryllis didn't answer. She had momentarily forgotten her injury and didn't want to be reminded. The noise was giving her a headache.

Villa scooted over towards the girl and smiled. "She wasn't elbowed by her boyfriend. She was elbowed by the UNLV center in a basketball game."

"You played against UNLV!?"

"Not the guys—the girls. We're the Exiles. We played an exhibition game with the women's team today and lost by one point. Our whole team is out on the town at this very moment trying to forget about it. Isn't that right Amaryllis?"

"Uh-huh," she responded standing. "Excuse me. I'll be back in a minute. I want to send a postcard to my mother."

Amaryllis found the hotel gift shop and slowly spun the display rack to chose from the predictable assortment: pictures of people with styled hair throwing dice down a crowded craps table, ardent couples drinking martinis in the privacy of wallpapered hotel rooms, senior citizens swinging golf clubs, lines of hotels lighting the dark desert night. Amaryllis found the tacky and the sad, the corny and the mundane, the old and the new. She bought a handful and returned to the bar to find Villa drinking another round and laughing aloud with the girl.

"Guess what? Emily has three tickets to see Buzzy Slater."

"Who's that?"

"It says that he's a comedian."

"I don't know if I'm in the mood."

"Come on New Girl. It's my treat."

The woman giggled. "Villa, you know those tickets were free."

Inside the casino, between the Keno and the dining area, a woman in a sparkling silver gown was finishing her review of favorite show tunes.

When she stepped off the stage, an electric sign changed from singer to comedian and a recording announced, *"Ladies and Gentlemen, give a warm welcome to a Vegas veteran and very funny man, Mr. 'Go Home' himself—Buzzy Slater."*

Thin and gray haired, Buzzy wore a bright red tie and a reasonably priced black corderoy suit. His face was wrinkled, but his smile was warm and promptly disappeared as soon as the act began.

"Go Home! Everyone, get up, go back to your rooms, pack and get lost. I'm doing you a favor. What's this? Nobody's budging? Big surprise. I've been doing this for forty years and not once has anyone listened. Why are you laughing? My jokes aren't funny. I'm dead serious. I'm giving you good advice."

"I've had a long career, but I still don't understand Vegas tourists. 'You get what you pay for in life.' It's a common saying. Yet every year, millions come here expecting to score money, sex, power and happiness for fifty-eight bucks a night. I'm sorry, it can't be done. Now you know, alrighty? Go Home."

"So maybe my act isn't top billing anyore, at least I'm honest with people. I mean look how you guys behave. When you come to Vegas, do you stay with friends or relatives? Do you find a cozy hotel or motel? No, you gotta sleep in an amusement park. Forty years ago, I used to take a shower, shave, get dressed, go to the club and work my act. Now, I cross a moat, hop over a volcano and run away from white tigers. I mean, you people outta grow up. You know, I'm a father of three and when my kids were small, if they were bad, I grounded them. Now listen. You've all have been very bad. You're grounded. Go Home."

"At home, you have responsibilities and duties. You go to work, and trim the lawn on the weekends. And you get knocks on the door, or ads in the mail, or telephone calls asking you for a small donation to help house the homeless, or for a few volunteer hours to stuff envelopes or maybe a commitment to come to open house at the junior high school. And what do you do? You hang up, throw the junk in the trash and slam the damn door in their faces. Sure, but when a TV commertial flashes some rip-off package deal to stay in a tasteless hotel, pour a months wages down some infantile slot machine, break your sobriety on cheap booze, then in the middle of the night, walk in a stupor down an endless fairytale carpet corridor to your tiny flower wallpaper room full of bargain furniture—what do you do? You flock here by the millions. We can't keep you people away. It's the fastest growing city in the country."

"And the sad thing is, you don't even know where you are. Let me give you a clue. You ever seen a picture of Freemont street-1905? What's in it? Baby casinoes waiting to grow up? A big sign-'Future Site of Tacky Gambling Resort'? No! Life's not a cartoon—it's a dirt road, two dozen gabled houses and a few mules."

"You know where you are yet? No? Alright, I'll try again. In 1910, that dirt road got a new train depot. Sure, there were banks, stores, restaurants and saloons, but the people still knew where they were. If they didn't fill their canteen in the morning they'd never make it back to bed at night. Nowadays, there are hundred foot signs: Dunes, Sands, Sahara, Mirage, Oasis. Do you people know where you are yet? Times up! Surprise, you're in the middle of a desert. You know like—I'm thirsty, I'm thirsty. They cut the lines to this place and it dries up forty-eight fours tops. Do yourselves a favor. Pack it up you guys. Go home!"

"And where is home for most of you? Let me guess. Vegas is the only city that can make you happy to be back in L.A. Smog, spread out, no center, soulless throngs of Hollywood phonies jamming the freeways—still at least Los Angeles has it's major industries: import/export, garment manufacture, entertainment. What's Vegas' major industry? Addiction. Some towns want their citizens to plant trees and have bake sales. For seventy years, we've encouraged ours to do nothing but drink and gamble. Chicago is powerful. D.C. is monumental. New York is impressive. Vegas tour guides can barely pull the bus away from the curb. *'In the twenties, little neon signs lit up what was just another railroad company town. In the thirties, gambling was legalized, the divorce residency requirement was lowered to six weeks and Hoover Dam was built. By 1940, three story brick hotels and casinos sat on downtown intersections and by the fifties, bright signs made Fremont a national tourist attraction.'* Who cares! Where's the craps table?"

"When I came out in '55, at least I knew who I was working for—organized crime. These days, the whole things gotten so big, you don't know who's paying you. But somehow I still don't think it's Goodwill Industries. So now they call it this corporation or that corporation. Big deal. You still lose at blackjack and in a fire, the money goes in the safe before they show you the exit door."

"Okay, okay, you say some people need a vacation, an escape. But show some style. In my day, we'd go out to dinner and dancing, soup de jour and a slow fox trot. Now, it's the $1.99 buffet, the topless joint and the superslide.

Even in the Sixties, things weren't this silly. I can still remember back then when they replaced that little depot with a hotel and a bus station. Resorts with bright signs started sprouting up along route 91. At first, it seemed all you needed was a loud casino on the sidewalk and a big bright sign with some vague cutural reference like Arabic style writing or pointy corners like Alladin's lamp or the Genie's shoes. But then, they started turning the hotels into circuses and temples and huts. You walked in and everyone's a Centurian or a Clown or a Tiki God. Now no one is happy unless you're King Tut himself inside his tomb, Dorothy in the Land of Oz, or Sir Francis Drake on his Pirate Ship.

Don't you see? It's all a bunch of one line gimmicks. Outside on the Strip, they'll do anything to distract you. They've got fountains and super-heroes and ocean battles and space ships. They've got full size replica statues from ancient Rome, rennaisance Florence and Easter Island. Yeah, outside, they'll steal just about any idea and inside, here at my show, the new comics dress up like tourists and take down my material shorthand. And you guys grab up the free tickets to see it. I don't understand Vegas tourists. What can I say to convince you? There's nothing here. Somebody! Please anybody! Isn't there a single person out there that'll listen. Go Home! Go Home!! GO HOME!!!"

Amaryllis nudged Villa. "I don't feel very good," she whispered. "I think I'm going back to our room."

Villa glanced over at her new acquaintance and then leaned towards Amaryllis. "You'll miss the rest of the show."

"Sorry."

"Okay. We'll see you back there later."

Out on the sidewalk crowds of excited tourists pointed, gawked and paced about.

"Oh my god," screamed a lady. "The volcano looks so real."

"I can't wait to see the underwater mermaid show," said a man.

"Is it true they have a live tiger in the lobby?" asked another.

"Where are the Knight jousts?"

Amaryllis grabbed a city bus to her motel. Stepping down, she crossed the street and saw a couple of girls loading up that same hippie van she'd seen earlier. Her mind went blank. She stood and stared.

"Hi," the taller one finally said.

Amaryllis spoke. "You're going out to Peace Camp aren't you?"

"Yeah," answered the other. "It's a protest against the resumption of testing. There will be a ceremony to heal the land and return it to the Shoshone. We'll have rituals and circle dances."

"I haven't been there in five years. I went with my boyfriend—I mean ex-boyfriend—when I was seventeen. I've never forgotten it."

"What happened to your face?"

"I was elbowed playing basketball. My team lost and now they're out drinking and gambling."

"Why aren't you with them? Does your head hurt?"

"A little. But that's not why I'm not with them. I just couldn't get into the Strip. I had to get away."

"If you really want to get away, you should come with us."

Amaryllis left a note for Villa taped to the motel painting. She stuffed a few things in a bag and hopped into the back seat of the van. It was a relaxing ride. The bright lights and signs quickly turned into a familiar scene of mini marts, stucco apartments and gas stations. Then, the city disappeared into in the darkness of the desert leaving shapes of mountains against the night sky. Headlights shone on scattered Joshua Trees standing like plumed roadside sentinels. The wind was warm but growing cooler by the minute. The old VW motor hummed loudly. A shiver went down Amaryllis' back. "It's getting cold."

"You think it's cold now, wait until tonight. But don't worry, our extra sleeping bag is the best. It would keep you warm in two feet of snow."

"Are you full time activists?"

"No, right now we're working in a winery. Are you a full time basketball player?"

"No, just for the summer. I'm waitressing part-time."

"How do you like it?"

Amaryllis stared out at the passing roadside. "It sucks. My boss is handsome but he's so manipulative. As soon as I let him know I broke up with my old boyfriend, he tried to hit on me in his office."

They passed an Air Force base to the east, then the bright lights of a prison to the west. "Yeah that happens all the time."

"It happened to you too?"

"Sure, the guys in the winery are always up to something. Why do you think I like to get away?" Another prison appeared and then a curvaceous formation of mountains. Then finally, they arrived at a grouping of tents on their left. They drove past, then doubled back to avoid the Highway Patrol car stationed outside the camp.

At the entrance, a dusty ragged woman tended a small fire. "Park over there and camp at the top of this little hill." Several strangers, mere shapes in the darkness helped them set up their tent in the wind. Before going to sleep, Amaryllis visited the camp center and drank healing herbal tea. In the medicine tent, a young woman applied balm to her jaw.

"What happened to your face?"

"I was elbowed playing basketball."

"You should take care of yourself."

"What's that you're singing?"

The nurse massaged Amaryllis' shoulders and blessed her with sage smoke. "A healing chant. It will make you feel better and give you good dreams."

Amaryllis found her tent and pulled herself into the extra sleeping bag. She tossed and turned on the ground until she was settled in. It had been a long day. Snug, despite the desert cold, she fell into a deep sleep under a black sky full of millions of stars.

It was day. She arose, sharp pebbles stabbing her naked feet. A road lined by eight tall Joshua Trees stretched into the distance. A crow flew overhead and a bus with her father, Flor, Patricia, Steve and the cooks seated inside stopped beside her. She boarded, then stepped down at an alleyway that led through to a downtown street. In the middle of the intersection, a campfire burned hot. Her shirt was unbuttoned and several people stopped to suckle at her breast. In a storefront window, Geo and Jazz, both wearing parts of her uniform, performed an interpretive dance. Suddenly, Gita ran by kicking a ball high into the air and up ahead, Terry blew her whistle and waved at traffic. On the corner, Villa directed her teammate towards the payphone. Amaryllis stopped, inserted her coin, dialed and put the static-filled receiver to her ear. "Play."

The door was open to room #27 of the Glass Pool Motel and Amaryllis was relieved to find her teammate and that same girl inside.

"There you are," said Villa

"Hey, how was the Test Site?" asked the girl.

Amaryllis sat in a chair and heaved a sigh of relief. "It was amazing. I forgot how beautiful that place was. I mean you wake up in the morning and all you can see are these majestic tan mountains. There were Native American drummers and dancers and this lady taught me how to cleanse myself with sage smoke. They served vegetarian food on recycled plates. I ate off a Frisbee. We all held hands in a circle and whoever wanted to say something could. I feel much better."

"Is this the same person I met last night," asked the girl.

"I'm not sure," said Villa. "You are Amaryllis aren't you?"

"Stop playing around. Where's the team?"

"They went back earlier. I told Coach about your note and that I'd wait for you."

"Thanks a lot for letting us have the room to ourselves last night. The slide is fun," said the girl.

Villa blushed. "What else happened?"

"Well, I went to an educational workshop inside a big tent. I would never have guessed there was so much political activism in Las Vegas. But there is. There are environmental groups, and nuclear monitoring groups and Native American rights groups and local unions. Did you know that Las Vegas had organized protests against the War in Iraq. And in 1992, when the police who beat Rodney King received Not Guilty verdicts, people in Las Vegas took to the streets. One lady was telling me that resort parking lots are often lined with picketers and the streets are sometimes filled with protestors. She told me about an animal rights group that protested in the lobby of the Mirage and a Pro Choice group that..."

At the train depot, Villa bid a fond farewell to her girlfriend and later that night, the basketball twosome arrived at Union Station. "It's late. Why don't you stay over and go home tomorrow. Or better yet, spend a Sunday in Boyle Heights."

After the noise of the casinoes, Amaryllis loved the idea of being in Villa's neighborhood. Music played out of windows, traffic brushed by on the street, children loudly debated the rules to sidewalk kickball, firecrackers banged, whistles blew, babies cried, beer drinkers argued, couples laughed and car alarms went off.

The next morning they sat out in the sun on the porch facing narrow old houses and well kept gardens. Power lines framed the sky; cars lined the streets.

"You hungry?"

"Starving."

Villa looked down the sidewalk, "They should be along any minute."

"You're having breakfast delivered?"

"You could say that." Minutes later, vendors passed by shouting their wares. Villa bought fruit, corn tamales, and *champurado.* She brought Amaryllis a tray, a napkin and a glass of fresh squeezed orange juice.

Amaryllis sipped her cup and took a bite of melon. "So what's the plan today?"

"Kick back. Walk to the park. Take the kids swimming or just sit here all day."

"Wait a minute. Take what kids swimming?"

A loud truck rolled by. A police siren sounded in the distance. Two little girls ran up and placed a basketball in Villa's hands. "Do the tricks," said one.

"Those kids," said Villa.

"What are your names?" asked Amaryllis.

"I'm Marisol," said the younger sister.

"I'm Rosa," said the older.

"Who hit you?" they asked together.

Villa spun the ball on one finger for them. "She got elbowed playing ball."

"You play too?" asked Rosa.

"Of course," answered Amaryllis. "I'm the star of the team."

"Are you as good as Villa?"asked Marisol.

"Of course I am," laughed Amaryllis. "In my dreams."

"Take us to the pool! Take us to the pool!" the two girls begged.

On their way, Amaryllis, Villa, Marisol and Rosa followed the shade as best they could. Big trees lined the sidewalk in front of quaint old houses one of which had concrete pineapple capitals on its gateposts and a Spanish fountain under a palm in its courtyard. Dogs barked,tires screeched and in the distance, a bell tolled in it's tower.

Surrounding the Roosevelt High School olympic pool was a wall of glass windows, some busted, jammed or bullet pierced. Trees lined the fence and a huge bush dropped sweet purple mulberries onto the hot sidewalk. In the water, screams and shouts all but drowned out the whistles and piercing reprimands from the two lifeguard towers. "Get off his back! Stand up on the ramp! Let go of the ropes! WALK!"

On one side, staff parked their cars. On the other, parents watched the swim team from metal bleachers. Families sunbathed on the concrete under a half a dozen fifty-foot light stands. A line of clowning divers waited behind the low dive.

"Watch," shouted Marisol before doing a cannon-ball.

"Look at me," shouted Rosa before doing a belly-flop.

"Here goes," shouted Amaryllis before walking off the end of the diving board as if she didn't know it was there.

By the time they returned to Villa's cottage, the lunch vendors had arrived. After making her purchases, Villa set rice, beans, *chile rellenos* and a glass pitcher of Tamarindo on top of her lace draped table. "Sometimes, I think of getting a place to myself, but I'm afraid I'd be too lonely," said Amaryllis.

"It does get lonely. Even with all these people. It's funny, I was so anxious to leave home, but now sometimes I miss it." After lunch,

Amaryllis took a nap. And after the nap, they took a walk to the Youth Center. Filled with kids—boxing, lifting weights, and playing three-on-three—they waited their turn, then won six straight as the line of challengers grew longer; each team anxiously waiting their chance to take on these women with "Skills".

That Monday, Amaryllis felt refreshed and relieved when she arrived at work eventhough Jimmy seemed genuinely concerned.

"What happened to your face?"

"I got elbowed playing ball."

"You better put some make-up over that bruise. Don't let Steve see."

"Why not?"

"He'll fire you is why not."

"Stop kidding around Jimmy." She looked over at Rosario who looked back at her worried.

Things went well during her shift and afterwards, she changed her clothes. As she was leaving though, Steve appeared. "Amaryllis, I'd like to see you in my office."

She punched out and reported to Steve's office. "Steve, I have to tell you—"

Steve sat on the couch. "Would you sit down a minute?"

Amaryllis sat. "I've been meaning to talk to you anyway. It's about—"

Steve stared at her face. "That's a bad bruise." He came closer. She backed away. "Will you relax? What happened?"

"I got elbowed playing basketball." She backed away again. "Steve, that's what I wanted to tell you. I want our relationship to remain professional."

"Me too. And it's my professional opinion that Chez Bernard waitresses can't show up looking like prize fighters."

Amaryllis went home, slept and then packed for her trip to Tijuana. Arriving at San Diego Train Station, the team walked across the street and boarded the trolley south to San Ysidro. They crossed the border bridge with the crowds then caravaned in taxies through the streets and boulevards of Tijuana towards their destination—*El Auditorio.*

The Auditorio de Tijuana Fausto Gutierrez Moreno is a white dome building in between the river and the race track in the El Prado area of the city. Unloading on the concrete foyer, the team walked down the main ramp and into the stadium while Flor spoke Spanish with the director in the office.

Inside the main auditorium, the entire team was impressed with the beautifully shaped dome. Their marching feet rumbled echoes and the first bouncing ball sounded back five times like distant gunfire. The intricately ribbed ceiling formed an intriguing background to anything overhead, the backboard, the expensive scoreboard or the game ball itself.

Patty was first inside. "Woah, mini King Dome."

Then came Daisy. "Hey, Echo!"

Then Villa. "It's going to be loud in here."

During warm up, Terry waved Amaryllis over. "You should get some playing time today," she explained. "Probably in the second half."

The team warmed up as the fiberglass seats of the stadium filled with groups of students and teachers. By the time the game began, the noise was deafening—a rock concert. Terry gathered the team together and referred to her clipboard, jotting down quick notes on her prospectus sheet as she spoke. "Take care of the ball. Pass it around, keep up the pressure, control the boards and box out. This will definately be an uptempo game. We're going to start with the 1-3-1 and try to run them. They're in good shape but they'll still get tired."

"On defense, know the location of the ball and the position of the players. Predict the direction of play. Stay on the balls of your feet, knees bent, legs apart. Stay between your man and the basket. Block the passing lane."

Terry looked over at the other team, tall, strong and disciplined. "Now, Villa step up on Marino for the three point bombs. Patty, you stick Davila or she will run the floor then stop for the set shot. Neruda will drive, but always to the right, so Peggy, don't give her the base line. Everyone put in their hand and let this crowd know that the..."

Each put in a hand and shouted, "...Exiles are in Tijuana!"

Amaryllis began walking towards the bench and nudged Villa. "I may get some playing time."

"Of course. Didn't I say so. Now get ready."

"Look at this crowd."

In the first half, the crowd was loud and the game was a constant give and take. The score was high and by half time the Exiles were only leading by one basket. By the second half Iris badly needed a rest and Terry leaned over to Amaryllis.

"How's your jaw?"

"Okay."

"Want to keep #6 from getting the ball for a few minutes."

Amaryllis smiled. "Yes, Terry."

Amaryllis took her position on the floor. She leaned against #6 and got ready. This opponent had a hook shot that was accurate from under ten feet, but Amaryllis quickly found that if she attacked the ball low, #6 could never get it off. Twice she slapped the ball free and once stole it cleanly. She kept her scoreless for four minutes and this time kept her hands up to keep from getting hit by an elbow.

When she sat back down, Villa was taking a rest. "We're going to have to make a run for it afterwards. Stay with me okay? I want to show you something after the game."

"Whatever you say," said Amaryllis.

When it was all over—Exiles 62, Tijuana 58—the team pulled on their sweats and tried to make a quick exit. The din of shouting followed them outside where they were caught in the middle of a crowd of kids chanting for autographs. They made their way to two station wagons, but there was not enough room and Flor sent players to the border in additional taxies with instructions to take the trolley back and meet by the train station.

Villa spoke with Flor briefly then returned to Amaryllis. "Come on," she said. "We'll meet them later. I want to show you one of my favorite places."

They crossed the street and hailed a taxi. "But there's already someone in this one." said Amaryllis.

"That's how it works here. Get in."

Passing streets and people, monuments, gas stations and marketplaces, they drove in silence as the old Buick stopped repeatedly to allow new passengers in or out. Once they arrived at Via de la Revolución, Villa paid for both of them with a single dollar bill.

"Wow, that's it? Why can't we do that in L.A.?"

"It's down this way." she said and headed off on a quick walk pulling Amaryllis by the arm. Four blocks later, they arrived at Parque Teniente Guerrero, one of Tijuana's many quaint city parks. With rough topiary, a green hose for a fountain and a central plaza filled with kids and clown, the Parque looked like it came out of a favorite children's book. Villa bought them each a roasted ear of corn and picked a good spot to watch the show.

"Thanks Villa. This made me really happy."

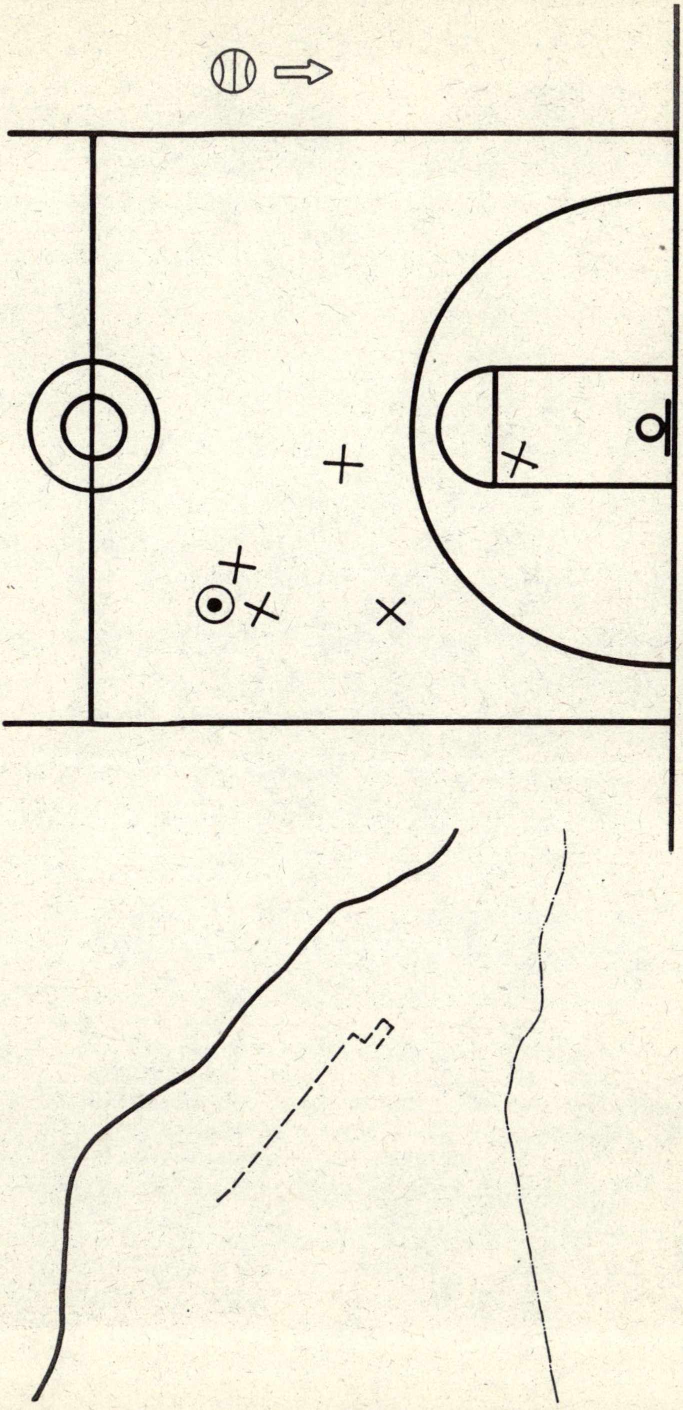

GITA

Stone Oranges and Stained Sidewalks 8

Taking the stairs three at a time, Amaryllis came to the Shalom Village third floor. She walked through the orange carpeted lounge and down the flower wallpapered corridor to her Grandmother's room. The door was wide open, but Gita nowhere in sight. She brushed aside the wind blown curtains to check the balcony. Still no sign. Just then, she heard the toilet flush.

Waiting for her Grandmother to come out, she took a seat and a few moments to survey the disheveled room. What strange things the old woman kept. From her old apartment full (Full!) of forty years of collected treasures, Gita had chosen six items to accompany her in the new home. Now, where were they? Lets see, to begin with, Amaryllis was sitting on the spiral pattern knit pillow—Gita had made it herself during her husband's final stay in the hospital. Also, on the dresser, was the "Lady in the Moon" porcelain statuette, an expensive antique purchased on installment from the dealer in Culver City.

These two items alone brought back a flood of memories. Even as a ball bouncing youngster, Amaryllis had marveled at the living room stockpile of knickknacks and artifacts. Candle holders, lamps, plates, vases and books piled on sofas, crammed together on the fake fireplace mantel and stuffed inside the antique display cabinet. Later as a teenager, she had heard stories of the old woman's move into the nursing home. The truck loads of furniture and heirlooms driven straight to the Medical Center Thrift Shop. The transfer of ownership to charity and the estate sales that had not come far from giving everyone a stroke. "How much for the Limoges China? Let me ask you this, how much do you think its worth?" Then after the answer had turned her showroom smile into a fire sale frown. "Yes, maybe during the depression, but how much you think its worth nowadays." Then after the argument. "Yes, you're right, I do sell the old-fashioned way. You see, I'm old-fashioned. Did you come to buy or maybe you're a social worker. It's too late for a foster home." Then as the customer turned to leave. "*Oy, mein* back *tut mir vey*. Excuse me, I don't feel so good. I have to sit a rest in my Williamsburg Rocker. An original, not imitation. Oh yes, I feel better already. Only $150.00. Okay, I'll give to you $120.00. Take the china too. $80.00 for the set. Of course you'll take it, it's worth that three times."

Out of all that, though, six treasured belongings, could not be parted with at any price. There, on the bed, wrinkled and torn, were the matching yellow spreads and linens. Outside on the balcony, the stained glass wind chimes. And by the mirror, the fourteen inch certified collector's item Barry Manilow "Copacabana" ceramic piano music box (everyone is allowed some extravagance).

That was five. But where was that last one? It was always the hardest. The photos in the new frames didn't count. The charity awards and certificates weren't part of the game either and everything else in the room seemed foreign; lacking her grandmother's charm. Aluminum walker, rubber catheters, steel oxygen tank, plastic bed pan, paper incontinent pads, canes, pill bottles and wheelchair were all concealing the puzzle's last piece. Where was it?

Sounds of running water came from the bathroom basin. Gita's face appeared in the doorway. Then, just as Amaryllis was ready to resign from her little game, she spotted the last item, hiding by the window all the time—the little Japanese Bonsai. How had something so small and delicate survived that monumental move, much less that merciless selection? Why would a woman attracted to life's *gute zachen* be so attached to a crooked little tree? A large fern, a potted palm, maybe, but the *Boimele*?

"Well if it isn't Little *Szvartze Oygen*," said Grandma Gita. "Do you remember, we used to call you that? Who'd ever think Miss Dark Eyes would reach six feet tall. And all from your mother. At least that good I can say about her." Gita sat down. "Now this, you won't believe. At breakfast, I choked on the oatmeal. You would expect a chicken bone or a cracker, but at my age, it can be anything. One little cough and it's into the wheelchair and back to my room."

"Grandma, they fired me."

Alarm gripped Gita's face, "You spilled the soup again?"

"No, it was the manager."

The old woman wagged an accusing finger. "So what did you do that the manager should fire you?"

"How can you even say that? He fired me because I wouldn't go out with him."

Gita frowned, then grinned. "Okay, here's what you do. You have to trick him. On the outside, you go back and apologize. But, inside don't forget, be careful always and watch out not to be alone with him. And when he argues, you just agree."

"What are you saying?"

"The manager is not as smart as he thinks. Be good. He probably wouldn't do it again."

"Wouldn't do it again? I can't just go back like a good little girl and apologize to him. How can you give me advice like that? It's so...so...backward."

Gita sighed. "Backward." She looked into the TV as if it were a window. It's true. How did you know? Backward from a backwards village. I was even born backwards—a breech baby. If it weren't for the midwife, I would not have breathed my first breath. A premature birth too...small, only three pounds." She poured tea into two cups.

Amaryllis rolled her eyes and sighed. "But Grandma, I—

"Did I get much bigger either?" continued Gita. "No. Maybe a six-footer like you would look down on me, but in my backwards village, envied was my small size. Blessed were the stunted girls that the soldiers would not notice. When they searched the houses, my mother would dress me up like a baby and put me in the crib. But pretty soon, small as I was, I wouldn't fit."

"Grandma!" interrupted Amaryllis, "When I go back for my check, I'm going to file a suit. I'll tell him—"

"Darling, please, *zay shtill.* Wait until I finish." Amaryllis slumped back in her chair as Gita went on. "You think you have problems. How would you have liked to live in a place were nothing made sense. In this country, young girls pray for a pretty face. In my backward village, I asked God to bless me with one so ugly it would turn away even the most desperate intruder." Gita stood and brought a round tin down from the shelf. "Would you like a cookie?"

Amaryllis yawned. "Oh, alright—the sprinkly kind."

"The *bashpritzte.* Yes, of course." She placed a glass plate of cookies on the table and the tin within reach. "Now, another surprise I'll tell you. You think sports only comes from your mother's side. No. I, too was athletic. I kicked the ball some days until it was dark. Watching me, my mother called, 'You're twelve years old. A young woman can't play with boys.' Then just as I slouched away with my head down, her eyes lit up like candles and she jumped like a bee had stung her bottom. 'Dress her like a boy—she runs like one. Cut her hair. Put her in pants. The soldiers will never guess.'"

Amaryllis' face lit up. "You played soccer? Was it fun? Were you very good?"

"Too good. And what started as a blessing, became a curse. Even with the task of being a boy in the morning and a girl at night, I was still the best twelve-year-old in the village. With each goal I kicked, they became more jealous. I watch through the *Yeshiva* window while they studied for hours what I was not allowed to see for a minute, and still, of me, they were jealous."

"What about the soldiers, did they discover you?"

"My mother suspected the boys would tell on me anyday, so she took us all to New York City and made plans to marry off her *kleine wilde chya.*"

"Did you play sports when you came here?"

"Oh yes, a game I played on the Lower East Side—fourteen hours everyday—sewing."

Amaryllis made a screwed up face. Somehow the story didn't make sense. "But Grandma, why didn't you just take some time off?"

Gita slouched and let out her breath. "You are a strange one. Beautiful mysterious dark eyes of a woman, but the *neshoma* of a spoiled child. Hands as big as my music box piano and inside, the same tiny tune. You, a girl who was allowed to play every night until after dark, who belonged to leagues and played in tournaments, who received letters from coaches and who now, studies in the university and chooses her own boyfriend. A girl given the gift of freedom, yet, everytime something goes a little wrong, she comes crying. Why can't you even understand a simple story? The heroine right before you eyes." She leaned forward gripping the sides of the table. "They wouldn't let me! Don't you see. It didn't matter what I did. I was a good sewer too. Would they let me be supervisor? No. They wouldn't let me grow—anyway I went—that way was a dead end. I want to be a big girl and talk to the soldiers. They dress me in baby's clothes and lie me in a baby's bed. I want to be beautiful like my mother. They cut off my hair and send me outside to play with my tormentors. I want to be a boy and kick the ball between the tree and rocks for a goal. They call me back inside to save me for marriage. I want to be married. They send me to work all day, married to a sewing machine. I want to be the best by my machine and get a promotion. They tell me I'm a "dumpling" and grab at me like the Polish Soldiers back home. Darling, what you have, I've worked for all my life and even now it has been taken from me."

Amaryllis ate another cookie. "What's that supposed to mean?"

"I guess you don't know you're talking to a court certified meshugena. I worked for my savings all my life. But now, you're father has me declared in a court of law, too old and crazy to handle my own purse. Even my own will, I couldn't change, if I wanted.

"He had you declared senile?"

"I fought as best I could, but the judge was with him."

Amaryllis paused momentarily. She looked into the wrinkled face. "Aren't you angry?"

"What's the *gevins* in being angry? They say old people know themselves. It's a lie. I don't know myself any better than I did when I was a little girl in boy's pants. I'm still going in circles, tied in knots. The only difference is now I know to distract myself." She lifted her tea cup and took a sip. "By the way how was Las Vegas? You win or lose?"

"I didn't gamble."

"You see the show?"

"I walked out."

"You stay in a big hotel or a little one?"

"I slept in a sleeping bag in the desert."

Gita leaned her elbows on the table. "Backwards parents...backwards children. When I was your age, I too, had a will of my own." She leaned back and yawned. "And where do you play next? Anchorage, Alaska?"

"Exposition Park."

Gita stretched. "There I haven't been since the old days." Her head sank. She lifted it. It sank again.

"Speaking of the old days, I visited Boyle Heights. It was great. My teammate lives there. It's funny. Relaxing a little, did me some good. I feel like I found my roots. I went to the pool and the library and the Youth Center." Amaryllis sipped her tea. "I know just what I'm going to do now. I'll go pick up my final paycheck." Her fingers grasped a sprinkles cookie. "Then I have to get ready for our last practice of the season. I'm going to jog at least six..." She brought the treat to her mouth and looked up to find her Grandmother breathing rhythmically, eyes closed, peacefully asleep. Amaryllis stared at her father's mother and smiled for just a moment. She washed the two tea cups, called the nurse to help her put Gita to bed, then, filled the potted Bonsai with water from the bathroom tap. There in the mirror in front of her was that same reflection. It was the same face she'd seen on that first day on the bus, but somehow different too. Tense yes, but alert as well, pensive and aware.

The Patriotic Hall Gym was sweltering. Terry, a whistle hung around her neck, wiped the sweat off her brow with a towel. "Our last game of the summer is this weekend. In preparation, we're going to practice our pressure defense."

"But it's hot."

"You're right Patty. It is hot." Terry continued. "In a full court press, the in-bounder is not covered. Instead, the first—"

"What time should we show up?"

"Show up for what Patty?"

"The final game."

"Do you remember when game time is?"

"Of course, two-thirty."

"An hour before game time like always." Coach picked up the ball. "Instead, the first player to get the ball is double-teamed. Everyone else cuts off the passing lane. If the ball crosses—"

"So it's one-thirty."

"Right Patty, one-thirty."

"We're going to get our asses kicked anyway."

"Maybe. Please stop interrupting."

"But we can't play a women's pro team. They're all olympic medalists."

Peggy leaned over. "Be quiet, Patty."

"Yeah Patty, shut up."

"I was just trying to—"

"Come on, Patty."

Patty smiled. "Alright, alright. But we already know this drill."

Flor piped in. "You can still practice something you know."

Patty stood in front of Terry and performed her immitation for the team. "If the ball crosses half court, Iris—or whoever is playing center—drops back to guard the key."

Terry kept going. "Thank you Patty. Because of the intensity and the distances covered, everyone must be in top shape and be ready to sub in or out. And remember—"

Patty stepped in. "Avoid fouling. Slap up, not down. Keep your arms moving."

"Right, Patty. Nice delivery."

Amaryllis tried to listen carefully and was ready when Terry blew the whistle and the ball was thrown in. Playing defense, she pounced on the first offensive player to stop with the ball—Villa. Villa ditched it off to Patty. Patty lowered her shoulder and slammed into Amaryllis' chest. The contact slowed her down enough for Dahlia to block the other side—

trapped. Patty pivoted her husky body and threw elbows. Amaryllis tiped the ball just slightly, then Dahlia knocked it entirely loose. Patty dove and retrieved it. She tried to pass. Terry blew her whistle.

"Why did you stop play?" objected Patty.

"Let's run it again," said Terry.

"Why? They didn't get it from me."

"You traveled."

"Traveled? You're crazy!"

"It doesn't matter. Run it again."

"But I didn't travel."

Terry blew her whistle. Iris inbounded to Villa. Villa dribbled but was stopped and passed it to Iris center court. Iris lobbed it to Patty who was trapped again. Amaryllis' arms looked like wavying branches. She tipped the ball free again and threw it to LaRhonda down court.

Patty stood with her mouth open. She was mad and wanted to object, but just smiled instead. She looked at Amaryllis. "Good hands," Patty conceeded.

"Thanks," said Amaryllis. She offered her hand and Patty slapped it easily.

They ran the drill again. This time when Patty got the ball, she quickly bounced passed it back to Villa. Dahlia managed to slow Villa at half court until Amaryllis came from behind. If she could just manage to tap the ball free. Villa faked a pass, but retained the ball. Amaryllis slapped the ball, but Villa's grip was too tight and it wouldn't come loose. She tapped at it again. Iris hollered from behind and Villa managed to lob the ball to her. Releaved, she gave Amaryllis a sly look of recognition and resumed playing.

The heat was overwhelming and after the drill and scrimmage was over, the team stumbled to the floor for stretching exercises, then wabbled to the showers. Returning to the gym, they assembled on the concrete bleachers. "I have some announcements," began Terry. "As you know, this was the final practice for the summer. Our final game will be at the Sports Arena in Exposition Park—a home game at last."

"No more cheap hotels?"

"No Patty. Just be there on time."

"Will you?"

Terry ignored her. "All of you have tried hard and shown improvement. You deserve to be proud of yourselves."

Amaryllis rested a foot on the bleacher hand rail in front of her. Did she really deserve to be proud? The practice went well and she hadn't done too poorly in the last two games. That's while she was conscious anyway.

"Peggy will be retiring, Amaryllis will be going back to college, and lets all wish good luck to LaRhonda who was offered a contract with the new US Women's Pro League." The team congratulated LaRhonda, slapping her back and messing her hair.

Amaryllis smiled. She felt privileged being apart of the comraderie and playing with such high acheivers. Good Hands. The words echoed in her ears. Good Hands.

Under the hundred degree sun, Max stood filling the fountain with water. Amaryllis wet her hands then rubbed her arms. She studied her father a few moments before she spoke. "Max, Gita said you had her declared senile. She's not crazy."

Max sprayed away the dirt and old mortar caked on the inside walls of the fountain. "No not crazy. Just unable to handle her own finances."

"Do you have her money?"

"Don't jump to conclusions. I don't have it. It's with a conservator—for her own good. She was going to give every penny to an orphanage in Tel-Aviv."

"But it's hers to give. She worked hard for it."

"There your right. All her life she worked for it. And she was quite a good business woman. Yes definately, it is hers—hers for her old age. In fact without it, all the burden of her care would fall on me. She would have to come live here."

Amaryllis shielded her eyes from the sun. "Maybe she wants to come live here. Maybe she misses you."

"My Daughter, for years, all my mother has expressed is the utmost disgust for me. She doesn't want to see me. She doesn't even want to hear my name. It took me time to accept that. Now you're suggesting—"

"Come on Max. All summer, you've been telling me how sad the world situation is. If all that's really true, at least you could visit your mother before doomsday."

The water line came close to the top of the fountain. Max folded the end of the hose to stop the flow. "I'm afraid it's too late. All that was already resolved. I was in therapy for many years." A high pressure spray was beginning to escape from the nozzle. Max went to the facet and turned off the valve.

"You took her support all your life and now—"

"I gave support too. To you and Melissa. I never missed an alimony or a child support payment."

"And don't you want me to visit you? Look at her. Hasn't she made enough sacrifices?"

"She's made too many. It was a mistake to give her money to charity if she needed it herself. She taught me what was a good decision and what was a bad one. That was a bad one. I'm sorry you can't see that. But I'm her only child and your father."

Amaryllis wiped sweat from her brow. "But why did you keep that from me? Didn't I deserve to know?"

"I wasn't sure how you would handle it?"

"If I can handle hearing that the world is coming to an end, I can handle hearing about Grandma."

Max rolled up the hose and plopped it down by the wall. "I've been depressed."

"I know, but that doesn't mean that I have to be depressed too. Or do you want me too give in and say, 'I guess Max is right. There's really no point in getting up in the morning.' Maybe I should start planting a garden too. You should have been up front with me. I deserved to know."

Max sat down. "My mother used to say, 'Wait until you have children of your own.' You've grown up Amaryllis. And look what happened to me—I've become the older generation. When I was your age, I rebeled against my mother. Did Gita tell you that she wanted me to be a doctor?"

"Yes it's nice that a mother has high aspirations for her son."

"You don't understand. She *wanted* me to be a doctor."

"So?"

"I'm not a doctor."

"I know."

"I'm not a doctor and never was one. I tried to explain to my mother that I just wasn't the type for check-ups, examinations and surgery, but in her generation, the parents told the children what to be. I tried not to do that to you eventhough I wanted you to be even stronger than your mother or mine. I wanted you to be a vital, confrontive, active woman—a leader—the leader I gave up trying to be."

"Max, you don't know what I've gone through this summer. I look at my reflection sometimes and I don't even recognize it. Please don't lay that trip on me now."

"Maybe I can't help it. We try to be different than our parents, but what changes? I never dreamed I'd end up treating you the same way she treated me, but in the end, there's no getting around it. In the Sixties, we complained about the Generation Gap, but in some ways it's necessary."

Amaryllis sat down. "Can't you even try to patch things up? You could go back to the therapist again. Where there's life there's hope."

"Where there is life there are also limitations. Look at us. We've tried to make up for eight years of separation in one summer."

"Maybe if you don't want her to live here, you could compromise. Let her handle part of her money. Let her change her will."

"The last time I let her have some of her money, naturally she hired a lawyer to get the rest. She changed her will so many times it hardly matters. Anyway I'm finally satisfied where it all—her savings and the rest of her estate—are going to."

"To you?"

"No Amaryllis, to you."

"And this little piggy went Wee, Wee, Wee all the way home..." Karin was enjoying her little game of tickling her lover's vulnerable naked ribs. On top, Terry begged, pleaded, and cried for her to "cut it out" then finally lost her temper and pinned down the two offending wrists. "I said stop!"

Karin, looked her in the eye and pouted, then wiggled down beneath her until their lips were just touching. She tilted her head and kissed Terry's mouth.

"Shhh," breathed Karin caressing Terry's back up and down with maternal concern. "It was only a game. Don't be angry." Karin looked around the room. "Can we miss the first half of the concert?"

"You jerk," said Terry. "I knew there was a reason you were being nice."

"Please."

"Not a chance. Jean is only conducting the first piece." Terry threw on her clothes and grimaced until Karin did the same.

Eyeing the clock the whole way, they arrived at the Music Center. "Aren't you glad the season's over? Now we have more time together. How did your talk with Amaryllis go?"

"Yes I'm glad and the talk went fine. She said she'll keep in touch with us during her senior year." Terry looked at Karin's outfit. "You look nice tonight. I like the print."

"What else?"

"The necklace adds a touch of class."

"No, I mean, what else did she say?"

"She had a lot on her mind. She thanked me."

They rode up the escalator across the foyer and to the ticket booth of the Dorothy Chandler Pavilion completed in 1969 as part of the "redevelopment" of Bunker Hill. Short, gray and neo-classic, on it's opening night, it looked out over a wasteland. Nothing was left of the surrounding quaint and historically rich Victorian neighborhood. Not a gingerbread house, a buckled sidewalk, an old oak, a meandering vine, a well kept garden, a cracked curb or an overgrown bush. As if a redevelopment bomb had disintigrated the entire district, the neighborhood along with it's residents, were gone—vanished.

"Two, please," said Terry.

The ticket booth attendant looked up. "The concert has already started. You'll have to wait until the second movement."

Terry was annoyed. "Now what will we do?"

Karin was overjoyed. "Get some dinner? Go for a walk? Be happy to be outside?"

"Fine, which way?"

"There has to be a restaurant open somewhere."

The couple walked south past the ornamented buildings of Broadway and finally ended up at Clifton's Cafeteria. Inside: a stuffed buck, a fake moon, a redwood tree trunk, an indoor waterfall—what was once splendors, now just impressed the very young or young at heart.

"This is so folksie." Karin read a plaque on the wall. "Did you know this place has been here since the thirties?"

"It looks like it."

"The whole street looks like it must have been through a lot."

Broadway had been through a lot. A half a dozen earthquakes, several explosions, a couple of major race riots, wars, parades, marches, fires and more recently in 1992, it became a venue for public outrage.

"Guilty! Guilty!" shouted an angry crowd. On the night of April 29th, the usual quiet was broken by citizens protesting a "Not Guilty Verdict" for four officers videotaped beating motorist Rodney King. It was a group of about fifty protestors: women and men from all backgrounds, old and young. A spontaneous politcal event (a street corner off-shoot of the organized demonstration earlier at City Hall). Police stood blocking First and Spring. The sounds of shattering glass could be heard coming from the next block. People stood on the grass taking in the scene, much the same as they'd done a year ago during the downtown protests against the War in Iraq. A speech impared man gave an impromptu oratory. A fire truck drove by and was booed and pummeled with trash. Then from the north came a marching crowd of hundreds heading down Main and stopping to overturn a police car then set it afire. "Lets go shopping!" shouted one tall man. With the police blocking other intersections, the crowd headed down Broadway—a street they knew well. Rocking security gates loose, groups smashed store front windows and emerged with jewelry, CD players, musical instruments and from the cutlery store—two foot long antique swords. Office filing cabinets were set ablaze making an eerie orange glow inside the dark old buildings. Trash cans were turned over; magazine booths thrown into the street. A man lay at the entrance of a building bleeding, stabbed by a protuding shard of plate glass as he'd tried to run inside. Security guards of some buildings hid on the upper floors while others watched dazed. Hotel residents sat in lobbies discussing the verdicts and the public reaction while outside fire and smoke lit the sky and filled the air.

Karin sipped her lemonade. "How do you think Amaryllis will do when she goes back to college?"

"She has the potential to be a strong defensive specialist. But there are always obstacles too. Hopefully, she'll do well and come back next year."

"After having trained with you, she'll do well."

Terry ate her salad. "Thanks Karin. That's nice of you to say."

"I'll be right back." Karin stood and returned minutes later with two slices of pecan pie. "You know what. We both deserve a treat."

Terry smiled. "I thought you were on a budget."

Karin smiled back. "Not since Rochelle paid off our bet."

"Hello, Mr. Seltzer, you're only twenty minutes late today," said the psychologist drying his hands with a light green towel. "That's showing improvement. Now, what shall we discuss?"

"My daughter."

"Yes, and what else?"

"My mother."

"Very good. Well we got that out of the way. Now, how old was your daughter again?"

"Twenty-three." Max was already in tears.

The psychologist, a man with glasses and a trim beard, handed his patient a box of tissue. “Please continue. What about you’re daughter?”

“She makes me angry. She stayed with me for the summer. Now she’s going back.”

“Well then, she won’t bother you any longer.”

“But, I made an agreement with her.”

“An agreement? What type of agreement?”

“I agreed to see my mother.”

The psychologist sat forward. “Yes, and what is the problem?”

Max waved away a fly. “I don’t want to see my mother. I haven’t seen her in eight years.”

“Eight years.” The psychologist waited for the fly to land, then swated it with a rolled up journal. He sprayed the desk with antiseptic cleaner and wiped it off with a paper towel. “Will you keep the agreement?”

Max guffawed. “Is that all you can think to ask?”

“Yes, don’t you think that is an appropriate question?”

Max blew his nose. “No, I think that—this isn’t working.”

“What isn’t working?”

“Psychoanalysis. Freud. Jung. You ask me questions and I tell you what I’m thinking. You listen to my problems, discover my disorder and prescribe an anti-depressant.”

“Mr. Seltzer, you’re a little behind the times. The world of psychololgy is more practical now. Doctors and patients are partners not opponents. Lets continue to focus. Now, why don’t you want to visit your mother?” The Doctor stood and walked to the small basin above the mini-refrigerator.

Max got up and stared out the window. “None of your business.”

The doctor squirted liquid soap in each palm and turned on the water. “Listen Mr. Seltzer, when you first came here, you said you wanted to cure yourself of your addiction to videos. Then, you decided you wanted to finish your gardening project and get out of the house more. Now, it’s an agreement with your daughter about your mother—”

“But this isn’t helpful. I’m better off gardening and watching videos.”

“Mr. Seltzer, you seem hostile.” He hung the towel back on the rack.

“People come in here. Spill their problems out to you and its all you can do to put up a wall of professionalism and just say, ‘Yes’ or ‘Uh-hum’, until you can figure out a nice neat label that fits some textbook pattern you learned years ago. That’s not therapy. That’s doing a crossword puzzle.”

“How would you like me to be?”

“I want you to be calm and understanding. I don’t want to be analyzed like a specimen. I want you to proud of me for being the way I am.”

“But Mr. Seltzer, I don’t even know you.”

“That’s just my point. You don’t love your fellow man anymore than anybody else. How can you help me?”

The doctor sat down. "What type of help do you want?"

"I want to cleanse my mind of the past. I want to look at pictures of myself without groaning. I want to see hope. What does any of that have to do with my mother? What do you want from me?"

"Well for starters, I want you to pay your bill. You're two payments behind." The doctor stood, walked to the basin, washed his hands and took the towels back down from the bar.

"I don't need a referral for that. I can stay at home, not pay my bills and wait for the collectors to call. Couldn't you in addition to wanting my money at least be a little entertaining?"

"Fine Mr. Seltzer, you asked for it." He dried his hands and neatly folded the towel. "If you want to look at a picture of yourself without groaning, you might consider taking up photography again. If you want to look out and see hope, I suggest you go downtown and look South from Flower or North from Grand. And if you want to cleanse your spirit, I suggest you stick to the agreements you make with your loved ones." The doctor sat back down.

"Listen, I'll see my mother when and if I'm ready. Not before. Understand?"

"You're making progress Mr. Seltzer. Time is up."

"But we just started."

"That's what happens when you're late. We'll continue next week."

"Maybe," mumbled Max as he stood and walked out of the office. He reached the street and felt the sun shine down on his face. Max liked the heat. He smiled and thought about his tan.

Just as he stepped out on the sidewalk, he heard a deep commanding yell and was nearly knocked over by two police rushing towards a group of teenagers. Mesmerized, he slowly approached the scene of LAPD walkie-talkies and young men laying face down on the black asphalt street.

The shorter of the two officers turned around. "Something wrong with you?"

"No Officer, never felt better." Max rubbed his hands together. "Excuse me, may I ask you a question?"

"Who are you?"

"My name is Max Seltzer. I'm the father of Amaryllis Benjamina Seltzer of the Exposition Park Exiles. I would like to ask you why you are making these boys lay face down on the street. It's too hot for that. Don't you think?"

"Okay, you're going to have to stand back away by that building. Don't interfere with an officer in the line of duty."

"I *will* watch from here. I'm not interfering. May I have your name before you leave and please let those boys stand up now."

"My name is Chasen. See, here, read the badge, okay? Now Mr. sidewalk lawyer, take a step back by that building like I instructed you. Ernie, let those two stand up. Satisfied?"

Max stood in the shade by the building to observe the arrest. He took notes and copied down the arresting officers names. He then got in his car and began the drive home. He headed west on Wilshire towards the freeway but then suddenly made an abrupt U-turn and headed towards Fairfax.

Villa stood straight and stiff in the elevator, her chest inches from the pin striped executive in front. The heat of the panting bike messenger behind radiated into her. Her white silk blouse touched his back and her arm brushed his thick, hairy wrist. Nervously, her eyes studied the tapered hairlines of the surrounding men, some recently shaved and trim, others growing in descending patterns of wind blown grass.

For Villa, being cramped together with so many men, unfortunately, felt like a roust. Fortunately though, it did bring to mind an item she had not yet purchased for her upcoming trip—shaving cream. Once inside the pharmacy, Villa's compulsive shopping weakness took over and she wrote a check for two types of shaving cream, a travel toothbrush container and glycerin soap.

She'd been feeling a bit sad lately. Could it be she missed Amaryllis? No, she'd been seeing someone special and had been out and about big time. Her job was dull, but she'd still never had a cross word or reprimand and the supervisor let her travel freely. Her savings were small, but at least they were there—no debt. She was angry. That was it. She'd been that way since yesterday when Gilbert, one of the kids who sat on the steps, had been disrespectful and had called her names. She'd felt uncomfortable since then. But no, it wasn't that she missed Amaryllis. Couldn't be.

Opening the door and setting down her back pack, she surveyed the set of brand new suitcases, open and neatly packed. She threw the bag of toiletries on top of the folded shirts while she plopped down on the couch and stared at the palm tree outside her window.

The thought of San Francisco made her heart pound with excitement. So then why was she so down? Laying there, caught up in the usual funk, she stared at the trophy case. The photo from high school—Villa surrounded by girls of all shades, her own skin dark from the outdoors, hand on hip, ball under arm, trophy in hand, her smile, the widest of all. The air, heavy with the sounds of neighbor's televisions, Villa rolled like a log, out of bed and began repacking for the third time that week.

This trip was the start of an experiment for the Exiles. Each player would choose their own hotel and be given a set amount reimbursement. If they wanted to stay at a five star and pay the difference, or, stay at their cousins and keep the difference, that was up to them. Villa was thrilled and arrived in the Bay Area a full day early. She slept at a bed and breakfast and awoke early to jog past trees, grassy meadows, shimmering ponds and exotic gardens along the winding paths of the city's largest public space—Golden Gate Park.

After the jog, lunch, shopping and seeing the sights, Villa met Amaryllis at a little restaurant off of Washington Square. She reviewed the menu while Amaryllis stared out the picture window. Across the street, a scattered few occupied the grassy ground of Washington Square. The steeple of the Church of Saint Peter and Paul rose above the little ticky tacky houses and storefront apartments. Behind, a small forest of wind blown Monterey Pines on a hill formed the base for handsome Coit Tower.

"Are you coming to the game tommorow," asked Villa wearing a souvenir T-Shirt and a knit cap.

"I can't. We're playing U of A."

"That's too bad. Everyone would like to see you." At the bar, a couple of sports fans hollered loudly at the TV as a soccer team scored a goal.

"How is everyone?

"Okay. Patty has been pretty quiet this week. Terry blew up and told her off."

"How about Peggy?"

"They changed her bus line and it's hard for her to make weekend practice."

"It's funny. I never thought I could miss L.A."

"How's your season going?"

"I'm a starter."

"You're starting—that's great!"

"Who replaced me on the team? Are you helping her out like you did with me?"

Their entrees arrived. Red, green and yellow peppers garnished the Northern Italian style meal. "Two glasses of house red," said Villa to the waitress.

Amaryllis reached out her hand. "Let me see your fingers. Jam them again? Damb, that's really swollen. Does it hurt?"

Villa looked aggrieved. "No, it's not that bad anymore, but don't pull on it okay?"

Outside, the wind gusted through the dark trees. Muni buses picked up passengers and departed. On the park bench, a long haired man with sunglasses sat next to a Chinese senior citizen. Amaryllis smelled her food then carefully chose the grilled eggplant.

Villa chewed a few bites of Porcini Mushroom in cream sauce. "You look good. That's such a cool sweater."

"Yeah."

"It's so funny how you forget the nice people in your life. Its like I get so caught up, I don't even notice who's around me."

"I know what you mean. School is a trip. How can I make it through?" Amaryllis rose to go to the bathroom and after a while, returned grinning.

Villa smiled as she sat back down. "What's so funny?"

"The bathroom lock works for everyone but me."

Villa chuckled. "Finish your wine. I want you to see the B and B I'm at. It's nutty."

It was almost 10:30 when they finally unlocked the door to room #36 at the San Remo B and B. A small, small room, barely enough space to maneuver without bumping. Three oval pictures hung on the wall above the brass bed frames.

"You see," said Villa. "This is what I mean by staying in style."

A glass dish of potpourri sat on a carved wood dresser. A painted green wood floor had just enough room for a small white tapestry rug. A ceiling fan offered a cooling breeze and a white curtained window offered a homey view. A comfy, cozy small room. A room small enough to smell the person next to you in the morning. Not big enough to fit worries. Just the right size for courtesy. One queen size bed covered by a flowery bed spread and a heart shaped pillow.

"How adorable." Amaryllis turned on the flower stem lamp and threw her stuff on the bed. "I've been meaning to tell you something. You really helped me last summer. You were a real good friend to me." Amaryllis gave Villa a hug. "Villa, you're the greatest!"

At her game, Amaryllis played until there were six minutes on the clock. Paroni spoke at her as she toweled off her face. "I want you to switch with Rene and stick #37. Keep close and don't let her get off the three."

"Relax Coach, we're not doing that bad. They're completely worn out. We'll catch up."

"Alright, alright, but just to make sure—"

"Jack, I need a few minutes rest. You've had me out front the entire game."

Coach Paroni nodded and signaled a freshman to sub in. Amaryllis sat down and the bench congratulated her. She leaned back, spread her knees and toweled off her neck. Janis Tanichek leaned over. "They're really bending the rules tonight. My ribs are raw."

"Look at my jersey," said Amaryllis. "They've stretched it completely out of shape."

"Thirty-two grabbed me by the wrist and pulled me out of the key."

Amaryllis leaned back laughing. "Me too. Press her hard. You can shut her down. She's had it."

"We should go with the half court press pretty soon if it keeps up this way."

"Yeah."

"Paroni just doesn't catch on. Lets start it with two minutes left."

Amaryllis listened and nodded as she watched the game. "We'll come back. We always do better in the last minutes." She glanced over to Cheryl Fergueson sitting silently while Paroni remained on his feet. Amaryllis felt a slight pang of guilt. She had confronted the assistant coach at the beginning of the season. Yes, Cheryl should have told her why she was being sent down to Los Angeles. She should have warned her how rough it would be, but hadn't it turned out that it was for her own good? Cheryl had even apologized. An assistant coach apologize to a player? But that was Cheryl's way. Always doing what was necessary—responsible, helpful. Cheryl, help me stretch. Cheryl, we don't have towels. Cheryl, can you explain what coach meant? Cheryl. Cheryl. Cheryl. She was the one who loved the game—the elegant patterns, the graceful movement, the gravity and space, muscle and emotion.

True, it was the players who had recently gotten together on their own and decided to have a meeting every week by themselves. But until then, who had kept them in the top ten, been their emotional anchor, compiled their strategy, figured out what they lacked, chose Amaryllis to receive special attention and be groomed as a defensive specialist in Los Angeles last summer, and now, who needed an ally? Cheryl.

Amaryllis' guilty feeling slowly melted away as she looked out on the floor. This season would pass quickly, but in what was left of it, she would be loyal and supportive of her assistant coach. Who knows? Maybe they would even be friends. Amaryllis got up and sat next to her.

"Hi."

"Hi Ms. D? Had enough rest?" The Assistant picked up a corner of her player's jersey. "What happened to your shirt?"

"Ask them?"

"You ready to get back in there? Keep it tight. No fouls."

Amaryllis could feel that they would win the game, maybe even make it to the semi-finals. And after that, Terry said she could have another chance. It would take a lot of hard work if she was going to get good enough. How would she do it? Amaryllis stood. "Yes Cheryl, I'm ready."

List of Illustrations

Basketball Defensive Strategy

Place Diagrams

Unreinforced Masonry Studio
P.O. Box 33671
Los Angeles, CA 90033